# CADENZA

# CADENZA

**BY**
**RALPH CUSACK**

---

AN AFTERWORD
BY
GILBERT SORRENTINO

---

**THE DALKEY ARCHIVE PRESS**

LIBRARY OF CONGRESS CATALOGING IN PUBLICATION DATA

Cusack, Ralph
Cadenza.
I. Title
PR6053.U82C3   1984   823'.914   84-21372
ISBN 0-916583-04-X
ISBN 0-916583-05-8

THE DALKEY ARCHIVE PRESS
1817 79th Avenue
Elmwood Park, IL 60635

CADENZA: flourish of voice or instrument at the close of a movement. (It.)—*Concise Oxford Dictionary.*

Je suis la plaie et le couteau!
. . . Et la victime et le bourreau.
BAUDELAIRE

# I

LYING back in the chair with my head on its headrest I opened my eyes.

Over the fresh net curtain, through the large upper panes of the high window, I could see the sun catching the top storeys of the tall mellow-brick Georgian houses on the other side of the street; behind them fluffy clouds in a blue sky; in the sky a wheeling white gull, blown sideways by the breeze from the sea.

Once more I was returning; consciousness returning.

Once more I was returning to the world of my vision: of our vision; of *your* sight: of *our* sound. Dream and reality, once merged, were re-emerging separate once more.

Yes, I had returned from my many-wheeled journeys; from far-placed plodding feet; from young leapings; from old wheezings.

In space and in time, at will and unwillingly, long ago or far ahead, my mind had thus run, and I had run too.

I had followed myself: you, too, had been with me.

I had followed myself but was never alone, in this our excursion.

For my dentist was kind.

So he thought.

# 2

SMASHING the cheap teacup with one blow of his fist, he stuffed the resultant crocks, unbroken handle and all, gently but firmly into my mouth.

With his freshly washed soapsmelling fingers he then adjusted the pieces so that they lined and filled every cranny, using the handle and its still attached fragment of curve to pin backwards and downwards the tip of my tongue and the larger curved morsels to arch in my palate.

Although it was now quite impossible to close my mouth completely, he insisted on my closing it sufficiently to prevent the twenty-three pieces falling out on the floor, telling me to come back in two hours.

I looked at my watch: it was just half past ten and a clear sunny morning in May. It was a pity, all the same, I had nowhere to hide.

He had said it was better to keep to the side streets, as of course in such case it was essential to keep my mouth shut both physically and metaphorically or people might ask questions and I should be lost or discovered. Normally I should have gravitated to the nearest pub and, skulking in a dark corner, lowered a few mediums; but, alas, I was debarred now from this as the crockery could not be taken out and I was afraid if left in I might swallow it down along with the dark silky porter.

# 3

CLOSING the heavy door silently behind me I glanced right and then left in the wide sunny street and seeing a loquacious acquaintance, a poet of some standing, slouching towards me, made off at such speed as my trembling legs would carry me to the right, pursued by his peculiarly loud and raucous shouts now mercifully being diminished by distance:

'Hey! Come here you! What are yez up to at all? Come here, damn ye . . . I want a loan . . . (more distant) . . . a small loan . . . (still further) . . . God's curse on ye anyhow!'

Luckily an alleyway turned off again right, a place ill-lit by day or after dark, used in the one for stocking shops on the main thoroughfare through trap- and back-doors and in the other for the surreptitious meetings of forbidden lovers. For all lovers were of course forbidden unless they were well enough off to ride to hounds, attend hunt-balls in country houses, breed, own or train racehorses, contribute handsomely to the Society of St. Vincent de Paul, know the right people to drink with in the Shelbourne Rooms, Buttery, Russell or Dolphin, exhibit themselves regularly in the Right Theatre's stalls, wear *fainnes*. . . .

Such garbled ruminations, however, were my very first undoing, for instanter I had stepped on vicious air and landed a good three feet below on a piled gross of boxes of artificial finnan-haddy oozing orange dye. The place smelt of dead wood, the said finnan-haddy and cats. In the process I had skinned my right fore-shin, trousers and all, on the sharp metal edge of the turned back thick-glazed trap and a ribbon of cloth hanging forward and down as I trod on its tail now impeded my flight. For I was up in a trice belching back my crocks from mid-gullet, and away on, looking more where I was going and less into my head.

At the end of the alleyway it was right again into the old mews once peopled by horses with their brakes, dog-carts, *vis-à-vis*, shandrydans, barouches, Victorias and the odd private coach; now stabling those on the run from society, short of cash, full of money.

I had friends there too and rapidly debated whether to keep close under the wall to the right where most windows were muffed, risking thus a familiar knock-knowledged door being opened in my path all too soon, or stalk upright undisguised directly past the acetylene welders, eggsporters, arty furniture dives, disused billiard rooms and spent kips on the sunny opposite side.

I chose the former and was instantaneously rewarded by a tur-quoise door, numbered 26A in white, painted primrose yellow (for I knew it) on the inside, being opened in my face.

Choking back the crockery I stood still, as Moore on his plinth always did and does, and allowed the refugee from war and all else to throw out her toothwater and tampax tube, take a deep sighing breath of polluted spring air and retire. She was one of those people who look better out of her clothes than in the over-rural tweeds she affected in the city, whilst the same was the case for high heels on the bog: but her body was beautiful.

I then shuffled on until I stumbled over a pair of sad-trousered reversed male legs tipped by good shoes, all splayed in my way: my friend the abortionist, lying on his stomach tinkering with his coach-housed car, endeavouring to retrieve with the lasso of his pseudo-stethoscope some bolt or nut which had scooted too far under its oil-sodden carcass for even his hands to lay hold. Before he could get up, cracking his head on the differential case, filling thus his unctuous hair in approximately equal proportions with a mixture of burnt oil and the assorted muds of all twenty-six counties, I was again on my way and slid stealthily into yet another alley, still right, where the delectable bins of a high-classy restaurant were often besieged by the gastronome cats of the neighbourhood and where, Lord be praised, I had sometimes supped myself.

I was just about to dispute with a big tabby-tom the rejected remains of a copious fine dish when I remembered the crockery, averted my eyes, tottered on at a teetering trot.

Crouching below the walls of the crockery-monger's still used mews, its ampelopsis still light green, unsullied by soot, I decided I had had enough of this damned alliteration and put it back in my head for later use.

So I almost strode to the shadow of the clock-arch of the maternity hospital (which struck something), nodded to my friend the real impecunious doctor, his kind Jewish wife and five kids (an action which almost trisected my tongue) and slipped up the wide road through the hop-scotch players to the fine hawthorn-scented square.

The sun shone kindly on my purple bloated face; sweet bunches of clouds stood still in the pale blue sky; four delicious large drops of pearly water fell off a pendant lilac down my aching neck.

And I thought of Mrs. N.

# 4

I was there again all right some summer or such a similar summer or spring. The last time I had visited her she had thought I was my grandmother with her copious dirty-white hair hiding combs galore and most of the Bible by heart. We had discussed at great length many people long dead of whom I had scarcely ever heard and never even seen but in yellowed ageing image or not even that. Indeed a good many of them had probably never existed. But Mrs. N. and I soon put them in their places on the fading map and came to the conclusion that apart from having quite obviously married the wrong men, we had made many another lamentable and irretrievable mistake, for example in our dressing and deportment that day we were presented to the Old Queen during the garden party at the Viceregal lodge.

It was pleasant enough for a time to be translated in epoch and sex and very often afterwards we played this rare game; until I became so convinced when in her company that I was indeed Lizzie that inexorably I was drawn into overacting the part, and one fine sad day could not overcome the temptation of a visit to Gings, the theatrical outfitters, on the way.

On appearing at Mrs. N.'s in what I was convinced was the spitting-image garb of my granny—hair locket, pince-nez, starched cuffs, wig, reticule and all—you can imagine my chagrin when she greeted me affectionately by the nickname of my own eldest son.

# 5

ON that dreadful occasion I was compelled, to my great embarrassment, to carry on a lengthy discussion on his father, and I do not really know whom I maligned most, my son or myself, although I am often if not always polite and try to avoid telling lies.

But I had to admit that Daddy and his wife were both too fond of the bottle, indeed Yes; that Daddy made too many obviously unnecessary trips both to London and Paris; was too fond of young girls, even schoolgirls . . . (And here I blushed, I must say, for I wondered how on earth it was that he (but of course it was *she*) ever got it into her head to think of that.)

On top of all this Daddy bought far too many rare plants and bulbs for his garden, squandering money thus far better applied to his farm; should never have given up tennis and grown fat; subscribed to far too many newspapers and periodicals which he could not possibly read (I did, I mean I do, read them all); was getting gross, lazy and too fond of good food; and avoided by all ruses he could think of visiting Mrs. N. and her family, which, as it so happened I was there, I denied very stoutly.

Having braced myself as best I could with ten drops of Maria Theresa Koelnischwasser to a teaspoonful of multi-coloured coffee-sugar, both mercifully available on her side-table and of which she took no notice, being addicted that way herself, we then went on to a lengthy and detailed discussion of my then living father, his grandfather, whose morals (according to my part for my son) seemed scarcely any better than my own, my father and son's grandfather having died, according to Mrs. N.'s rather too circumstantial evidence, some years before.

Lowering her voice Mrs. N. then began to speak of my son's sweet children; but this essay into the future was too much for me entirely and picking up my skirts I took forthwith my leave, changed my clothes in the lobby bathroom and, my gladstone bag gripped firmly, left.

Momentarily not knowing who I was, I most mistakenly went to the match at Lansdowne Road (my son being a keen rugger man), had a terrible struggle back through the turnstiles to arrive late at the weekly concert of the Friends of the National Collection of Musicians and missing the Mozart Quintet, which I loved, had to sit through a boring Bliss. In future, I said to myself, you must keep your feet more firmly planted on the ground in space as well as time . . .

# 6

BUT that was all very well. *Now* I thought: the very thing: Mrs. N. will surely save me, crockery and all: for this time and place I would as soon be out of; I shall go and see her; she will just be up, fresh from her accurate dreams, ready for her hazy day.

It was a little nerve-wracking though: supposing, just supposing (and sooner or later it was bound to happen) she mistook me for myself! Even if it could not be called recognition, what then? Should I break down and accuse her, for once, of being mistaken? Embark pronto on the memory of the day Lizzie's cob ran away with her at the Ward Union meet? Bark out loudly that I wished to know nothing of him for of a certainty he was up to no good? Or, scraping out the crockery, embrace her as myself?

Any harbour in a hurricane, I thought, and jumped on the tram for the Zoo. It was not long, however, before I realized my mistake and inadvertently transgressing the enamelled injunction not to spit either in or on the car, dribbled a salivated whine of anguish from the corner of my mouth where the round base of the smashed cup, still almost intact, left a narrow gap to the outer air.

I slapped on the bell, clattered down the stairs and landed forninst the Rotunda.

Hastily crossing the street I reversed my trolley, making sure this time I was in the ten not the nine, and duly arrived, partly on foot, at the beautifully proportioned carved sandstone fluted pillars (painted to imitate granite) and fine teak door (grained to resemble oak) and the elegant brasswork and knocker (chromiumed to emulate silver) and the former fine fanlight (removed to eliminate dusting and now safe in Sheepstown, Mo.) of number sixty-seven.

'Is Mrs. N. at home?' I managed to mumble, an idiot but polite question, for except to go abroad she had hardly left the house since the Civil War, and Martha the maid, not since the Boer, when her lover had sailed with his horse from the North Wall never to return.

'Indeed and she is, sir,' mumbled Martha. 'Come in, sir, Come in.'

In the furtive dark hall with its worn sunk doormat and heavy brass rail, its immense mahogany table with its visiting cards on the old brass French tray, its faded Millais etchings and G. F. Watts in milk-chocolate aqua, I was besieged by fear. *Who was I to be?*

Never mind: it was too late.

I was shown into the upper front drawing-room in its exquisite faded blue and fly-blown yellowed white-and-gold. There sat Mrs. N. nibbling a Marie biscuit and sipping her long cooled coffee, crumbs of one and drops of the other falling alternately onto the first folio of Redouté's Roses lying open and half toppling off her narrow lady's lap: lent of course, and illegally, by the Provost.

She looked up: here it was.

'My dear Melchi. How nice it is to see you! It's such ages since you called; and how is dear Hetty?'

I was saved.

My Uncle Melchizedek had died some years before and Hetty his wife decades before that. We had always called him Melchi for short.

In gratefulness I opened my mouth wide to answer her, but shut it again like a trap just in time, adroitly imprisoning the tips of the crockery between my clenched gums, the base and handle-piece alone falling softly to the dirty bearskin rug, where Finn McCool the poor old rheumatic mastiff sniffed and spurned them.

Entirely unabashed or surprised by such earthy phenomena Mrs. N. reached for the brocade bellpull with her elegant veined-ivory hand and when Martha appeared asked her for a basin.

In due course she came, one of the larger Meissen finger-bowls on a crocheted mat on a palekh tray, a large leaf of *Lippia citrio-dorus* floating on the kitcheny water.

Into this I carefully placed my remaining twenty-one pieces, picking up the fugitive two from the floor. They sank to the bottom leaving a visible scum of dog- and bear-hair, dust and bubbly saliva next the sweet-scented leaf.

This was fine.

'Don't forget to remind me to put those things in again when I am going,' I said, with the joy of speech regained, 'or the crockery-merchant will be very much upset.'

'Ah, my poor Melchi,' said Mrs. N. 'What dreadful things they do to us these days. And such cheap vulgar china too; not like the time of the Valentines whist-drive. Indeed No.'

But I left her to go on, knowing nothing of that party, if party it was, and picked up the Redouté from the floor where it had fallen, brushing off as best I could with the back of my cuff the pawmarks of the dog and my own shoe.

# 7

S o I left her to go on and soon I was with her though I had not
played this part before, but knew some of the cues and a line here
and there well enough. We were off again to Western Argyll, to
that cold sea-loch, facing, but cut off from, the distant Firth by its
fjord-like length; half fresh, half brackish water; burn-brown in
colour after heavy summer rain.

The trouble was the overlap. For a score of years I had lived
there too with dear Uncle Melchi and all our brood, and a gnaw-
ing premonition warned me that at any moment, certain sure,
we should once again (this time through the valiant person of
Melchi my nearest and dearest old Uncle) be discussing my infant,
childhood or adolescent self, a prospect that filled me with horror.

At the moment, however, all was serene.

We were enjoying the time of the water-paper-chase to Loch
Long and how I (Uncle Melchi) had smoked the tea-kettles by
lazily building too much dried seaweed into the fires (though of
course it did help to keep off those frightful midges) and then cut
my finger so badly while splitting and oatmealing the mackerel
we had caught on the way out that I had been unable to row on
the way home and poor Hetty had had to take an oar, which had
likely been the beginning of her angina; and that anyway by going
too far we were much too late with the children, although of
course they had loved the phosphorescence on the way back and
slept so soundly, mesmerized by watching the green-flamed drops
running from the momentarily uplifted oarblades until awakened
by that disgraceful caterwauling of '*A boat a boat unto the ferry*' and
that dreadful man Duffy (Was it Duffy? Such a name) reciting his
vulgar version of *Lord Ullin's Daughter*. And how Mother (Whose
mother? I rather apprehensively wondered) had made them all
sing '*Speed bonnie boat*' and '*The Noble Earl of Moray*' to cheer
them up and stop them whimpering and snivelling all the way
home.

Which reminded her, Indeed Yes, of that day of the sports at
the Osprey's Falls in Glen Mor (the little one) when it rained so

heavily that she thought we might as well shelter under the falls, and the drenching sacks in the sackrace with all its false starts had given the children the most frightful colds, as Mother (Whose mother?) had insisted that the girls put their skirts *outside* their sacks as it was *not decent otherwise* and too like boys; and of course Dr. Shearwater was no use at all and never prescribed anything but steamed tripe and two drops of laudanum on a lump of sugar at bed-time with senna-pod tea in the morning.

Which reminded her of course (Oh heavens, here it was, short-circuited) of how that disgraceful Nurse Pettigrew had given that poor child nothing but laudanum, gripe-water and gruel for years and years and no wonder he had grown up so weakly and eccentric and died so very young. Indeed No . . .

At this point I decided not to listen any longer for the child was myself and I thought I was alive.

Our single track thus split; *there* between hills and sea: she on her own one, me on mine.

Mrs. N. prattled on ironic or gay, histrionic or soothing, whilst I went in search of that 'disgraceful Nurse Pettigrew'.

'Indeed Yes,' said Mrs. N.; but I paid no more heed.

# 8

N o w the time we were living in was, you should know, the time of *Carrick Castle* and *Lord of the Isles*, and I loved them both with their multi-coloured ringed funnels: broad black top, thin white band, thin black band, another thin white, then glowing vermilion all the way down to the silvered gratings round their hot oily-engine-smelling base; and copper steam pipes with bell-flanged lips and nearby leaking brass-plated sirens, enlarged images of Uncle's silent dog-whistle; and the harper too, forward of this, with his green baize harp cover and white-topped harper-seaman's golden-braided bogus hat.

But what was the use of the long white pennant with its *Lord of the Isles* in red? You could never make it out except in bits unless an impossible hurricane were to blow it out straight or the old *Lord* speed at thirty wild knots, her haystack boilers tied down at the valve: which would kill her.

Every day at the same time, if the driving rain or the Scotch mist was not too obscuring, my nurse would hold me up in the little bow-window that looked west over the mile-wide everchanging water, south to the far seas and Carrick Hill, north to the pale northern sky, Drymnsynie, Ben Donich and the village itself; and far away I could see that puff of smoke and sometimes in a ray of watery sunlight the scarlet streak of funnel; and after a while, an endless while, I could hear, if the wind blew right and if I could disentangle the sound from the fevered beating of my heart, the distant paddle-wheel floats whacking the glassy water, creeping louder and louder, thumping, thumping.

Then she would be abreast right before me and if there was no wind and the windows were open, no rain and the panes were not dappled with drops and above all, rarity of rarities, the sun shone down brightly; then, oh then, not only could I see the magnificent creature in all her apocryphal glory, the sleek black hull reflecting the feather-curved white foaming bow-wave, the stupendous black and gold paddle-boxes vomiting occasionally torrents of white spurting foam through their fan-like vanes, the tall gay striped funnels belching long trails of soft smoke and the flags flying (though not nearly enough of them admittedly) from the jack at the bows to the always brand-new ensign at the peak of the crown-topped staff at the stern and the whole foamy green-edged straight wide wake, but I could hear, *hear* mind you, the wheezing snuffling engines themselves, their oscillating cylinders creaking and spluttering as (so I thought, but it may have been later I thought it) the odd drops of cool condensed moisture fell sizzling on the crouched straining crankshafts below.

Then, gorgeous phantom, she would slide silently out of sight behind Cora point with its orange-hued fresh-watered seaweed and at that moment blow a piercing blast on her brass-whistle-siren, echoing and re-echoing in the mountain walled room of the loch so that Ian the piermaster knew he should ready his gang-ways.

I would struggle and push and wave my arms and dribble a little on Nurse Pettigrew's clean apron (for it must have been she) and then begin to anticipate, terribly too soon, the reverse journey, funeral of all hopes for the day.

After a while, a long while, too long a while (and if I had the fortune once more to be held up) out slowly stern-first would come the fine steamer, everything back-to-front; the rudder, hard-a-starboard, cutting with apparent difficulty the dark metallic water under her pretty gilded counter, the sternstaff wrongly raked, the ensign entangled and dead in its halyards, the funnels askew, smoke blowing full on the fore-deck; the mast a mere parody; flags furled invisible; wake before bow; jack abaft stern.

By this time it was generally raining and a small knot of people stood disconsolately about under black-slug umbrellas close to the refuge companionways, unable to sit down on the now sodden seats. Astern, at a point between Mayburn and Witch Wood, she rang full-ahead.

Slowly, very slowly, churning the water behind her, gathering fractionally a poor half-speed, she repassed by the window, beating on to the south, her smoke curling after her twisted by the fresh north-west wind, on into the constant Carrick rainstorms, out of sight.

My day was over and I longed for the sugar. I whined like a dog and was soon given it.

Every day I was encouraged by this pageant and I think it very largely kept me alive. Each day, if I was conscious and well enough, even if it was raining, I saw her; each day, that is, except that most awful God-accursed day, His Sunday, supposedly blessed. On Sunday, as Scotland was then, no boat came: the buckram blinds were drawn half-way, and rain or shine their little wooden blindcorded tassels slapped rapped or pattered against the window-glass, their rhythm according to the wind.

I hated Sunday: no steamer: only a brief midday blind-veiled interval in navy-blue twilight; a change of clothes if wet: a little gruel, an enema and no more.

The twilit ritual took place nonetheless at just the same time as on weekdays. It was good for my digestion to form regular habits, if I had had anything to digest except laudanum and sugar, and for my bowels to move if there was anything to move them except soap.

On week-days I looked forward to it: it was my whole life. But on Sunday I loathed it, hated everything, tried to clench the gruel spoon between my ragged teeth and if possible pee on Nurse Pettigrew's uniform as high up as possible all the more to drench her. It was a real victory for me if she had to change every stitch.

One Sunday when I was gritting my teeth on the gruel spoon which N.P. had been trying to extract from my grip, my heart nearly stopped!

No! No! I thought, it cannot be so: and my heart was drowning it all anyhow . . . but Yes, Yes; surely, surely, sound was never lying: surely, surely, Yes, incredibly . . . *Paddlewheels, paddlewheels!*

Instantly I released the spoon, regurgitated the unwanted half-swallowed gruel and let out the loudest scream by far I had up till then ever managed. I struggled with my whole body, kicked the enema, kidney-bowl and all, off N.P.'s table onto the floor and flailing my arms in the general direction of the window, sat up.

N.P. had heard it too: I think she actually smiled a little: she obviously must have had some idea of my lusts.

In any case she took me up at once, walked to the window and noiselessly, for fear of my keen-eared grandmother, raised very slowly the southern-facing blind. And there, wonder of wonders, not far away, coming towards us up the loch, *was* a paddle steamer! But Oh such a sad one, a black one, a gloomy one—a real Sunday steamer I said to myself in what words I don't know.

The vessel came nearer: I could see her clearly now: black hull, black funnel with a narrow white band on it, brown cabins, no flags. A white paddle-box, stained, faded, ungilded; her only colour pale salmon boot-topping streaked with dun rust scratching the grey water: *a real Sunday steamer*, I said to myself.

Just as she came right in front of the window she began to turn on her churning axles and around she went and away into the constant Carrick rainstorm: a myth, a hoax, out of sight.

I never saw her again nor heard of her either until many years afterwards I picked up a book about old Clyde Steamers and, turning the pages, saw a very bad photograph that rang a distant bell.

The caption beneath said: *Falcon approaching Kirn*—so to Falcon I turned in the tabulated lists: and there she was:

'*Falcon:* Owners Hamilton Brothers, Glasgow. Built 1882 by Morlay Fife and Co. 430 gt. 215 x 25 x 8: upright boilers: engined by Parrikin and Sackmore: 140 I.H.P.: 14 k. Services: a popular steamer on the Inellan, Dunoon and Rothesay runs where she plied for many years before the First World War. Experimentally placed on a Sunday non-calling cruise in early August 1914, the first of its kind. Withdrawn on the outbreak of war and requisitioned by the Admiralty as a mine-sweeper. Mined and sunk off Chios 17/6/1916. . . .'

So now I knew all about it: knew that *Falcon* had been there.

I also knew that that day was the first Sunday in August 1914 and if I had had a calendar of that year, could have looked up the date. I also knew that I had known Nurse Pettigrew, as no one else had been there at that window to observe, and if they had been there would never have noted; and in any case she herself had been sacked and then jailed but a few days later.

# 9

'BUT what could you expect?' continued Mrs. N., 'with his father so addicted to the bottle and his mother so neurotic with her German glass eye. He was doomed from the start for he never had a chance. Was he buried with the others in St. Fintans . . . ?'

'Excuse me, Mrs. N.,' I said, getting up. 'I am afraid I must be off . . . Excuse me, I must go . . .' And I stuffed the crockery back as best I could into my freshly constricted mouth, only wishing I had a shoe-horn or a glove-stretcher to help me.

'Good-bye, dear Melchi. Do come again quite soon and we'll have a good talk . . . .'

But I was off.

The hairs made matters worse for they bound the crockery together in a most villainous cross-woven pile and although I skulked for ages behind a privet in the park I could only get them partly and roughly re-arranged in their proper several places.

So I hurried on, ripping the ribbon of my right trousers leg from the turnup to the knee as I did so. Bending down I tore the piece right off and flung it over the hedge; but it stuck on the top looking rather new, and I wondered if I should have it sown in (or was it on?) again if I could only get it down. But no time was left for such idle speculation: it could not be helped. As it was I was almost too late.

A tram clanged past at the end of the street: I had missed one already and must hurry the more or the merchant would be off to his succulent lunch.

Down the square then I scampered, past the pub with the red leather seats, and the masonite front of the fishmongers, round the corner by the mouse-scented cake-shop and stores.

In ten minutes, there I was, back to the front of the back, at the door with its great belt of bells and the right one: ping ping.

'Yes, very good. Just a little off here: the handle perhaps and that curiously jagged fracture. Must have been an impurity in the kaolin; and Oh Yes, just a shave off that round bottom so curiously and perfectly intact.'

'Ouart! AUort! Ought!'

'It's all right. Don't worry . . . That's it: press hard! . . . Yes, there we are; come back tomorrow at three and don't take them out on any account unless they are completely unbearable.'

'They're unbearable now,' I half-squeaked, half-screamed, rattling like a trap in the process.

'I know. I know. But the longer you bear it, the sooner the steak! Hah, hah! Good day now. It's lunchtime.'

So I walked out again and by now it was dark though I thought getting light. For I had been off somewhere else all this while in the interval although no one, nor myself, could tell me its whereabouts. And I do not know yet if I ever found out or am likely to do so; although some say I did and others I will . . .

It could be, in my opinion, I was there in that bus on the high Corniche road to the village above; or in Skerries the day the sea froze in slimy undulent sheets on the foreshore as the tide fell.

I must ask Mrs. N. if she knew or if she knows.


# 10

THEY had put the lights on. It was that village on the hill, Cabris I think: or was it Barnacullia so early?

Anyhow, it cost me a hundred and forty francs return, which inclined me to the former though the wind from the half open door was icy, inclining me to the latter.

The drone of a plane, a Viscount losing height, BEA or AF routed overhead, pinned me to the village; but No: it was one of those damned diesel-engined Dorniers returning from the north. But No again: the vile soft thuds I had taken for bombs were nothing but a *cageot* of carrots and two of scraggy netted fowl being dumped before the left-hand emergency exit, permanently blocked.

Thus I followed the edge of the solid sea wall and the tide was full for some spray flew shorewards to ease my bloated face: and soon, sure enough, we were rattling over the causeway by the estuary where fine-beaked mergansers and smews were often my only delight or the new bridge (was it?) just below that desperate stream gushing from the base of those iron-stained limestone cliffs, now yielding no drop.

No: of course it was that causeway at Rush, Donabate or Malahide and I should never have come home in that spring of thirty-nine . . . yet neither perhaps, but that wooden-roofed, wooden-paved bridge over the muddy Inn between Flintsbach and Auer associated by me always with bloodless and untrodden snow and Isar (at least a tributary) rolling rapidly.

But wherever it was made absolutely no difference: my ideas in the matter were not at my mercy: the wheels of the train on the iron causeway, the fact that I had slept much, little or never, soon settled me down far away or elsewhere.

# II

IT was long before Hitler and his doings and his epoch on a white dusty road north of Ljubljana in a high valley of the rocky Karawanken: she was dark and dark-skinned and very, very supple.

We were cycling along and the cycle-wheels were spinning: spinning in the sunlight, sifting through a paling, backwards for a fall, forwards for the outing. I was looking out for plants.

I did not look much or care where I was going, only to be with her, cycling in her shadow, and several times ran off the fenceless track to turn turtle and collapse laughing in the moist soft green meadows. I was delighted with the flora, the sun and mountain air; intoxicated with spring, the stolen day, her throbbing presence, my own desire and the many green-stemmed *chasha* of cool white bouqueted wine we had taken at Rastlanka.

We passed through sun and shadow like fleas hopping joyfully over a piebald circus pony's pelt.

In the valley below clocks in the onion-domed church towers chimed some time or other, meant nothing at all. It was morning, still fresh. As we toiled up the road our desire toiled with us; exquisite goad.

Distracted and delighted, eventually I went and collided with her in full flight, buzzard on the wing to his soft-feathered prey, and we came walloping down on the fine sandy road in a tumble of dust. I may have been looking at some primula on a rock but my eyes and my senses were anchored elsewhere; on the warm rippling muscles, on her taut sunbrown legs.

Not much harm done: handlebars twisted, mudguards askew,

an oily hanging chain, and our knees nicely sandpapered, red blood between us.

We collected our breath, dumped the bikes in a ditch, and set off down a path to find a clear pool to wash our grave wounds.

Through a small thicket to a rock-tumbled dip and there it was: perfect.

Deep and transparent, a few trout darting: concentric rings of sunlight expanding on its sparkling pebble bed.

Trembling we undressed as quickly as we could, tearing at our sweat-clinging garments, fumbling with their fastenings, revelling in the blood-hammering sight of each other as we did so, her still blue eyes swallowing mine, her released body encompassing me in its warm echoed embrace, each part of her to my part of me—and flung ourselves, soon swimming, into the icy cold water. We dried ourselves on ourselves and ourselves in the sun and made love closely with gay urgent passion, clutching at each minute and moment with the vice-grip of insisted arrested escaping time, there, on a great bed of gentians, so that for my love and myself all else was sky blue; and our eyes. Until finally we were chilly and hungry for food and we had to dress up to go on.

We came to a big inn hidden in a side-valley under full blooming chestnuts, tables and chairs set out in their dappled shade. There I saw a few hens which whetted my appetite for I love roasted fowl and adore fresh eggs. We tucked into a huge platter of rich golden scrambled with raw smoke-cured ham. A litre of Croatian hock washed it all down. Then we had glasses of apricot brandy. This was our meal.

It was much hotter now: noon was passing, critical axis at the turn of the day.

We set off to make the most, to lose the least, to keep part of it, still up the steep valley, the sun drawing rivulets of sweet sweat tickling down our ribs ready to be washed and loved off again, this time in a great cauldron foaming below a waterfall in full sun, a misted spectrum of sunsplit colour ephemerally dancing around her splayed swimming limbs and buoyant breasts, until I dragged her to the land, and the prickly grass and golden carline thistles added sensory grist to our roaring mill.

Over and over again we bathed that day: over and over again we swam, made love and kissed. And after each bathe our love was ever firmer, more vital, more serious, more desperate—obsessed. We held each other gripped more closely: at times there were times we had time by the throat: so we thought, but he always escaped us: so we thought, but no damn clocks were stopped.

We played in other pools: ran in many meadows: lay in other woods. Under pines, northern, sad-phallic, threatening: under hazels, cracking our nuts: under beeches, fangreen, sunwaving, the mast in their dried leaves distracting too much: under larches, lacy, sun-scented, rough rooted: beneath alders in deep shade: next oaks.

Then the dusk was upon us with its comrade sadness: layers of dead still scented wood-smoke straddled our path, and as it would by the calendar a great weeping moon, poking its face through the love-laden woods, consoled and confused us. Always there would be moons; always also lovers. But not us.

It was over, but caught and nailed down: it was over, safe stored in the head: it was over, inimitable, gone: it was over, filed in the cabinet, filed in that damned thrice-accursed metal cabinet, fire-proof, jemmy-safe, incorruptible, uncorrodable. Filed in that damned filing cabinet I had paid far too much for, filed for future reference if only I could open it when I had found the bloody key: and pinched my fingers in it: and kicked and hammered on it . . . much good that that would do me. If only I could hear myself above this dreadful racket . . . God damn it all to Hell, what on earth was going on?

# 12

THAT hateful clicking of wheels upon trackways, snuffling and coughing and many scraping feet?

It all smelt of cattle and public convenience in an ill-kept rain-soaked country market town . . .

So it was.

And so it was.

I was furious.

I've had enough of this, I thought, and remained firmly seated whilst the train emptied itself of its passengers to the last leg and ferrule.

They all disappeared, bustling or traipsing into the sooty maw of the soiled-glass station, right down to the end of platform number one where Mick the begrudger, safe in his cubicle, nodded at seasons and snatched at the others.

But I sat on: I much preferred the musty smell of the crude-grained upholstery, the dust, the dirt and purple NO SMOKING. The carriage was an old one with no corridor, the compartments separated by tongued-and-grooved wood; their only decoration a chapter of repetitive insults scratched or scribbled roughly by obscenely-minded orangemen, addressed for the most part to an Italian, the Pope; whilst the defenders of His Holiness, somewhat cramped in their style, could only beg the Almighty to forgive the first scratchers and sign themselves with swastikas in German: F—— the King.

Some enterprising character, supported on enthusiastic shoulders, had wildly pencilled on the curved, once whitish, ceiling, 'To Hell with Hitler. Down with Dublin. Up Kerry all the Time.' And lifting my cap figuratively (for I had not yet put it on) I could but agree with these noble sentiments; for moored as I was to the platform of Amiens Street railway station, I refused to get out, hated the house-painter heartily, and had very pleasant memories of Woodford Bourne's Brown Label in the Harp or O'Connels at Cahirciveen.

If I refused to step out, I leant and looked out, and was greatly dispirited by the doors of the carriages hanging listlessly open like the wings of dead birds used as scares. I decided at once that, retaining my ticket, I would wait for the train to take me away, I did not care whither. For I had come too early anyway and what should I do until far-away three?

There was dead silence: coal was very short, passengers very plentiful.

The war was on. Why should the railway company fritter away

its dividends? 'Time enough,' they said: and by Jove I was with them.

So I relaxed my head against the scratchy cushions and stared blankly across the circumscribed space between myself and the planking opposite. I then noticed that some biped creatures had taken the trouble to bore holes here and there between the boardings, no doubt to observe, *faute de mieux* (or the landscape) the antics of fellow travellers in the next box. The train was always very crowded or almost empty, having to fetch back commuters where it ditched them, and I supposed that at times there was excellent sport. There were holes everywhere; above the racks, below the seats; the latter big enough to admit a large cat and much draught.

I saw with delight how fanciful could be the views enjoyed from a handy embankment:

FIRST COMPARTMENT: No one at all, evidently: but in fact Jem the plumber prone on the floor, his eye jammed between the cold hot-pipes and the seat bottom, watching, in the SECOND COMPART-MENT, in semi-*flagrante* demi-*delicto*, some buttons open here and there (but not all, for they were protestants), Jill and Jack Hamilton having a ripping time together, watched also in the THIRD COMPARTMENT by Muriel Missie the convent schoolgirl, busy and schizophrenic in a two-front war watching Jack and Jill but afraid that the Rev. Fr. Candlestick in the FOURTH COMPARTMENT might take to watching *her*. In the FIFTH COMPARTMENT, seeing nothing from one hole but a pair of black clothed leg bottoms and from another a hairy red ear and a missal open at page twenty-seven, two young rampant rascals, their legs only visible from the rail-side, clung to the rack and watched in the SIXTH COMPARTMENT Philomena and Fanny, tentative crushers, show each other their new knickers from Cassidy's, suspenders from Geoghan's, bras from Beverley's and no doubt during the long run from Raheny to Portmarnock, trying them all on, whilst in the SEVENTH COM-PARTMENT, also agog with their mannequins' postures, knelt poor Colonel Smasher on the soiled soggy seat, his eye glued to an advantageous aperture: lost to the Black Watch, found by the Louth Hounds—as kennelman. In the EIGHTH COMPARTMENT . . .

but I was tired of the game and the couplings came anyhow for it was the end of the coach.

I was beginning to wonder why, at any rate, the train had not backed out to some sanitary siding, as the station was terminal and the engine just wasting its hiss between the buffers and the book-stall, when who should come along looking straight ahead but peering in sideways (no doubt on the lookout for losable lost-property or a dog-eared copy of the *Drogheda Independent*) but Mick the begrudger himself.

'What in the name of God are yez doing in there, sir? The thrain's in this long time an'll be off quite soon.'

'Where to?' I snapped, for I had been enjoying my solitude.

'To Balbriggan again, sir, but first to number three. Are yez all right, sir?' said he, sniffing rather pointedly, 'or can I give you a hand?'

'Never mind, Mick,' I said, 'I'm stone cold sober. But I have decided to stay here. I came in far too early. I'll try again later; maybe much later.'

'Have you got your ticket?' said he.

'I have,' I said, 'and I intend to keep it. For ages. It's a return and I needn't give it up until I pass a barrier, need I? Or only for inspection anyhow. I am staying here.'

'All right. Very well. Just as you wish, sir, just as you wish. But it's not allowed really you know, sir. I'm sure it isn't . . .'

'Look at this, Mick,' I said, producing my beige morsel of stiff cheap cardboard printed on one side with black names and a red R and on the other with all manner of disclaimers. 'Do you see this starry hole? Well, that's the ticket punch at home, you know, and there's no other on it and you're not going to get it and I am not going to pass out the barrier at home either: and you're very likely not going to get your clipper at it either. What time is she due back?'

'About two, sir: two-twelve, sir: after dinner.'

The talk of dinner worried me, for I was mighty thirsty and had an idea I might be hungry before two o'clock. I saw also that Mick was getting anxious and, unless I was careful, might go and fetch help. He clearly feared the worst for he knew me since childhood.

'Come here, Mick,' I softened, tendering a dollar, one horse and one head. 'It may seem very queer to you, but, believe me, I have no wish either now or later on any account to get out of this train. Unless I have to I am not going to step out on that platform,' I shouted, pointing between his feet (he looked down), 'unless I am stood on it: for the longer I stay here the less I'll be in Dublin.' I bellowed. 'But,' I said, softening again, 'it's only a question of food . . . and of drink, of course, too,' I concluded in a confidential whisper, 'and the opposite.'

Before he could regain his wits I brightened up suddenly and, producing a doubly identical offering in cash (but four horses this time), spoke out confidently:

'Listen to me, Mick. Please be so good as to go along to Miss Mixin in the station buffet and bring me back three stouts by the neck, three baby Powers, three ham sandwiches, two hard-boiled eggs, a slab of railway cake and some salt wrapped up in an *Irish Independent* or two. And something for yourself of course, Mick; something for yourself,' I grinningly ended. 'Not a word now, not a word, Mick,' and I placed a conspiring finger vertical to and alongside my nose.

He went off greatly puzzled, rather afraid we might get into trouble, but to my surprise was back before long carrying a large goatskin bag, bought by my mother the year she went blind from trachoma in Sidi-Okba, which I habitually used for such rations and borrowing books. I had left it in the buffet whilst passing by the counter (so Miss Mixin said) some days ago; and now it was just what I wanted. The fool had brought three *Independents* as well.

I placed the bag tenderly on the seat beside me.

'Tell me this, Mick,' I said, lowering my voice. 'Supposing I stayed in this train for a day or two, where would I go then?'

'My God, sir, are the guards on ye? Because if so I am having no truck with this at all. It's against the regulations, I am sure it is, and I have my wife and the kids to think of and Maureen as well; and long as I know ye, sir, I won't be taken up in a police-case, sir, indeed and I won't.'

But I knew about Maureen, and he knew that I knew.

'Ah, not at all,' I assured him. 'It's just like this: I don't want to go home and I can't stand Dublin nor any place between the two of them either or at all. So where better could I be than in this train or some other, suspended between the north and the south like a star in the sky and not touching this earth: like a homing pigeon with no home, twisting and twirling, like a peregrine. . . .' But I saw he was looking askance and alarmed so, curbing my eloquence, began once again:

'It's all right for you, Mick, don't you know it yourself? Don't you know what I mean? You are always in and out of them but I am not. Don't you see the rest and the peace of it, all sight and no contact? Doesn't a field look lovely racing by, with no work in it at all, the horses at the ploughing as easy there as wink? And that muddy boreen with the blue sky reflected clear in its endless oozing puddles, as tasty a track as you ever walked? And all the houses from here to the border just skipping by, everyone busy and happy singing in them? No roofs leaking or taps dripping or burnt griddle bread or henshit. And at night each glowing lighted window a lovers' warm haven to be sure! The sea still and blue and the birds undisturbed; curlews and oystercatchers wading and feeding, snipe in the marshes, swans on the inlets, cock in the woods; millions of pintail, tufters and teal grazing on the sea a stonesthrow from the windows, fistfuls of widgeon all over the place. Whisking over a bridge a glimpse of a cyclist: no notice at all he is wheeling a floursack. And those awful fruit-orchards, back-breaking to work in, flowery patterns curving and capering. Silent cars, people out walking, men in back-yards knocking for an entry and beautiful girls you can look full in the face they are so fast gone, very probably ugly. Don't they all look fine out of a train? Does not everything look fine out of a train? If it bores you, it's soon gone. If it's evidently lovely there's no time for disappointment until the way back when you've forgotten all about it. Who wouldn't live in a train? Any train! But this one particularly in view of my circumstances. Mick, I am going to live here. I shall need all your help!'

Allowing no pause for either of us to consider anything I went on like a fast goods, tendering a brown fiver:

'Here,' I said, 'buy what tickets you like. I leave it all to you. But only the odd one will surely be really necessary when old Mulcahy the punch-drunk travelling puncher has it looking like a wafer with all his triangles and no more reading-matter at all. . . . And, Mick, there's a good chap, do three other things for me: see at once that I am supplied with the following: Firstly: plenty of drink and the odd spot of food: pork-pies, calvesfeet, crawbeens, oxtails. That sort of thing. I dislike them all and if I cannot muster up enough hunger to eat them can at least have the satisfaction of flinging them out of the window into the estuary for the johnpike and mullet. Secondly: a list of all stations, their average time of halt, and the location of their accommodation for Gentlemen. Thirdly: the running schedule of this carriage'—I looked at the number on the door—'304D, for the next few weeks. Now, Mick, not a word: do you hear? If anyone should ask you where I am,' I added as an anxious afterthought, 'just say *I am on my way*. That's it: "He's on his way": "in the train on his way". On his *way* now, mind. No talk, if you please, of where to. Do you understand?'

'I do, sir. Yes. I do: but it's very irregular. With the housing shortage there is, wouldn't every train be full, sir, and overfull, if everyone did this?'

'Indeed, I cannot think why they are not. A most excellent idea: I must start a train-agency for them; "*TO LET: partly furnished period third-class compartment between Dunleer and Ardee. No modern conveniences aboard or en route. Low rent. Season arranged at reduced fee.*" Splendid. But in that case, Mick, I should at once get out: even there at your feet,' I pointed, he looked down, 'for I don't want any company at all at any price.'

'I see, sir, I see.' He ruminated and after a pause and a look at the fiver held lightly in his fist, which he then tightened, 'Well, all right, sir. Very well, but it's against the regulations. Oh Kay!'

So I undid the belt of my re-proofed oil-stained raincoat, put on my cap, re-tied my bootlaces, drank a baby Power and settled down *in situ*. There was no hurry now. Time enough. Plenty of time enough.

Then I thought of the crockery-monger anxiously awaiting

me, took out the brown paper sugar-bag from my pocket, placing it carefully in the rack above my head. There, I said to myself, it can stay there until I am ready for him; for it was increasingly obvious I had mistaken the day, or the week, or the month, or the year . . .

# 13

THE old creakers were moved, two engines puffing, one freed later, from number one to number three and I had my first views from my new residence. I saw the sidings and engine-sheds: a great tank of tar: Fisher's *Palm* from Newry: a pigeon fancier's back-yard: lettuce in another: the curve of the loopline: and cattle for the lairings on the North Wall driven dribbling and harassed on their way to their humane killers overseas at Birkenhead. I was delighted.

Every man's home is his very own castle and so he must make it! I quickly extracted a hack-saw blade I providentially had in my mackintosh pocket wrapped up in string, shallots and creased cards, and putting it down into the slot where the window rattles always on its sooty leather strap, in a few thousand tiring strokes severed the outside handle from the inside lock, so I could get out and not a one in. I should have to do the same job on the other handle for the up runs, I thought. But time enough now; I was safe.

I must confess I was overjoyed with the idea: address: somewhere between Dundalk and Dublin: but neither would find me. Of no fixed abode but never a vagrant. Resident in fact in carriage 304D: non-bogey, three axled, wooden; sometimes on sidings, sometimes on the loose . . .

To return to precision however, I wish to list here those honourable individuals who left or leave some impression of lasting affection, detestation or nothingness from these or those days of permanent quasi-elation. To me they were very important. They are now and they should be always, for they collaborated in allowing someone alive to be dead, someone dead to be alive and

I, this certain person, to escape from this earth for many long weeks. All power to them then: mark them down well.

Mrs. Annie Mahr, carriage-cleaner of 67 St. Joseph's Road, North Strand. Kind and courteous: never cleaned me at all. Mrs. Delia Wynn of Prague House, Aloysius Street, North Strand, Dublin: similar attention; and all their nieces and sisters on holidays: all the above maladvertently bombed by fate, subsequently grudgingly white-papered as possibly tired out Luftwaffe personnel: even more subsequently flooded by the Tolka which should have known better, being partially nurtured by drainage from the coffins of our national heroes in Glasnevin. Captain Nathaniel Gusk, R.N. Rtd., D.S.O., M.C., 'Mimosa', Arrolstown Road, Castleknock: Herr Friedrich Gutt, D.Ph., D.Sc., U.C.D. . . . but I see I have got to the wrong page of the directory and the kind of people who helped me were not in that category at all; insufficient influence, insufficient money, and no credit at all for the Dep. of P. & T.

To be precise with this list: the stationmasters, ticket-men and lamp-boys (all coinciding, all one and the same) of the following stations and halts: Clontarf, Killester, Raheny . . . to continue consult current or lapsed timetables for the Dublin–Dundalk section of the G.N.R. (Ireland).

The following footplate and firemen: of Tanks (2–4–2): 4, 6, 11, 22, 48, 72, 120, 121. Of tenders (0–6–0) all. Of Beyer-Peacocks (4–4–0) the whole lot.

And everyone and anyone that was ever any good.

As you see it was a large engagement: too large and too final in the follow up.

But I am grossly anticipating: I shall set it all down.

I am grossly anticipating, I shall show it all up.

# 14

TWENTY to seven on the morning of Monday, January twenty-fourth, nineteen forty-eight: that, as it happens, was the time. But it could just as well have been any other day, thereabouts, further away or nearer now.

And the place? A bus stop twenty-eight metres westwards from the Place Emile Rostand just outside the village of Saranon, Var. The square itself was in summer a favourite spot for *pétanque* and *boules*, those volcanically demonstrative games of the Midi, when the protective plane trees made a green leafy canopy and the shiny metal balls leapt spinning in the hot patterned dust. Now the leafless trees were festooned only with the strung-together golf-balls of their seeds, subsequently disintegrating germanely into wind-borne wisps of pale yellow fluff.

There were nine people waiting at the bus stop indicated by a no longer legible inscription on a short rusty metal pole. The nine had their backs to the roofs of the village down below.

Those roofs were old, lichened, earthen-hued, Roman-tiled, concealing. School and bakery, church and grocery seemed all of one age; part of the red soil, cut from the grey rock.

I was standing most miserably tired, confused and shivering at the side of this road, my face towards the mountain, my mouth full of pain. Although I was not speaking I was trying to think: of what I must do in that day stretched before me: in the day stretched in front up that road in the bus.

It was early.

It was early in that day which I am telling you about.

For the time and the place it was not a bad morning but it promised little. The sky looked dangerous; there was too much wind. Mistral was leaking in badly from north-west, Tramontana from the east. The sun was being frustrated by nasty looking strips of opaque cloud from hoisting itself out of the Corsican seas.

Ages we waited and ages it was, for this vehicle had contracted the bussy habit of sometimes arriving ten minutes too early, yet leaving invariably fifteen too late. As we waited the wind dropped, the air changed and relaxed; out of a pale yellow and dove grey, salmon-slashed south-east the sun struggled, agitated, swirling, but the conqueror.

I propped myself somehow on what was left of my legs and

supporting myself by clinging doggedly to the sleeves of my own old coat, settled down to enjoy the kind stillness. Snoozing or half-snoozing I rested an instant in a still pool of time.

Unawares, agonizingly, to my near complete undoing, a chaffinch spurted his song from the olives; this chromatic stuttering, maybe tuneless, certainly timeless, I could hardly endure. His cheep-cheep and cheep-cheep and its following abandoned torrent of pale glittering promise unbuttoned my heart, over-burdened my body and I sobbed, then I belched, very sadly that moment. I knew then that that day I would have the greatest difficulty in holding on or up or out. *All birds that don't sing make me hungry: all birds that do make me sad.*

He began again; and yet again, repeatedly.

Do you know how he goes? Do you know?

Like a pale twittering torrent; gentle yet a torrent; a little torrent with a great crescendo; a little torrent with a great fall as of pebbles rolling downwards, sideways, hesitating, over the bared strings of an open grand piano; various pebbles, rough and smooth ones; marbles and walnuts, oak-apples and acorns; and all small round things—rabbit-droppings, beads: from the treble downwards, from the heart inwards, from the mind upwards, heavenwards from the earth.

Listen to him!

The mute queue stood still in a body, ailing in mind. They did not hear the chaffinch: so much the better or worse. No chaffinch impact: no chaffinch undermining; no chaffinch heavenwards; *no chaffinch at all.*

Blind Jean with his white stick, who was also quite deaf, searching vainly for the steps of the anticipated bus to grope his way onto them; another day's treatment safely useless; another day over without Mr. Chaffinch; another day onwards towards his son's new war's blinding.

Young Meillan the plasterer, late for his time-punch, dithering in his carpet slippers, easier on the roof ridge; easier in winter on the canted wet tiles. There was always next Sunday.

As for the itinerant clock and wrist-watch seller, little did he care. His camel-haired overcoat was now all but paid for, his watch stock more than half pledged: two thousand down and the rest in easy payments. What was their time-telling or paying compared to his liver-time eaten by cancer, his too close companion? With any fair luck they would see him well down.

A pretty young honey-skinned girl with her unwanted dearly loved baby, adored him: hated him: asked for he who loved her to love him: hated him too. She should have smiled sad-bitterly, but unable to manage it, smiled. Carrying her treasure she readjusted the fine proud stance of her overstretched pelvis to the trigonometrical necessities of her wide-standing legs for his weight; and smiled again; to herself and the baby. Perhaps she had heard the chaffinch? I rather think she had.

Nothing could be helped.

Madame Artubis, always too late and ten minutes too early, arrived breathless and bursting twenty too soon, stuffing her over-eager duck's necks clumsily back into their efficient death-basket. It was all she ever asked for; there and back without them; money in their place.

Nothing could be helped.

Mademoiselle Viviane the typist was fed up: not because of anything but because of everything: the daily come and go. Her primping boss in his scented office, scented letters and scented machine; the constant stink of smartness and elegance and her own self smelling to high heaven too. Housewash before and housework after, always the same, rinse or dry; always the same, her mother and lover demanding, *demanding*, at the end of the day. Always the same type-twisted letters, always the same shallow flirt on the bus. Always the same each day and Sunday, the ride to the office or ride in the wood: coffee always grinding and her mother grumbling 'You should be content or no one ever could.'

Nothing could be helped.

It all added up to a life of repetition: repetition inevitable, sure of content, not con*tent*. It all added up to something quite miserable, deadly automatic, treadmilled, spent.

Perhaps it was the chaffinch? I am certain that it was . . .

Nothing could be helped.

Then there was the dark shadow: Vara Alsacescu formerly of

Cluj, a hideous creature in innumerable dimensions, no side of her mind or her body related to its kin, obscurely French-speaking, clearly German thinking. In her bedroom hung a framed photograph of the house they had built in Sibiu-Hermannstadt, a fine house with a fine big steep-angled snow-shedding roof, no glass in its windows yet, but a beribboned fir-tree tip tied to its gable-end and down before it all, facing the snapshooter, her husband, a crowd of gipsy fiddlers, taragatöists and 'cellists celebrating the great day with *Hora* and *Doina* and many a good downing. By God, the Fuehrer had soon seen to all that oily riff-raff, stripping them forthwith from the silver Banat Saxons: it was good to be at rest in much despised France where the people were lecherous, loving and lazy. She could ply here four-squarely her corrosive cartomancy, her cretinous mind and stale sweaty grip holding in thrall not a few of the stupider rentiers of the town and its suburbs, less power to them both.

Two other men were there, hunter and hunted, known one by their arms the other by their eyes: Mr. Early-to-Rise and No-where-to-lie-Down stood uneasily together thawing in the sun.

And myself.

And myself and the chaffinch and very much more . . .

The whole ridge of the hill, the oaks and the olives.

The oaks and the olives and the still pale sun.

The still pale sun, the chaffinch, a wren, a blackcap and a chiff-chaff.

The still pale sun on the green soft grass; blue morning woodsmoke; old ochre houses.

The still pale sun on the rich red earth and grey-silver artichokes as classic as Acanthus.

The still pale sun standing guardian to the morning, to the crowing of bantams, coo-cooing of pigeons, dead standing stalks of last year's sweet corn.

And the chaffinch again.

And the bus.

The bus: homely, inhabitable, usual, its kindly smoking driver bidding us good-day; a wild rush canalized and curbed.

In we stumbled.

Then up the hairpins, twisting and turning, the strengthened sun now blazing in to left, then right. Zigzagging, I sneeze, the dazzle of it catching me.

Up we go, gears grinding venomously; up the great hill to Cabris, above cited.

The journey is on, all journeys are on; I've been there often and I'll tell you all about it.

It's a grand fine journey; and all of it, each time, new.

As all journeys should be.

As this one was too . . .

The sky was a link, my body a bone: of contention to gnaw at or bury like a dog.

And all the world's others both near and so distant, omnipresent, tender, lonely, dastardly . . .

There were multitudes with me during these and other journeys.

I carried my companions.

I was never alone.

# 15

I HAD managed the change over and was deeper in that day.

I sat close to the window with my head resting on the cool trembling glass.

Outside I saw the café begin to move and people standing uncertainly on the brink of their work.

I saw the sun glinting on the sea.

I saw the fine rich plain below.

I saw the tumbled blue mountains and a blue curve of bay.

I looked hard at reality and it simply was not there.

I looked hard at reality and it was not there that day.

Or maybe ever.

Yes, there were houses.

Yes, people waiting.

I looked hard at reality and it was not there.

And the train had started.

# 16

TRAIN or bus, for a week or day only; whichever it was, it was well to be off.

These three-cyclindered jobs were comparatively even, but they pulled you all the same at the start-up with their crankheads, rattling over the points as we tackled the rail section leading off to the docks by the muddy canal with its three-island black-funnelled *Palm*, my crockery jangling in its brown paper bag on the sooty net rack.

One of these days I must keep my appointment: return to him with apologies but most certainly, I thought, and to Mrs. N., too.

But meanwhile I thought I was free.

For some reason the prospect now pleased me far less—this endless to-and-fro up and down familiar rails.

There was, to begin with, little or no advantage in being off the earth in this ambulant *pied-à-terre* unless I used my favoured fortune to look out of it, look into it, or both.

I looked out.

We were joggling past the slob.

To the east the tide was full out; seven soiled swans stood incongruously regal in a rivulet carved by a drain in the crapulous mud, their bright orange beaks dipping and guzzling in the brackish slime, their leathery black feet finding stance amongst the rusted cans: only Mutes, no Bewicks yet. Here and there an ignorant fool of a wader probed with long beak for lug or lamprey, his companions long flown to the Bull or beyond.

Three clouds of dust carried on the sharp south-west wind: from the silo, the fertilizer factory and the East Wall dump, smelling each according to their ability, maybe need.

Far away towards Dollymount the sailing club dinghies lay scattered on their sides, masts slanting this way and that as the ebb tide had left them; pale sunlight leaked through the clouds, glinting on wet patches.

Westwards over the damp grey-green wilderness of Fairview Park, its trees all of an awkward age struggling with the wind and the trunk-twisting children, I could see the trams, old favourites these and still inviting, to Blackbanks and Howth and the freshest herrings for tea: a small remnant of Victorian housing; a rash of developing development; the crazy-tilted asbestos roof of the new flashy cinema; and Edge's, the edge, as it always was for me, of the town. For when I was a child the town ended there and I thought the brave merchant had named himself appositely because of it.

I looked again east, as the train crossed the road, with its silent impersonal traffic concerning me no longer except as an image, at the backs of depressing hauntingly respectable suburban houses and their miserable pampas-grassed gardens, a small clear stream surprisingly confined and incongruously winding amongst them from the fresh greens of the nearby golf-course to the ooze of the adjacent polluted sea.

Clontarf station and Garry's place: many things with it. I was nearly off with them all to Kerry; off from this refuge of train or any bus. I was hesitating here and halted there at the point we were at but would never quite reach. I was just about off, was just taking flight; but before I could fly it was flown for me.

# 17

I SAW a fine cock-pheasant and this fellow stopped me.

He was strutting on the headland of a stubble-field to the west as it rose in parabola, the windowed shadow of the train sliding over it.

This exquisite Chinese fowl delighted me.

He flew off to a thicket, and I flew in him.

I could hear our sharp call and the battering whirr of our fresh-startled wings. I flew in him through hazel and through fronded sapling ash, my eyes his eyes, ringed with scarlet, glimpsing along my opalescent green head the nutty sharpness of my arrowed beak, gliding on stiff silent wings to Duffy's field over the hill's edge where my speckled hen sat, clear to me only, on our coffee-brown eggs, warm, rounded and polished, hatching our errant chicks in the tall half-withered, some sprouting, grass; last year's dead leaves in this year's leaf-shadows.

But suddenly I saw crouched behind some thorn bushes a man with his gun following my flight. The poacher fired; I fell back into my seat.

I collapsed into myself, cannibal that I was! Hunger for roast pheasant—Cannibal that I am!

I reached for Mick's sandwiches to quell my shame at once.

*All birds that don't sing make me hungry: all birds that do make me sad.*

# 18

THE train had run on.

Through the close eastern wood the sun flashed in snatched intervals, an up train doubling with its syncopated counter-point. A dozen blurred creatures, upright in their carriages, swept by at our fast combined, low separate, speeds. Taut phone wires were plunging, not taut at all.

So we came to Burrow Hill and bridge seventeen.

Burrow Hill, grey and flaking as always; it never seemed to have had a fresh coat of paint, nor ever properly to have lost its last one applied when the Boer War was the Big War, then.

I breathed it and its tennis parties twenty years over: one quite particular, one out of them all——

One of those awful tennis parties. Does any one really, *did* anyone ever really like them?

Tennis? I suppose so.

Parties? Of course.

But tennis parties! Surely, oh surely, I hoped . . . ?

My hoping was nonsense.

We both hated tennis parties, their attenders and all that went with them: but we had to go.

It was done.

It was not done to do what was not done.

We had to go.

We had to go but we tried to undo it whenever we could and to find an escape.

Besides which we liked other things very much; painting (door and canvas), and gardening and walking, and swimming in that cold grey sea. We were children though—thought of as children—and need not be watched so very closely yet.

So we made our damp hay whilst the sun palely shone and were glad of it.

Our escapes needed fine acting, careful managing. They could always be suspected but never, *never* known. No matter whether we were partners or opponents the essential was subtly but surely to sabotage the set, to make everyone apologetically beg us to stop and never dream of asking us to play with them again that day at least. It meant carefully botched shots and services: 'sorry partners' in bucketfuls, deliberate, infuriating: slips, slides, 'nets', 'outs' and the occasional well tried wild one that sent the ball flying out over the wall down the bank onto the railway where the 'children' were not allowed to retrieve it since the day Mrs. Huke's spaniel had been mangled to bits by the four p.m. down whilst heroically fulfilling this very duty.

So we were most *frightfully* apologetic, most *frightfully* sorry and after some while they had all had enough of us and a new box of balls was produced for our followers.

Now was our chance: we disappeared separately at well spaced intervals, she housewards (ostensibly to help with the tea), I round the corner of the laurustinus hedge (ostensibly to relieve myself, which I did).

We had tons of time now. After another few sets there would be tea and chat, followed inexorably by chat and tea; whiskey for the gentlemen, sherry for the ladies, lemonade for the rest.

We always used to meet in the big walled garden (I could see one of its walls that very moment along the top of the cutting) either near the derelict frames where in its season the gorgeous yellow grey-leaved garlands of *Tropaeolum polyphyllum* trailed in unusual and riotous profusion or, later on, by the tumbling down greenhouse with its ingrained emanation of green-mouldy flowerpots and (if there were any that year) luscious odour of warm ripening peaches quickly being devoured by hordes of vicious wasps. They always went together: with the plum crop too . . .

Delighted with ourselves and in the highest spirits we were lazily laughing, doting on our tactics:

'Really, you know, you are knocking rather too many out, aren't you? They are expensive and I doubt if they can afford them.'

'Never mind about *them*, let's hope they cannot afford *us*—and the sooner the better!'

We roared and rocked with our silly drowning laughter.

She was looking so gay and fresh, flushed and bubbling with life. Only recently we had become conscious of seeing each other thus; of seeing each other at all this way. We started on our usual garden streel, always a very great delight to us; for there were many fine specimens of rare shrubs and plants we had grown up with and learnt to love under the insistent instruction and repeatedly imparted scientific hammering of our mothers' botanically esoteric learning. It was something we treasured secretly between us.

There was an enormous *Sophora tetraptera*, a regular tree of *Chimonanthus fragrans* fully forty feet high with a great bulbous base, splendid Paulownias and Judas trees strung with *Clematis macropetala*. There was a great *Gingko* which had sown itself in several places on the top of the half crumbled wall and in warm corners at their right time rare species of South African gladioli, nerines, acidanthera, cypellas, zephyranthes and, most exciting of all, a small patch of *Tecophilea*, the Chilean blue crocus.

I do not remember if that day we discussed or admired any of these, or whether or not they were in bud, leaf or seed; but I do know that our hearts were not in it or with them and that our rather high-falutin' botanical chatter became less and less important until it ceased altogether. We found we were holding hands and though we had often walked thus, now a heightened tremor threaded through our finger-tips like the feel of a telephone pole in a high fresh wind. Our voices lowered slowly, softening towards conspiracy.

When we came to the corner under the hanging cloak of ivy we faced each other and knew. Knew that moment of that very day. We had kissed here before and we kissed here again—tentatively: a stuttering recognition from and by our lips. Fire burnt in us as fires are thus kindled. I laid my hand on her blouse, on her pulsing young body and she liked being touched and shivered at my touching. We were both of us trembling, trying to look deeply into the mirrors of our eyes, first one, then another; for alas, we soon found, you cannot look in both.

'Let's go to the paddock,' I said.

The paddock, cut off from the rest of the garden, was entered through a once-green door in the high old red-brick wall. It was overplanted with fruit-trees, mostly pears, and several hives of bees buzzed there productively on warm days. As if by pre-arrangement (though we never had been in there together before) we walked over to the corner furthest from the hives where, beneath a huge fig-tree trained against the wall, we were sheltered and close. The grass was rather coarse and long, and a few rag-weeds grew here and there, but there was room for us too. We were wrapped up safe. We were all-feeling.

We were just going to plump down on the grass when I realized we should ruin our fairly immaculate tennis clothes and find it hard later on to account for their staining.

'Celia,' I said, ' what about our whites? We'll ruin them, damn them anyhow. You know how the grass always greens them.'

'Let's take them off then! Why not? No one'll bother us here. Come on!' she replied, commencing to unfasten her skirt at the side.

I was filled with excitement but at the same time a curious anxeity, a new shyness, began to bother me. It is easier, so I thought, for a girl to take off her skirt than a boy his trousers; shirt-tails are so very unreliable a covering as you know at the strand; if only I was wearing underpants, that would make it easier.

But Celia went right ahead—easier for her though—stepped out of her skirt, folded it, put it aside and stood there unabashed in her neat cotton knickers.

'It's all very well for you, Celia, *I* have no pants on!'

She laughed most mischievously.

'All the better then. Come on, hurry up, can't you?'

'I will not. I won't unless you do it, too. Why should I?' I found myself bargaining as once I did at school. 'And what about your blouse anyhow?' I drove my lead home.

'All right. Let's take everything off. It's fun, Oh what fun! Just think of those old fogeys. If they saw us they'd have a fit, wouldn't they? And a good thing, too. I'd love to shock the wits out of them if they had any to shock. Come on!'

She unbuttoned her blouse and threw it from her, kicking off her knickers to follow it. There she stood, bewildering and blurring me, naked and so white in the sunshine, smiling and natural.

There was nothing I could do but lamely to imitate her, and I covered up my nakedness by catching her in my arms and holding here there pressed very near to me. That way I felt safer than standing in round air: but that way too, soon, my head was gone dancing, my body was leaping.

Afterwards we were lying beside each other on the rather prickly grass; we knew each other better now and there was great peace between us. We did not notice time passing nor the sun wheeling but whispered to each other lost and drugged in the pearly shell of our love. . . .

Abruptly doom struck: struck with Colonel Feather's outraged spluttering voice . . . (How long had he been peeping at us? I wondered long afterwards):

'Celia! . . . Desmond! . . . DIS . . . DISGRACEFUL!' he half choked, half roared through his apoplectic gills. 'I . . . I . . . GET DRESSED AT ONCE!'

We leapt miserably, and oh so very nakedly now, to our feet. Colonel Feathers made a wild swipe at me with his shooting-stick, luckily missing me by its vicious point's length. Beside him stood gallant Mrs. Huke.

'We came in here to have a look at the bees . . . and *this* is what we find!' he rampaged. '*Dis*graceful . . . outrageous, MONSTROUS!' Then maudlin, 'Oh my God! . . . your poor dear mother. My God, if she knew; if she *knew* she would turn . . . and as for you, sir,' he flared (Celia was fairly well dressed up by now), 'as for

45

you: get out of this house, I mean place, and don't let me ever hear of you again. I'll have you run out of the country. Get out of my sight this instant. *Disgraceful.*' He was purple and cruel.

We stole a hurried timid longing look at each other, Celia and I. Tears stood welling in our eyes; our smiles were gone; our laughing throttled.

I never saw her again. That night they sent her to a convent down the country where her mother's sister was Mother Superior. Some years later, when the big war had started, she escaped to the North, enlisted in one of the women's services and was killed in an air raid on Belfast. No doubt while doing her duty . . . like the dog.

# 19

THE train had rattled further.

I was glad to have moved on from the ribbon of that wall, out of the cutting onto its consequent high-flown embankment; clear away in the brightening sun.

Eastwards amidst various tillage stood wind-blown salt-ravaged beech trees, beyond them the tip of the Bull, Shielmartin and the long narrow ribbon of the blue bay itself over white sand. On the blue ribbon, headed for the Poolbeg, part cargo from Halifax N.S., sailed the half-laden cargo ship *Inishowen Head*, whilst at the other limit, leftwards, *Hopper Number Eight* of the Dublin Port and Docks Board rounding Red Rock, was bound beyond Baily, there to spew her Liffey mud safe in deep water, a great widening circle of stuffy brown in the bottle green seething open sea.

The rash of bungalows, spreading from the defacing tram-chimney at Sutton, had not then crawled over the alluvial fields, and seagulls were wheeling by late ploughing, early landing. Kilbarrack and Blackbanks were alone with their widgeon and pintail; and shelduck waddled near their burrows in the bank.

Inland were farms dominated by huge red-painted iron Dutch barns as ugly and out of place as they were large and useful. No hint of functional beauty here or near it; for Fingal loves all things hideous; cement its favourite colour; cement Institutions its favourite consolation.

Second grade bullocks, their haunches matted with dried dung, grazed apprehensively, raising their heads as the scudding smoke of my engine shadowed them, whilst further inland stood their long whitewashed stalling, and their owners' farmhouses where life, long partially atrophied, was now carried on in the eternal triangle of cattle market, bank account and church.

A few displaced small dwellings, plucked long ago from safe Edwardian suburbia, sat sadly in obscure, now tarred, boreens, protected by privet, monkey-puzzles and laurels from life and the landscape; occupied precariously by failed turf-accountants, retired gombeen-men and poor old ailing priests; whilst the last loved homes of the moribund gentry stood neither spick nor span in their forsythia and fust.

Now I could see the white gables of the old house peeping from the line-engraved tree-shapes of my mind, its bulging lime-stone walls now as then (walls and mind too) evidently in imminent danger of collapse; still surprisingly upright.

The tall feather-tipped deodar waved over the sycamores and the rigid pinsapo, so useful a basis for the little crosses my mother used to make for Evans's blighted children, concealing, no doubt as usual, the lazybones nest of many a fat pigeon. Over the garden walls many shrubs, now trees, flaunted their flowers and multi-coloured leaves.

# 20

As we crossed the narrow roadway and the flounder-bearing Maine I saw the piled concrete of the grandstand on the racecourse and remembered once more bitterly how I had earned my 'big money'—the shame of it racing to keep pace with my pride.

It is not a pleasant story. I retell it with reluctance.

I have always hated horses except as steaks in that stuffy little restaurant off the rue Vaugirard; fresh and succulent they are there and then from the neighbouring slaughter.

47

And it was not my fault if I was given a new airgun for my tenth or twelfth birthday. I did not ask for it. I always disliked firearms, being a rotten shot.

I could not hit the provided target, kept missing also the telephone insulators, and after a while the odd shot at my mother's tin wheelbarrow, posted near her as she knelt gardening, bored me and scared her.

I was far too fond of birds to want to persecute them, although I daresay if I had known then how to pluck and draw a fowl I should have been tempted to pot one and roast it over a fire in the end backfields; anyhow I was afraid of the feathers giving me away, as foxes were few and the fowl often counted.

I was on the best of terms with our cattle and on no account would frighten them, and the poor old donkey had enough to put up with as it was. What more natural for me then than to turn, *faute de mieux*, to horse-shooting?

I felt I would get my own just a little back on these beasts I disliked so much, and indirectly on those who liked riding them. I thought of the miserable chatting meets of the Fingal Harriers and the Ward Union Stags, of the side-saddled harridans on their great fat cobs, the nice young girls jodhpurred on their nasty pretty ponies, the masters and whips astride their great hacks.

They hunted hares or stags: *I* would hunt horses.

So I took myself off down the back fields below Kelly's bottoms where on Sundays and Saints' days draught horses and ponies were put out to graze, and found little difficulty, given close enough range, in peppering their backsides with slug after slug.

I don't think it did them any harm; but it goaded them into action so that they began to gallop round the big field in an unruly bunch, finally, to my delight, leaping the hedge into Burnham's spring wheat.

I returned home well satisfied with this new sport, determined to perfect it as opportunity offered.

A few Sundays later I was caught in the act.

My Heaven, how they flayed me! With ashplants handy from the ditch! Merrigan, and LeFanu too, whilst Norbert looked on or held me at their mercy. They confiscated my gun (for which I was thankful) and said they would tell both my father and the guards (which frightened me badly).

Then they went off leaving me miserable and shaken.

How on earth was I going to explain these vile antics? To my father? To the guards? I was horrified at the prospect indeed.

I watched them departing across the wide, cropped, wind-blown grass but it was not very long before they stopped, evidently arguing my fate, handling the gun and glancing back in my direction.

I felt trapped. A sprinkling of larks sang loudly in the wide sky.

They started to make back for me, and I decided to make a bolt for it through O'Neill's ditch for the Flemings who I thought might protect me, when what did I hear but one of them shouting:

'Come here now! Come here! We's are not going to harm ye. Come back here now, come back!'

I stopped as if frozen by a ferret.

They approached me, smiling nastily.

'How would ye like to be out away in that reformatory beyant in Glencree?' leered Merrigan.

'And get twelve good strokes of the birch or the cat?' snuffled LeFanu.

'Or be put in a right proper jail all your life?' added Norbert. 'You will be if we tell on you, you know that, don't ye?'

It was final, I thought: there is nothing I can do. In a land of horse-worshippers I was an outcast, a pariah: a horseshooter in horseheaven!

I began to weep.

'Ah, don't do that, Master Desmond,' said Norbert, 'don't do that; sure we mean you no harm at all at all, do we, men? Only— lookit here—You tell him, Peadar man.'

'Well, now lookit, it's like this,' piped up LeFanu. 'If you's'll do what we's want you to do for us, maybe we won't say e'er a word at all—will we, Matt?'

'Indeed that's so: that's the very way: that's the way all right: that's a good lad. Now listen.'

And they began to propound the most fearful plot that filled me with horror, excitement and shame; revolting me on the one hand, on the other, alas, fitting rather closely to my scarcely latent feelings.

When they gave me back my gun and a shining half-crown and promised to tell no one of my exploits and further to reward me if I did my job well, I agreed half willingly, partly resistant, to their plans, and rubbing my badly bruised buttocks very gently went home and into the house by the side garden-door. When I looked at myself in my mother's long mirror I saw I was bruised black and blue. I went to bed and lying on my front, fell asleep. I had nightmares and woke often.

Three weeks later, suffocating with a mixture of excitement and apprehension I waited sleepless in my bed until two o'clock at night when my mother and father had at long last stopped blowing the damp wood fire with our huge old creaking bellows.

Then I got up, and, dressing quickly and as warmly as I could, crept downstairs with my airgun in one hand, my boots in the other, and out by the back door into the yard, where I put them on. I cut across the front lawn and fields to the Bridge o' Maine road, out through Finn's iron gate and along the river's edge to the railway (just there, where I am looking, was the spot) where Matt and Peadar were waiting for me as arranged.

They gave me my final instructions. We had already rehearsed the whole business in detail again and again, but not, so to speak, in the field. Now all this theory was being forced into practice and I felt like a daring criminal. Little did I realize that in fact I was one, even if by now far more frightened than daring.

We crossed the railway under bridge twenty-two, then the fields to the eastward and finally the Maine itself at a place called the flounder-leap, which brought us right up to the back of the racecourse.

It was still quite dark when we reached the arranged spot: a small group of gorse bushes near the inner rails inside the great oval of the track.

Very rarely spectators came here: it was fully five furlongs from the winning post; just nice, said LeFanu, the field would be likely spread out.

I had to crawl into and under the largest thickest gorse bush: it was very prickly inside but there was quite good shelter from the cold night breeze off the sea, and the boyos had stocked up quite well for me: sandwiches, hard-boiled eggs, chocolate, sweets, fruit, seven copies of *Tiger Tim's Weekly*, a bottle of milk and another of old Tawny Port, if I was cold: it was to be a long, long wait.

The first race was at one-thirty, and I had to note all this on a bit of paper which I was to destroy later on, or in an emergency.

FIRST RACE: Blue and maroon, maroon cap. Gold and green, green cap with gold peak: blue, cut red, red and blue cap: purple and orange, orange halved cap.

SECOND RACE: Scarlet and yellow, yellow cap: green, blue sleeves, striped cap—and so on, and so on.

To each race its colours.

Not the horses' but the jockeys'.

Not the jockeys but the horses: I was to be sure it was the horses, as many as I could, low down, anywhere. For God's sake keep it down, right down. *No* jockeys, mind: the surgeon would find it.

They had worked out some complicated arrangements themselves with their tic-tacs and cronies, they said, and were sure to make thousands out of it one way or another; but this was only by way of an experiment for it was difficult to anticipate the reactions to my slugs. They might speed the steeds on, seriously slow them down, or turn them off the track altogether in the end up.

A multiple gamble with heavy odds on their side, that was the long and the short of it; and next time—next time, having carefully weighed the matter—there would be no limits altogether, we should all be worth thousands and thousands. Meanwhile a fiver for the best I could do: otherwise a good hiding.

They said they would come back for me well after dark, the next dark: not to move a single inch meanwhile; and good luck to me also; and went off.

I felt as lonely as adrift on the ocean, and the wind made a queer little cricking noise in the dead underside of the thorns of the gorse bush as of goldfinches crunching thistleseed in still isolation on a remote sunny day. But the darkness was abominably complete, only the faint glowing reflection of the city in its late deadly hours and the revolving reflected flashes of Poolbeg and Baily could be seen even when my eyes were well used to the night. The isolation and opacity exaggerated all senses: I thought I smelt the warm homely breath of a grazing milch cow, heard the thin grass-padding feet of late-night feeding birds, turnstones or oyster-catchers maybe, the seashore being too hard for them. I thought I saw a black-winged Pegasus, black and after me, gobbling what was left of the stars in a cloud-gap, a shower of them falling like sparks at a smithy from his voracious silent-champing teeth, and a fleet, long unsailing, of dark furtive luggers threading the channel from Baldoyle to the Eye. I thought I felt, crawling beneath my stomach, an army of ants, or small hard-cased beetles, pursuing their inevitable or inherited route, attending their dead, burying their new born. And inspectors galore, of course, whip-swishing, efficient, probing the race-course for me and the rabbits who had scuffled little holes in the sacred sandy turf.

When the breeze rose a little it howled miniature terror in the prickly rigid branches of the thick standing furze.

The sea, heard in a shell, poured out and engulfed me.

The soft rising squall menaced with great rollers.

Though not cold, I was cold: not trembling, I trembled fearfully.

It was not yet false dawn nor yet the last darkness.

I lay there paralysed in paralysed time itself.

I hardly thought I could miss them not ten yards from me: there, there beyond the tape of paler railing. But the whole situation confused and infested me with worry as indeed it well might.

My grandmother had once cautioned me to beware of sharp needles: if they stuck in you they entered the conduits of your veins, creeping maliciously along them until they pierced your very heart. So it was with these horses, these slugs, the whole thing of it; surely it would pierce me; surely I was done for; whichever way I turned the whorl of horror had me. Whatever way I fired, I fired at myself.

At last it began to lighten: the miserable dawn, unable to make a proper entry in the east, infiltrated the four corners of the compass with water-sodden grey. So I started on *Tiger Tims*.

But I happened on a story, lavish in coloured detail, about a young crook caught red-handed who was duly, frightfully and very justly punished, and my morale, which I had thought had already reached rock-bottom, took a further great plunge to geological strata I had not hitherto conceived of as existing; very hard, merciless grey damp stone.

I had great difficulty in relieving myself in this cramped recumbent position but somehow I managed it, setting myself apart from my own pitiful excreta, all the time frightened of shaking the bush now that I had waited until daylight of a sort. The sun struggled up finally and the course was at last and truly inspected. I was convinced they would certainly find me lying there, I could see and hear the stewards so clearly. I crumpled up the instructions, stuffing them into my mouth ready to swallow, rehearsed the stupid story about poaching lapwings; but they did not see me, scarcely expecting to find a young horseshooter at this time or place. I ate some sandwiches and drank half the milk, straightening out the saliva-wet instructions as best I could with the side of my hand on the smooth paper back of a bar of milk chocolate.

The morning improved: a filtered warmth began to penetrate the south-easterly side of my spiny hideout. Larks were at it hard, and stonechats knocked pebbles endlessly together, one a foot above my head. I read the pictures of *Further Adventures of Sindbad*. The time, the terrible time, was now at least passing; by my pocket Ingersoll it was twenty to one . . . ONE! . . .

Each minute dragged now horribly. My courage, or such little of it as had flowed back into me during the last sunny hours, was fast and furiously ebbing. I thought I would just get up and run out and mix with the crowd, but then I remembered the threats of what they would do if I deserted my post, and my fear of the reformatory and cat were far greater than my present funk: they kept me where I was.

At last I could stand it no longer—I turned, somewhat hopelessly, to the port, took out the ready loosened cork and gulped a great swig, then another. In a few minutes I was glowing, purposeful, certain—a conqueror, if a Dutch one. It was my first real comfort taken from a bottle since the laudanum and by no means the last.

I could hear the distant wind-interrupted murmuring of the race crowd assembling: the hum and hoot of cabs and other traffic, all mercifully fairly removed from my lair. They had been right in choosing this part of the course for my lurking ambush; no spectators came anywhere near. The expectant buzz of the crowd grew louder and raised itself in tone and I thought I could hear away behind me the horses getting ready at the starting gates, the odd hoof and whinny. How I hated those brutes!

'They're off!'

The idiot cry transfixed me.

I clasped my air gun, loaded it and put a dozen more slugs carefully by my right hand on a smoothed-out sweet paper.

They came thundering. Thundering. I could feel the ground shaking with their hoofbeats beneath me, nearer, nearer . . . Terribly and absurdly there splashed into my mind lines once learnt then forgotten: *quadrupedante putrem sonitu quatit ungula campum.*

They were before me.

Their twin colours flashed.

I fired and fired: low: low down: all the slugs; the sharp little phut of my gun drowned in the torrent of horse-hooves resounding. They were gone. They had passed.

I breathed in the air, the sweet air, again.

But not for long; scarcely three or four breaths. For now that air was distantly buzzing with cheering and shouting, catcalls, booing and high-pitched whistling. It all sounded very dangerous to me there in that gorse bush. I knew nothing of horseracing, nothing at all, for this was the first one I had ever attended; I knew nothing at all but wanted to know less, rapidly, permanently, just as soon as I could . . .

I do not know yet how I managed that day. It turned out one of those half-and-half summer-promisers with scuds of cirrus gallivanting in a pale cool sun; I was practically crazed with anxiety and port. From then on, for the next race, all the races, I blazed away as best I could; all the instructions and all the fine jockey colours spun in an imperfect disc to a cool blurred neutral grey. Several times I wished I held in my trembling hands that old dusty German hand-grenade that stood on the chimneypiece at home converted to a never-used ashtray: but loaded: loaded and all and just ready; the pin seized in my chattering teeth—to throw at the next lot and be done with it for good.

I must have fallen asleep in the end for when I awoke it was dark and rain was dropping rhythmically, strained through my furze-needle canopy onto the nape of my neck. There was still some port and varied sodden wrapped articles left.

I consumed everything.

I felt sick, had a violent headache and was very inclined to cry. Which in the end I did.

I was sodden with self-pity, rain, and very real despair when at last they showed up well the worse for booze themselves in so far as I could take in anything.

'Well, the grand boy! The grand boy himself! Come out, master, come along out now. You're the great boyo altogether, come on along out.'

But I could not move at all; so they dragged me out and stood me up.

'Isn't the poor child dead with the cold and the drouth, isn't he?' said a new voice. 'Come on wid me, laddo, the great fine lad. Indeed yiz are, be the Holy Fly altogether. Indeed so. Jasus knows it surely.'

I stumbled off with his arm round my shoulders. They had a car, and I dumped myself into its warm badly-sprung soft-clothed back seat. We drove west along the estuary, hither then thither, to some shebeen in far Swords where we knocked for an entry, slithering in cattle muck; chinks of light widened to sizeable triangles; with his nailed boot someone closed the long-warped door. The place was packed with people; I was welcomed as a hero.

The warmth of the car and multiple backslapping, both physical and spoken, had encouraged me. A new trickle of life had begun to percolate me, and I thought I felt able, in a meet bragging gesture, to face a great plate of greasy rashers, two eggs and tomato. Instead of feeling worse I felt very much better.

Begod and BY GOD I was the hero of the day: they were drinking themselves into fits by, with, and for me!

I was far too exhausted to make out much clearly but the upshot of my exploits seemed to represent a fortune; for everyone was flush.

They gave me twelve good clean green pound notes all to myself; never had I held so much money in my hands. But they horrified and scalded me, and I held them like a very hot handleless cup. I shuffled and twisted them, then put them away.

What should I do with them? How could I account for them? The so longed-for wealth tore a hole in my coat.

They drove me home to the second back field hedge. I clawed and scrambled through the ditches, fetched up at the tall iron gate, climbed the rose trellis into my room, vomited and fell asleep.

I awoke to white terror.

What had I done? What was I doing?

I must stop this at once.

Now.

I got up and dressed fully, weary and miserable. With a clammy cold face-cloth I did my best to remove what was left of last night's half-digested banquet from the artificially smoke-scented weave of my Bradford-woven Harris Tweed coat. I did not eat the porridge cooled to a slimy pancake but picked it up, plate-shaped from its mould, and flung it into the ever-sizzling damp-timbered fire from which one of our half-starved healthy terriers gingerly extracted it to the accompaniment of the smell of burnt fur.

I went straight to Kelly's bottoms where I knew Merrigan would be working at a field drain.

'Good man yourself, how are ye?' he greeted me. 'Me own fine fellow.'

'Merrigan,' I said, 'I'll not do it any more. You can do what you like, I just won't.'

'Aha! So ye won't, will ye not? Then let me tell you what'll happen to you,' said he. 'Far worse things than ever I can tell you, me boyo; far and a long way worse. For myself and Peadar will straightway tell the guards on ye: and not the horse-shooting only but what about the races? They'll have the horses examined and they'll find your pellets in them and it'll be life-long you'll be jailed and thrashed every day of it and they'll give you nothing to eat at all or maybe hanging it'll be easily if e'er a man was hurted, and disgrace to all your family, the disgrace of the whole entire world. Yiz might as well kill yourself and the whole bloody lot of ye for if ye do not go on, for sure we'll quite ruin you. We'll drag the howl lot of ye into the dungheap where ye belong, you and your mammy and your daddy and your dothering ould uncle, the howl bloody lot of them. God's curse on ye all, ye filthy little bastard.'

He raised his great spade and I thought he was going to brain me there and then.

So I fell on my knees in the black mud and watercress and begged him to forgive me and I'd surely do anything and everything he wanted this time, if no more, and for the Love of God to say nothing and I'd do anything he wanted, anything he wanted.

'That's the good little man, that's the good little man,' he said. 'Come here to me now.' And he put his left arm round my shoulders and with the other began to fumble with my trouser buttons. He put in his hand.

'That's the good little man,' he said, feeling me horribly, his hand shaking, his breath gasping, 'that's the good little God-fearing little man.'

I never felt so low and so miserable; never surely before and seldom ever again.

After some long minutes I found I was still alive.

Unfortunately.

I went back to our garden and I wandered then in it as Schumann with his Heine on that summer morning my mother loved to sing of: but the flowers I loved so well meant nothing at all to me now.

Only the birds singing: singing: piercing.

I felt as I was, soiled in mind and body. I wanted to die but was afraid to. I went down where deadly nightshade often used to grow amongst leafless starved brambles, and there were its polished bright berries. I wondered how they tasted.

Abruptly I plucked a handful, stuffed them into my mouth and swallowed hard. They tasted of nothing very much, raw potatoes perhaps; slightly faded; cunningly insipid.

I stood quite still. Why was I not dead?

A thrush sang: a blackbird: nothing at all happened.

I decided I would walk all round the garden, then go to my bed and lie down to die.

Now under my own sentence I saw the earth more clearly at my feet. I saw it with infinite clarity: each grain of worn-down rock, each small-bundled tilled morsel and lump: the infinite stalk-like tinsel of humus descended from grass through the ruminant's stomach pressing along its rod-like line the miniscus-held globules of assuaging water, the dampness of growth and purveyor of yield.

My head was a microscope, macrocosm, lens: through the tiniest capillaries of the hairbroad rootlets I could feel, I could see, the pulse-sap flowing, gaining, rising to feed and feed the flower and its pod; its pod and its seed. I saw each plant living and moving; moving me. Houseleek on its stone, caltha in its pond, each plant with its forbears and progeny stretching to the ends of the earth and of time; *Iris chamaeiris* I had found with my mother not far from Fréjus that very last year, growing on the aromatic sunbleached *garrigues* over the Argens where the water-meadows swayed with heaven-scent narcissi near the stream.

I could see them all now; all clearly: the cellular structure of their delicate petals, the veins decurving in their gently-breathing leaves.

I lingered over them, walking over the soft mossy grass under old copper hazels, their bases thick with the marbled leaves of neapolitan cyclamen excavated from a hot wall near a mulepath above Sforzi, round by the snobby sunk garden, its aristocratic herbs spicy in the sun, to the shady peat beds where lilies, azaleas and cerulean lithospermum ensigned their bright colours.

So I rambled and wandered, and I do not know now for how short or how long; for I was seized of a sudden by an iron claw in the midst of my guts which twisted and constricted me and drew me like a chicken. I screamed out with all my strength and started to stumble and run—but oh, not to my bed: not at all to my bed: not to death: nor to die. Oh God, No! No! No!

I burst into the kitchen, 'Mustard!' I screamed. 'Mustard!'

'God's mercy!' screeched the cook. 'God's Holy Mercy, what's up?'

I staggered towards the dresser, and there like a beacon stood the lovely yellow tin.

Seizing it, I ran to the sink where an unwashed jampot stood steeping in dishwater. I tipped in the mustard as death screwed me tighter; I mixed it with my fingers and stuffed it down my throat: gobbled it, gurgled it: down, burning, burning . . .

It seared me, scalded me; my vitals torn one way then another, now to light now to dark.

I whirled and I span.

My brain and skull opened and shut like my Brownie camera's shutter when I peeped at it from inside: occluding, admitting.

I swallowed more mustard, I gasped at the air: a fountain of vomit mounted to my knowledge, cascading on some teatray. I departed elsewhere.

I was in a strange bed under a strange ceiling with quite different cracks and lightplays. Several faces leant over me with tubes, cylinders, squelchings. I opened my eyes and one face smiled.

It was enough, I was alive! Even a little, I was alive!

But after a little while I remembered it was all no use: not worth recovering: not worth re-breathing the iced air through my scalded mouth. It was far worse to recover but I was too weak to care, and sought refuge in weakness, surrendering to my night.

Three weeks later I was in my bed at home.

'It was a near thing,' said Droves, 'if you hadn't taken the mustard your number would have been up! As it is you have just a badly scalded mouth and gullet which will mend themselves given time.'

'I can't think,' said my mother, 'how you could have been so stupid as to swallow *Atropa belladonna*. Even *you* know it's not a native but a nasty introduction. I must say I never knew my own son was such a fool. What ever were you thinking of?'

'Other things,' I croaked. 'I am sorry for all the trouble.'

The doctor asked my mother to go downstairs with him and I thought I heard voices raised in anger. Some time later she came back again and asked me if there was anything I would like.

'Yes,' I whispered, 'some ice-cream. It's easy to——'

'You know very well—— oh all right, dear,' she said. 'I'll send Evans for some to the Burrow. I believe they have some in that nasty wooden shop.'

'Thank you, Mammy, thank you, I feel it might be easy to swallow and cool my throat.'

The news had got around that Master D. was nearly after poisoning himself. When at last I was better and able to go out I took the airgun and all the slugs and threw them into deep water in the tiderace in the South Channel near Maldowneys.

I burnt the twelve pounds on the bent-grassed sandhills, kicking their ashes to the fresh north wind.

I found seven plover's nests.

I walked ages in the garden.

I walked always in fear.

I kept to the garden until my holidays were ended and I had to go back to the school in Llanfach.

I was glad, terribly glad, to be leaving Ireland and the receding bay was a heavenly landscape, the smell of the mailboat a putrid delight.

Holyhead: the sight and sound of the North-Western carriages, pale grey and rich chocolate in the sea-shimmering station and their balanced trundling on the slow run to Llanfach far better than the one I am in this very moment.

Valley, Rhosneigr, Llanfaelog, Tycroes: the Anglesey place names were wholly delightful and the Welsh mainland better with more sea between us.

I was caught up in school life, a pummelling palliative. I had terrible nightmares, sweeter than reality.

As the term went on and the holidays drew near once again I was re-invaded with fears: I longed to go home but was terrified of the prospect. Would LeFanu be about and Merrigan and Norbert? All waiting to entangle me and browbeat me again?

I had decided, painfully, to make a clean breast of the whole matter to my father if they did. Better far the reformatory than the never ending stress. I had decided this after setting down the whole story in slightly changed form, and presenting this to my

English master as a free essay: as I wrote it for him it ended with death, not recovery.

Mr. Young, whom I very much worshipped in true schoolboy fashion—for he had begun to teach me to like poetry, even bad and hackneyed poetry, for which beginning I am ever grateful—was rather upset.

'This is a morbid story for a young fellow like you to write,' he said. 'Don't you think so? And anyhow, why on earth did you let him kill himself? Depressing and silly.'

'Well, sir, what else could he have done?'

'He could and should have told the police or his parents about it all at once. He would not have got into any serious trouble. Don't you see?'

'Yes. Thank you, sir. Thank you, sir. I see all right.'

I went out wonderfully reassured.

And when I got home I immediately felt there had been a great change, not only in myself, but also outside.

After a few days I casually (but still rather tremblingly) asked Evans: 'How are Merrigan and LeFanu? I don't see them around. And Norbert?'

'God, sir, did you not hear? They was all took up when you was away. Race gang over at Baldoyle they was: killed a man and all: someway in a fight beyant at Swords. All in for seven long years and more; some of them for life.'

I went shaking indoors.


# 21

THE train was rumbling on: we had flashed over that bridge and were deep in the cutting when we stopped at the station. I looked out and was most thankful that I need not get out: never: never ever again.

Some vaguely familiar faces, aged or more ageing, glided past as the train shuffled on. Wait till next time, I said; wait till next time and I'll tell myself more.

304D was jiggeting northwards, its engine's white smoke puff-shadowing the eastern fields, its west windows reflecting the slight bright sun onto the heron's nests in the dark branchless fir trees in the swamp down below. The trees were now dying but the herons still fished there. Once all this swamp had been fine ploughed up land.

304D was carrying me onwards and backwards and all ways——
And so was the bus.

We were somewhere on the road between Maganosc and Rouret. The passengers bobbed and bounced, swayed and lurched in idiotic marionette-like unison as the bus span onwards on the heat-shimmering tar. I had my head resting on the cool trembling glass. I sat close, still closer, to the window.

Outside bright green Aleppo pinewoods fled by. There was an ochre village clutching a hillbrow; there were people working in the vineyards, chatting at the washplace. There was reality, the reality I looked for. It had not been there before.

I raised my head and looked again. Next me sat a frowsty woman reading *Der Urschrei des Volksherzen, ein Roman von Eva, Graefin Rippelheim.*

Heaven, oh Heaven, here indeed was reality.

Across the bus just in front of me sat a pretty girl, her pigskin briefcase bouncing merrily on her smartly skirted lap. She wore very little make-up except a little magenta lipstick and, intriguingly, a small black painted horizontal stroke from the outer corners of each soft brown eye.

I looked at her for a long while. She was remote yet very near.

Yes, there were houses.

Yes, people waiting.

The bus was slowing down.

I fell asleep.

# 22

IN the train or the bus a dichotomy of feeling, the addling or hatching of some ambivalent egg.

On the morning of that morning as of all new mornings, a schizoid uncertainty.

How will the day run? How the capering?

It is not there yet, but behind and outside those half-unwilling lids.

Nothing has yet moved but the brain within its senses (or without them) has stumblingly returned from the far side of the deep dark ditch.

Ah, the mornings of anticipation, joyful and firm! They are rare and young or old and seldom and the sun's angled measuring in the windowslats can mar them entirely or make them supreme.

Which way runs the straining dog? Whereto scutters the bounding hare?

It's a daring business anyhow to wake up or to die; very likely wisest to shun both like the plague.

The cow goes to its water meadow, its pinkly sprawled udder warm on the cool dewy grass, chewing its lush cud—to be robbed in its turn of its calf and its milk and its breath—all for Daisy and me.

Ah rails! Rails! What curseable usable certainty!

Here they are on the map: they proceed surely and safely, by increments incrementing, by excrements excrementing, day sure and night doubly certain, with a holiday only for the gallbladder's gutting, a staff presentation of silver or salver or windpipe or engraved acid-stainless catheter: a good chap, you know, in his day.

Interruption at night from the baby within you: this heaving and flocculent curving, is it old or is it new? Does that river flowing warmly from your breast to your womb carry urgent demand to be let out to die? Is the heave and swell of the distended drum of your resonant belly, its navel now a nipple, the beginning of the end or the curtain rising on accumulated ages? Should she wake? Should he wake? Should they all three awaken?

Has the hour now struck?

What hour is it at all?

Dragon-fly larva in the mud in the depths of your pool; should you scrabble towards the spearing sunstreaks or relax to the carved dimlit depths with their soft, caressing mosses?

Is it really worthwhile hoisting your rackety ill-jointed body up that disappearing pipelike stick to the incandescent light, there to hover and dazzle with your iridescent wings?

Your comings and goings over water and marsh marigold, by alder and flower-shedding elder, in the blinding treacherous shatter of refracted light from the surface of that pool: what do they amount to?

Every thing or *no* thing?

Hunger affirms, desire endorses: *no* thing is nothing——Every thing insists.

Every thing aspires.

Every thing lives——

—to die.

Open your eyes then and think if you can't help it!

# 23

As usual this time: Ward six, Block A.

But not quite as usual.

Always too early, of course, with that wretched prying matron and for ever ambulant night-nurse; someone next door coughing their guts out, and in again snufflingly. I could not say I liked it.

No, I could not.

There was not much difference really except for the Op. I remembered it now: that was for today.

It had been decided upon gravely between the sure surgeons, the specialist and my own dear G.P.; not very serious in itself and by way of a probably successful experiment, simpler than pneumo-thorax and safer than more drastic incisions, a then new but generally effective manipulation causing little aftermath and heal-ing itself in due time: a Phrenic Crush.

To be done under a local: that would be interesting, not least to myself. I rather relished that, for it added to experience, avoided re-awakening, and the mornings were sufficient without added false dawns.

I could face it all right. Simple and clearcut the day stretched before me, secure as could be in its own sweet way; though with no doubt at all some unpleasant surprises.

Sure enough; there was the maid!

The pink maid with the pink dress, pink face and tits (when you could see them) and pink hands and heart and faint smell of pink sweat, offering me just a cup of weak tea—no more today for those for the Theatre—pink jokes and pink smiles.

I sloshed the grey tasteless tepid liquid down; liquids were worth stowing, so I thought.

A long sunny pause followed: it was March or October. Out of my window I could see the grey freshly rain-wetted slate roofs of the main block reflecting the pale spring or autumn sun, a curved pipe like Tenniel's flamingo-mallets protruding out of one side of the shabby newish building spouting clouds of white steam, initially downwards, to rise up in a reassuring curve against angry clouds; eight-tenths, about three thousand feet. This steam, I had been told, was a sign they were sterilizing the theatre: maybe they were. It filled me with no apprehension but puffed away chuffily like the train I was in: or will be in soon.

I read the paper and fiddled with my nice clean blanket. I made as sure as I could that my sexual organs were intact and hoped they would remain so.

In came the blue nurse:

She was as blue as the maid was pink, as sweatless as she was sweaty; her tits (which you could never see, oh dear no, but only imagine) blue too, her starched white cuffs on her short blue sleeves, her stretched white collar below her bright blue eyes, her starched white cap above them, as white as the shiny enamel kidney-bowl and basin she had set on the snow-white cloth on her little preparation trolley as she wheeled it to my bed. Blue blood flowed through her veins and was pumped by her true-blue heart.

'Now, Mr. D., it's time to get you ready,' she said, leaning over me and helping me off with my flabby flannel pyjamas.

I liked her leaning over me: she was close and very distant. Her body was held tight in the blue nurse's uniform, her breasts pressed flat beneath her blue twill dress.

65

I liked being 'prepared'; it was a regular ritual, scrubbing with alcohol, shaving and scraping: shapeless warm clothing and long woolly stockings, all of which I felt sure were whipped off as soon as they had you spreadeagled on that table. This time perhaps I should find out.

When she had finished her preparations she proffered, to my surprise, a couple of capsules of sedatives or suchlike—to keep me easy, so she said.

'I am not in the least anxious or nervous,' I objected, 'and I don't at all want any of your dope. I want to see this thing through with my own eyes and enjoy it.'

'Now, now, Mr. D., none of that,' she wagged. 'Be a good boy and swallow them all up.' So, to please her, I swallowed the things down.

In the hazy light of that spring (or autumn) morning I sank into a vastly comfortable haze myself, waiting between patience and impatience for the anticipated circus's fanfares to begin.

Her insistence on the capsules had slightly disturbed me; but I conjured no doubt there would be nervous sideshows it would be as well to take good care of for the present.

The wait prolonged itself interminably; as it lengthened I lay further in stupor. Eventually the block sister came in, apologized through my muffed ears (to my amazement) for the delay and proffered the excuse that Mr. Harrick the surgeon had been held by an exceptionally complicated case but would be ready for me shortly.

I snoozed then awhile and was brought back to half-life by the incursion and appearance of the two lanky trolleymen, their somewhat soiled waistcoats and spotted creaseless trousers in which they wheeled the dead ones to the chapel late at night (for I once, roused by my bowels, had to greet them in the passage), concealed by ill-fitting spotless white overalls buttoning to their turkey-like necks.

They slithered me off the bed onto the taut canvas of the blanketed rubber-sheeted trolley, and we proceeded by way of the Ronuk-smelling passage to the clickety lift and the ground floor. Perhaps it was as well I had been given the nembutal for I did not greatly care for this avian pair of Jakes; nor their lift; nor their

66

trolley; nor our subsequent obsequious ride across the sooty tar-macked courtyard between A and the Main block.

A fine cool drizzle was falling and they spread an undersheet over me to keep off the drops.

But soon we were in the main passage amidst hurrying and scurrying, brightly lit, warmly cheerful, to the big hall itself and a short jaunt in the heaven-ascending silent cage. They took off the mac, and I was ushered in gaily to the Holy of Holies: very warm, very bright.

The Jakes then transferred me to the high holy altar as adjustable and twitchable as three dentist's chairs, where I tried to sit up and be helpful and lively but was firmly if quietly admonished to lie down. Under me were warm woollen blankets; above me a huge cluster of most brilliant lights gathered in a vast muffed-glass sphere. On all sides peered unrecognizable pairs of eyes, their faces yashmaked like harem inmates in a painting by Delacroix, whether males or females I could not know.

Go ahead, I thought, go ahead; I am going to enjoy this.

Whereupon an almost opaque white cloth was laid over my face and all I could see was the central ball of lights shining as the sun through a heavy pall of mist. I did not like it. I wheezed and coughed and spluttered and I raised up my right hand and removed that cloth.

There was mumbled anger; someone with a pleasant female voice said:

'Now, now; you mustn't do that; just relax and leave things to us. Please.'

'But I want to see exactly what goes on,' I whimpered. 'I want to *see*. What's the use of all this local business if you're going to half throttle me with that stuffy bloody rag?'

'Now, now. Relax, my dear chap. Come on now,' said a strong man's voice. 'It wouldn't be very pleasant for you to see but in any case you must have a cloth over your face as your breath might infect the open wound. It will be quite near, you know. Please now, there's a good lad, pull yourself together.'

I was furious at being thus babied but could do nothing but submit. I was glad now I had had the sedative and lay back to relax and ponder. Shadows criss-crossed between the bright light and my cloth-covered eyes. There was hurried low talk and the snapping and tightening of rubber gloves or aprons.

I was fed up now.

I was just waiting.

They began, as I expected they would after all that dressing up, to dress me down. They were undoing my clothing at the neck, slipping off one sleeve.

Queer, I thought, queer.

I was rather numb by now and very tired and found it hard to think clearly or be bothered to do so. Why bother anyhow? Leave it all to them.

Then I felt the cool evaporation of alcohol or ether being rubbed on my skin and its coldness raised me nearer to the surface of my thoughts. Curious, I said to myself, they are cleaning me on that side; surely it was not on that side the nurse had prepared me in our distantly sexual, closely practical, earlier encounter?

I began weakly to remonstrate, though I did not really care very much what they did, and I knew that they would think me increasingly neurotic, and either regret they had not given me a general or give me one by injection or respiration pretty quickly.

But suddenly I was convinced: and as my conviction grew my fear grew with it. It was urgent, very urgent, and I was badly scared. Sweat began to spurt from my armpits and run down my sides. Under the brilliant lamps, under the stuffy white cloth, my face became a steam bath and my eyes stung with the salt of my panic. Fear and terror cast out and off the effects of the dope, and I saw my miserable future with the wrong lung resting, my only good one, and the other rattling away like a worn out accordion to a gradual, slow, if fairly painless end. The basic struggle to survive, or at least not to permit myself to be polished off so stupidly, took charge.

I began to struggle and shout beneath the stifling white cloth. I tried to snatch it off but they had strapped both my arms to my sides. I could not sit up although I tried.

'Take it easy, old man, don't excite yourself.'

'Leave it to us——'

68

'Now, now. There, there! Don't worry——'

'It's not going to hurt——'

'——general, what about a general? —general, general: What about a general——'

I was beside myself, pinioned in this nightmare. I began to screech and I can screech very loudly. I was a maniac now.

'The wrong side. Stop—stop! Idiots, you'll kill me! The wrong side I tell you—— Stop it!'

Suddenly there was silence. Had I deafened myself, shrieking in my sack of sweat? But I heard again my own doctor's friendly soothing voice.

'Now, D., look here. You are always imagining things—people always do on the table here anyhow—like this. I am not blaming you. But why on earth get such ideas into your head?—Though, as I say, it's common enough and I know very well it's all a nervous strain. Would you sooner have a whiff of something and let us get on with it? There's a good chap now, don't think wild thoughts. It'll be all right soon—all over quite soon.'

'It's the wrong side,' I choked, 'the wrong side, I *know* it is. Take the cloth off me please, and I'll tell you. Take it off me for a minute *please*, and I'll show you.'

He did, oh he did, and at last I was back—to some kind of nightmare not under that cloth: the oval of masked faces, their eyes peering objectively at the object I was for them, their voices quite muffled now that mine was at last free . . .

I had it! Suddenly, by God, I had it!

'Why then did Nurse shave me under my right arm this morning? If you say it's left, tell me why did she do it? Answer me, answer me! Why?' I renewed my screeching.

The oval of faces turned towards each other: inwards, then outwards, their eyes slightly questioning.

Someone came forward and, pulling back the shoulder of my garment or garments, revealed my bare armpit to their ever-shielded enigmatic gaze.

There was a new silence: I could hear steam hissing somewhere: I could hear water running and a clock or a meter of some sort faintly ticking time. I was in a lather of sweat.

'Go and get the X-rays,' said someone commandingly.

I was at least reprieved.

No word was said: no one moved. The silence increased, the weight of the waiting with it.

After an eternity an envelope was brought. The radiographer held the negatives to the battery of light. There was some rumbling guarded talk. Nothing was said to me.

A general post ensued: the assistants with their paraphernalia moved round to my right side: the lights were readjusted. I thought I heard a slight sigh, of relief or of boredom: it may have been my own. I was too flattened to do anything or open my mouth in any thanks or curses. I lay shivering and drenched.

More blankets were piled over me. They began *da capo* their scrubbing evaporation: this time there near my right yoked collar-bone.

They put a thinner cloth over my head and through it I watched detachedly shadowy hands about their business. Disinterestedly I felt activities connected with me: the tiny first prick of the hypo-dermic needle, shallow at first, carrying its anaesthesia with it, probing further, pausing, a little more pressure on its shiny plunger. It all took some time.

Soft orders were given, silently obeyed; they had buttoned up a very tightly-fitting high-necked jacket around my upper torso and throat; it held me together and prevented the threatened dis-integration of my body and brain.

After an *entr'acte* they began cutting off me the suit they had so carefully fitted on: there were several layers. I could feel the stitching giving way at the seams, hear the buttons flying and hopping, first off the outer jacket, then the waistcoat, shirt and vest. On the way they had snatched at my braces and cut them in two with a pair of strong pliers and the trouser-holding tension of them over my right shoulder slackened suddenly and died. I felt I could hear the two ends of the overtaut cable fly swishing through the air cutting off some small twigs from the nearby hawthorn hedges which smelt sweet.

Finally they did me all up again, re-stitched the parted seams, and with an old-fashioned buttonhook, a shoehorn as its handle, re-buttoned the re-sewn-on buttons. It was all nice and neat but my braces were severed and I knew that when I stood up my trousers would fall down in a pile around my ankles.

The cloth was taken off my face.

Several known faces smiled down at me: they had taken off their masks. I tried to smile back but I could not or would not.

'That's a good lad,' someone said, and I was moved, more gently this time on account of the fresh sewing, onto the taut canvas of the trolley, out by the double swing-doors through a roomful of taps, running water, sloshing water, enamel rattling, vasty washing up; down the lift, along the corridor, over the tarmac, palindromically to my own bed where I fell into an uneasy waking sleep.

And the surgeon never sent a bill.

There were some people in the room: two or three. They were real and they were kind. I saw evoluating on the wall pictures of peacocks and parasols in dull and subtle smoky purples and sun-shadowed mottled olive greens, the colours you see if you press your fists into your eyes, holding them there firmly and long.

There was hammering going on, or a thunderstorm maybe, or hail on the galvanized roof, unpredictable yet regular; and when I opened or tried to open my eyes I saw people as trees moving and trees as fine people gracefully and gently revolving.

And then I saw that it was neither, but the heavy-hanging elms near Trumbull's lodge and there I was, if I had ever left it, back again in 304D.

# 24

A HUGE log fire blazed in the enormous brass grate, flickering on the Italianate chimney-piece from Sundays Well, Cork.

The oil lamps, although the very best patented Hampton and Leedom's could offer, and carefully trimmed by my mother's own hand—as usual, as always—much inclined to smoke.

The candles, although the very best patented the Army and

Navy could tender—as usual, as always—dribbling and dripping from the semi-circular sconces and rococo chandelier in the centre.

It was all gaiety: the Christmas tree smelling dangerously combustible, even faintly in combustion, dangling its improving presents from its somewhat exhausted arms; Alphabets, Aesop, *The Pirate, A Tale of Two Cities, The Lady of the Lake, Marmion, Quentin Durward, Ivanhoe, Kenilworth*—all in the cheapest then available editions—weighing them mercilessly down.

The Curate was there, the Leslie-Coultersons, Lady Cotten de Grief, Errant-Harrows and all. Tom Cobley was conspicuously absent; not so Mrs. Brentgoose reeling out her repertory on the old Blüthner, valse after valse.

We had had *Nuts in May*: we had had musical chairs selected from *Carmen*, the *Quaker Girl* selected from nothing and a *Beautiful Blue Danube* as muddy as can be. *Oranges and Lemons* proved equally sour.

We were now in the throes of *Sir Roger de Coverley*, Brentgoose's speciality: she had been known to keep at it without a second's pause for nearly two hours, once. Up and down, criss and cross, fling the toes out, jigging and shaking, row facing row. All the same rows, the same repetition; mawkish peep and inviting, arm-clasped, diagonal swirl from the far other end. Jiggety-jiggety—one foot forward: jiggety-jiggety, then the other: jiggety-jiggety *ad infinitum*: bemused in the end as foot-soldiers drilling, packs on their backs, lead in their boots, nothing in their heads.

On went *Sir Roger*, Brentgoose goading him, as Rumanian gipsies fiddling out a *Hora* till they fall down insensate, having given of their all. But Brentgoose gave nothing but the hammers of her fingers and the hollow of her heart.

Personally I hoped it would go on until we all *did* collapse, for the next and to me most excruciatingly painful item was laid down to be a solo song by myself entitled *I want to be a Soldier and Fight for the King*; and both king and soldiers were alien to my sentiments; nothing could have been more. Musically—but it was not music; it began 'Every day at morning my Daddy says to me'—Need I sing more?

I was just turning over with immense distaste the diabolical prospect stretching immediately before me when I saw, out of the corner of my forever jiggeting eye as it swirled around arm-crooked-in-arm with someone or other's sister, one of the maids come into the room and call my mother out earnestly and hurriedly. Owing to Brentgoose's grizzly din I naturally heard nothing of what passed between them. On we went:

> Rumpty-tumpty, tum-titty,
> Rumpty-tumpty, tum-titty,
> Rumpty-tumpty, tum-titty *tum*,
> Rump-titty tum titty.
> Rum rum rum titty,
> Rumpty-tumpty, tum-titty,
> Rumpty-tumpty tum-titty *tum*,
> Rump-titty tum-titty . . .

Brentgoose played it straight, strictly *senza variazione*, yet not with the grinding precision of a mechanical piano—oh dear no. For she stumbled here and there, botching the time, necessitating thus a sudden and disturbing readjustment of our twitching feet which might otherwise have been happily left to carry on their paranoid jerking by themselves.

A tremendous stretch of time having seemingly passed I saw, again out of the corner of my now badly addled ill-focusing eye, my mother return through the heavy matt-Vandyke-brown white-spotted door, crimson in the face and very, very, stern-looking.

She went over to Brentgoose and suddenly, in the middle of a tum-titty, *Sir Roger de Coverley* stopped dead.

There were gasps, an uneasy silence, a few stifled sighing yawns or yawning sighs.

My mother clapped her hands rapidly and loudly five times together; then twice, more loudly, more slowly, menacing toastmistress that she was.

'Children! Friends!' she began (it sounded ominous all right). 'I have an announcement to make to you all . . .

'I have just been subjected to the most frightful and unendurable insult imaginable. I was called to my own front door and there stood three common-looking young men with masks—dirty black masks—over their faces. "Madam," they had the effrontery to say, "we have come to ask you for a subscription—*subscription*, if you please—to the Irish Republican Army." *Can you imagine such a thing?*' She was trembling with rage and foaming a little at the corners of her mouth. 'And they gave me a dirty little piece of paper with some kind of writing on it. I tore it up and threw it in their faces. They were furious, and I told them to go away and steal some stamp paper from the post office' (the local P.O. had in fact been burgled the night before) 'and stick it together again. "We didn't rob the post office!" they shouted. But of course I am sure they did. "You'll pay for this, wait till you see!" they screeched at me. "Go away," I said, and banged the door in their faces and bolted and chained it.'

My mother was exhausted and indeed felt insulted, but one way or another I had little sympathy for her.

I probably knew these lads, as I knew everybody thereabouts, and in my heart felt far more on their side than on the side of ourselves or our friends or our family.

My mother was going on now in a rather sanctimonious voice which I did not care for at all.

'My children! My friends! In this appalling moment of utter degradation, when these dirty Sinn Feiners dare come to this house to ask for a subscription from *me* for their gang of murderous brutes, I want to ask you all, as a troth of loyalty to our Gracious Majesty (she bowed her head as in the Creed in church)—King George of England—(some very weak "hear hears") to sing with me our glorious Hymn of Loyalty'—and in a quavering soprano she started it:

'God save our gracious King,
Long live our gracious King . . .'

It was dreadful: somewhere inside me a great anger began to brew. It brewed and boiled, rising up from my stomach, invading my chest, burning my heart, bubbling in my brain. This damnable sanctimonious claptrap with its mixture of a god in heaven and a bearded gorgon on earth—This!—a Hymn of Loyalty? What rubbish!

I did not feel this was loyalty but disloyalty, traitorous to those who lived and worked around and for us. For I knew scarcely one of them that did not feel an absolute unity with the cause of freedom, for freedom for Ireland, then a glory and a wonderful goal, subsequently, so it seems, so utterly wasted. But then, yes *then*, only the rich and the snobs, the bigots and their bootlickers, could dream, or ever dreamt of anything else. Now there are other rich, new snobs, a new generation of bigots with other bigotries and a new army of bootlickers: and they are satisfied: mostly satisfied: and they never dream at all . . .

But anyhow at that moment, as the dreary hypocritical verse tottered throatily to the heights of 'lo-hong to reign oh-ho-ho-ver us', I caught Robbie's eye.

He was scarlet in the face and trembling: his mouth was tight shut.

When the last notes of the anthem arrived (not quite all together) at their unconvincing 'King', there was a strained, pained, silence. My father and the Major swallowed audibly.

Swallow: more silence.

Swallow: it was whiskey.

Robbie, who was standing near the piano, suddenly struck the top of it with the flat of his hand.

'Up the Republic! Long live the Republic!' he screeched in a frenzy, and I found myself joining him.

'Up the Republic!' I yelled, and before we knew where we were we had struck up, he in his half-cracked adolescent tenor, I in my choir-boy treble:

Up De Valera the hero of the right,
We'll follow him to battle with the orange, green and white.
We'll beat old England and we'll give her Hell's delight,
Up De Valera, King of Ireland.

The effect on the party was terrible. They looked horrified to the point of fainting; even terrified, as if they half expected their God to strike down such infamy with a flash and the smell of brimstone. This last not occurring, they then rapidly passed into a state of violently embarrassed shame as if they had had a chamber pot poured over their heads, or had all found they had dog-dirt on their shoes which they could not get rid of.

They looked sideways and downwards, neither at us nor at each other. The silence was solid, desperately anticipating.

All at once, mutually certain, my father and the Major began to push their way resolutely through the crowd of gawkers from where they had been comfortably installed near the fireplace, whiskeys in their hands, enjoying all the fun.

'Follow me, you two,' my father managed to hiss through his clenched teeth. 'Step to it!' he burst, safety-valve at its limit.

We obeyed sheepishly.

They walked us straight out into the hall, down the turkey-carpeted passage, past the two drawing-rooms to the front door.

My father unlocked, unbolted and unchained it.

'I have nothing, there *is* nothing, to be said to people of your kind. You are unfit to be my son, you are both unfit to mix with decent people. I want to hear nothing either now or in the future of either of you.'

Turning the latch, he opened the door wide.

'Get out and stay out. Go to your so-called friends!'

And with that they flung us out with all their force into the dark, our faces in violent contact with the cold sharp gravel. The door slammed behind us: the brass knocker knocked itself loudly. They re-locked, re-bolted and re-chained that same door.

It was silent but for heavy drops dripping off the ilex.

Then Robbie was swearing and cursing at them madly, almost inarticulate.

'The swine, the filthy dirty swine. I am glad I did it. The dirty beastly swine.' He spat copiously back through the darkness at the dimly lit house. 'Our fathers are nothing but swine; by God I'll soon kill them, I'll kill them, both of them, the swine.'

I was thinking: there's a curfew soon, only partly let off because of Christmas. Where should we go? What should we do?

'Daddy's not so bad really,' I said. 'It's not his fault. It's Mother makes him like that, she's . . .'

'Well, why did he put you out then? Why didn't he tell her to shut up that awful churchy God save the King muck? The dirty stinking bitch, I hope the IRA get her and serve her right too. I hope they burn you out like they've done lots of you so-called gentry!'

'But, Robbie, I supported you!'

'Yes, all right. I know. But you didn't really feel it. You like those damned horrible people in there.' (He spat again.) 'Don't you?'

'They are my friends and I know them best but I do *not* like them. What can I do about it? Tell me, what can I do?' I paused. 'Where shall we go?'

'We'll go to the Flemings; they're decent people and will take us in. They'll help us. The others might think we were spies and rightly so, knowing where we come from, but the Flemings'll take us in.' He paused, thinking things over, aware of our predicament. 'We can't go by the roads, though; there are ambushes and mines and blocks and they'll shoot as soon as ask. We'll have to cross the fields and go by the brickworks swamp. It's a long way that way, but we shall have to take it; we'll go to the Flemings and they'll hide us. They've tons of room, and tomorrow our damned parents'll be in a real good funk about us when we don't show up. They'll be expecting us to knock at the door any time now and beg and whine to be let in and sent to bed without supper in disgrace. But we'll show them! We won't crawl to them, the dirty swine! They'll have to look for us. What time is it now?'

By my much-prized luminous Ingersoll it was just half past six.

'No curfew until nine tonight: we've loads of time if we hurry. Come on!'

We set off.

Set off! Such an idea; such a description; such a misnomer . . .

We stumbled, our hands groping before us, as far as the end of the gravel where it met the avenue at right angles. By the sound of our feet we knew we were on the gravel and by the feel of the bushes against our hands and faces we knew we were off it.

It was totally dark, and a fine trickle of rain was soaking us steadily. To the south the dimmed lights of the seething city cast a faint glow on the low clouds, and as usual these days in two or three places on the horizon buildings were burning with fitful reddish glow.

We decided to keep parallel with the railway and to the west of the road. We knew the ground well but in the inky darkness the only means of gauging where we were was to stare up at the netted tree branches when we heard them grumbling in the night wind, trying to identify them, black against blacker in the deep winter, from perhaps having lain down beneath them for shelter from a rare hot summer sun.

In the middle of the larger fields it was easy enough to lose all sense of direction, no light or star for a clue; and once we must have made a circle over the sound-absorbing tufty wet sod for we fetched up almost where we had set out, near a large rotting elm which we both knew well. We decided we had better keep near the hedge or ditch-side within arm- or sight, or sound-length of them, and this we did, getting viciously lacerated, scratched and clothes-torn by the briary tentacles of the hedges, and plastered with a mixture of cowdung and mud in the ditches, when our feet broke through the thin layer of ice left over from last night's freezing. We were soaking now, and our cuts stung. Half a mile from home we were very nearly lost.

We resolved to make east towards the sea and the road, guided by the reflected flashing of the coast lights, none of them easily visible as they revolved, all concealed largely behind hills or far away. Penetrating a hedge with our heads down, pushing and butting like obstinate goats, we felt hard macadam and heard our feet on it. As quietly as we could we hurried across into a waste of frost-browned nettles, some of the stings still active on their brittle wintry stalks: then through rusty barbed-wire overgrown with spiking blackthorn, across a deep muddy-watered ditch frequented by moorhens, whose sharp alarm cries unexpectedly startled, into the huge forty-acre sheepfield beyond, near the line.

Now the going was easier, there were fewer ditches. The place was open: too open perhaps: for on one of the cart-bridges over the railway line was a sandbagged machine-gun post, and Laffan the gunner all too easy on his trigger after dark.

We crossed the line stealthily further on, hopping from sleeper to sleeper, avoiding the ballast.

But nothing happened.

We had some great frights from sleeping cattle rearing up like steaming mountains as we stumbled in or on to them, and the demolishing clatter of wood pigeons disturbed from their roosts in ivy-throttled thorns; and when a startled mallard flew up almost into my face near the bulrush-edged swamp he made me jump aside up to my thighs in cracking-iced bubble-gushing bog water.

On we stumbled. I, for my part, despondent, sad and troubled, the whole background conflict and strife that had us out thus in the night revolting me; the distant fires, anguish and death, all to no real purpose; the refusal of friendship and common ground on the common fields beneath our common sky to a common end and peace, unexplainable and cruel.

We were sloshing along in a deep sunk cart-track in a morass of emulsified half-frozen mud, the stony bottom once laid there and clear only discernible if we stood still and allowed our bootsoles to settle to it. We were mounting the east slope of Malahide Hill, hoping to descend to the estuary and Fleming's haven on the other. The darkness seemed to have become even more opaque: as in Egypt it almost could be felt. We spoke very little, contributing only such knowledge of the hedges, banks, thickets, ditches, boreens and bushes as might guide us on our way.

We slipped across another narrower road and made on gropingly to the rather indefinite, most uncrestlike, crest; as we approached it I could see somewhere beyond it yet another fire-glow, another structure flaming; or maybe it was a hay shed or straw stack.

We came to the top and there, sure enough, near the edge of and reflected in the quiet-watered pent-up estuary, flared another beacon, another bright candle lit in the name of something-or-other someone-or-other had convinced himself was right. It appeared to be just where Fleming's house lay, just exactly there; but of course it couldn't be. Luckily, thank goodness, it could not be theirs; for they were on the *right* side, on *our* side, on the side of the ordinary people and of friendship: so it couldn't be them.

We descended the sloping fields; it was easier going now with that beacon.

Down there, down the very steep high railway cutting just before it became an unscaleable cliff, to the twin singing rails (exactly where now I was passing), once again hopping the sleepers, up, scrambling and clawing, to the southern side of the demesne beechwoods, sheltered as always from the north-east winds which made man and beast miserable hereabouts in unwilling sulky spring, along the little track, deserted as always, towards the western dimness, Feltrim, and the road across to Swords, the thick tall woods moaning dejectedly in unison on our right, not letting through though a trickle of the northern coldness.

We would keep going thus until the woods ended and then turn right towards Yellow Walls on the other side of the main Dublin road, continue through the rich fields to the estuary's edge, follow its shingly shore to our goal.

We were exhausted now and for the first time, and by unspoken mutual consent, sat down, our backs against a damp supporting bank surmounted by a thick clipped hedge.

'Why do you think it's like this, Robbie?'

'Simply because your lot are swine,' he recommenced, 'dirty filthy swine. I am so glad to see the fires: best thing to do is to burn 'em all out; like wasps: and I hope they burn you, too.'

He was seething whilst I was sad, unpleasantly bored with the whole nasty business. I thought of my home, and with affection too. How should I not do so? If familiarity sometimes breeds contempt for living people, it breeds affection for places and mute things, so that the merest muddy duckpond becomes a glittering ocean when the breeze blows and the sun sparkles; an old familiar crock of a bicycle, its ballbearings grinding, part of oneself, flying ecstatically through the lanes; the meanest street corner with its fly-blown grocers and its chalk-scrawled walls an unsurpassable kingdom, a happy place to be.

How should I not think of it with affection?—With the winter sun striking low at teatime on the grain like a waterfall from the dark polished table, sending coloured spectra tiltingly dancing from the cut-crystal droplets of the greasy chandelier? Or the old mongrel dog, heraldic on the window-seat upholstered with embroidery from a fair-day at Kolosczvar, with the same sun scorching from behind his rather mangy, rough-to-the-face, brindled fur so that it glowed like the haloes in the pictures of the Virgin my mother had dragged me far too often to see on wet Sundays in Florence? Or when it struck, too, when I was sick in bed, onto the pink ceiling of my room, so low was it in the south in the winter's afternoon, suffusing the whole place with a spurious rosy glow, the fluorescent cut glass in the back of the old French white-and-green wicker chair striking a monstrous colour contrast in the sad declining light?

Then, at that bank, it all seemed as summer: we had come, not across miles of sodden bog, ploughland and grazing, acres of squelching mud and by ill-kept bramble-ridden lanes, but over fields golden with buttercups, watermeadows studded with spotted orchis and brown-flowering rushes, where the hay-mower sang but the corncrakes ran panicking to fall silent and twitching, their legs sliced off neatly at the first joint by the oscillating blades of the horse-drawn machine . . .

I thought of all this and the unpleasantness of my boredom at Robbie's words increased. Resentment took the upper hand; resentment in a maze. A futile maze like the laurel one at Villiers'; some hedges broken; holes here and there; cut to see over; more difficult thus to penetrate or return from the ferngrown pile of stones and Victorian lovers' seat in the middle . . .

Must it be so?

All burnt? All burning?

Yes. Burn it down; burn it down!

Burn everything down; burn everything!

Then recommence: start all over again: build up and burn!

New convents, new monasteries, retreat-houses, brotherhoods, churches, presbyteries, seminaries, asylums!

Then set the match again! Set it once again!

Surely a fine fire?

BURN . . .

By now the bank's reeking damp had seeped an extra ration of moisture through my already rain-soaked back. It was neither summer nor hell, but full Christian winter. There were no flowers now but phallic candles on the pagan tree-of-trees for the so-called *son* of benighted wretched men.

'Come on, let's go. Let's get along to Flemings'. They'll warm us anyhow and give us a cup of tea.'

'I hope they burn the whole damn lot of you out.'

We struggled to our feet, eagerly reluctant. With some concentration, mastering our aching stiffness, we managed to put one before the other, the newly-cooled areas of our sopping clothing unwelcomingly caressing our still slightly warm flesh in places that had hidden themselves cunningly hitherto.

On again: some leaden steps further to the end of the wood; across the hard road on which drops from the high trees fell deadly; right and northwards to the shore, where the freed north breeze blew chain after musical chain of inch-high ripples amongst its seaworn stones.

Before us the glow shone ever more steadily, forlorn and comforting as the flickering reflection of an unknown fire on the uncurtained ceiling of an un-named room in a secret house in a city at nightfall. We rounded Swan Point, itself low and featureless, the Bewicks asleep, but both showing well in the stronger orange light.

My God! My heart stopped.

It stopped beating entirely.

It was Fleming's, Fleming's!—there could be no doubt about it.

There, against and in the mounting greedy flames, stood the outline of the house I had known so very well.

There, with a great lisping tongue leaping through its window, the spare room I had often slept in.

There the familiar gable-end which crumbled as I watched.

What had happened?

Who had done it?

Why?

I could see figures silhouetted, waiting isolated. We began to run over the rising unploughed field towards this frightful warmth.

One of the figures turned: there was a spit of yellow flame and the snip of bullets near us. We cried out and dived for the nearest hedge and lay panting and terrified in its concealing shadow.

'We'll crawl and see what in hell's name's up. Keep down, keep down, you fool, can't you?' said Robbie.

So we did: on the cold repellent grass.

We came nearer and I could see Anne and Richard now: they were standing rigidly a little to our left watching the pyre of their house and home. Dotted here and there stood men, firearms of some sort slung over their shoulders or at the ready in their hands.

We got to our feet and raced to our friends.

'Anne! Richard! What's happened? What's happened?'

They turned and when they saw us the horror and anguish rampant in their faces doubled: they stared at us and it redoubled, twisting away all kindness.

They looked us up and down.

'What are you doing here? Why the hell are you out at this hour? Go away. Go away at once!' Richard screeched, verging on hysteria.

We could not move, nor could we speak. What could we say?

'We came to . . . to . . .'

'Well, out with it! What is it?' he snapped.

Never could I have dreamt of him speaking so to anyone.

'. . . to . . . to . . . to ask you to . . . it's no use now. I'm sorry.'

'Out with it!' he roared, beside himself now.

'Robbie and I were put out at home, put out last night because we, because we . . . we . . . it's all no use. Why did they set fire to you? Why? *Why?*' I wailed.

'Who? What do you know about it? Out with it, or I'll kill you both.'

I was paralysed with dismay. I heard Robbie speaking.

'We were put out for shouting "Up the Republic" . . . We thought you might put us up and help us. We thought you were the only people who knew us and could help us. We walked all the way by the fields . . . It's awful . . . and now we find you like this. Oh, Richard, I am so sorry. What on earth has happened?'

'I'm sorry, boys . . . sorry, boys. I didn't know.'

Anne was sobbing.

'I didn't know, boys. I don't know, boys. They came and burnt us. *Us.* No one we knew, all masked. I don't know who they were: we called up the lads; there they are around us. I don't know who they were or why they did it. These new Tans, I suppose. It's breaking our hearts. It's all breaking our hearts. It's misery.'

We all stood silent, the flames cracking and throbbing, soaring and hissing in the old house. The great chimney with its never-counted pots fell with a muffled thud amidst a pillar of vituperant sparks.

We could not speak, nor could we move.

On the lawn stood a huddle of household oddments, a table, some cushions and rainsodden books. The rain fell gently on them. It was a pattern too often repeated, and to be repeated, both here and elsewhere.

We moved closer together: the flames were now lessening, they had had their rich fill. Gratefully and ashamedly I enjoyed the warming glow from the piled-up embers in the perished filthy remnants of my Christmas-party suit.

'Stay with us,' said Anne.

# 25

THE sun was warm through the quivering glass.

It was the bus all right, curving and dipping on the contoured road, the same people in it, the student and the frowster; all the same people, perhaps even myself.

If I opened the emergency door beside me I should fall out on the road, my head would surely burst on it, it would tear off my ear and part of my clothes, spattering bits of me on the sun-soaked stone. It was hard, that stone, as hard as stone—not plaster or pillow, but a fact.

I had no intention of doing so.

If I moved away from the Rippelheim reader beside me, stumbling clumsily against her knees, treading inadvertently on her feet, and over to the girl with the eyestreaks, I could put my hand in her lap under her bouncing pigskin briefcase and feel her warm thighs there and the buttons of her suspenders, or put out my right hand to cup her now green-nippled breast. But I do not think she would have tolerated all this and most likely there would have been a row: possibly I should have been put out: less possibly arrested.

I shall never really know as I did not do it. I feared the consequences yet they might have been worth it. I had the desire but the will for it failed me.

I had no intention of doing so.

If I walked calmly towards the exit near the driver and whilst passing him wrenched his steering wheel to the left, we should plunge off the road down those steep rocky banks through the aromatic rosemary, lavender and thyme to the dried-up torrent far below. We should all end up mashed or roasted at the bottom: but I shall never really know.

I had no intention of doing it.

Not only my own but the destiny of all of us lay thus sometime hanging in my hands through my head.

I do not know: nor can I now, ever.

The girl might have liked to have been rummaged and assaulted, the passengers in hospitals or coffins far safer: and it might easily have been better if my brains had bespattered that sunny stone wall.

But I shall never know; nor anyone else either.

For I had no intention of doing these things, nor any other antic.

So temporarily I was free.

I decided to get out.

By the ordinary door, next the driver.

I stood up.

I said 'Entschuldigen Sie mich' to the frowster, trod inadvertently on her feet and knocked, by mistake, the Rippelheim off her knees. I said 'Vielen Dank', but I said it too soon. I picked up the book: page one-eighty-four was soiled by my footmark and spit.

I said 'Entschuldiger Sie mich' again and gave it back to her.

'*Aufwiederseh'n,*' I said and I should not have said it.

I squeezed past her and out into the central gangway.

I moved forwards.

I came next to the eyestreaked girl: her briefcase was bouncing on her lap. I began to raise my hand with vague ideas forming in its autonomous fingertips when the bus gave a lurch and I fell across almost on top of her.

I was profuse in my apologies and whilst struggling to get to my feet, managed to lean momentarily on her warm left thigh. I was profuse in my apologies (the suspender button was there all right) and whilst further attempting to attain to the vertical (inadvertently) brushed the back of my left hand across and against her green-nippled breast which was also no illusion.

I apologized even more profusely, and she gave me an odd and rather frightened look. I tried to raise my hat but I had not got it on. She gave me a consoling, condoning smile: she must have had weak-minded relations and been used to it.

So was I.

So had I.

I thought I was making a mistake to get out: here it was and I could play this further. I should have sat down next to her but misfortunately I had failed to notice that the seat was already occupied by an elderly gentleman with a hearing aid upon whom I was still leaning or lying.

What a pity that the girl was next the window!

'*Mille pardons,*' I said, straightening myself up at last.

He looked furious, his hat was askew; I straightened it for him.

I should not have done that: he looked even more furious.

'*Dix milles pardons,*' I said. I should not have said that. He was fit to explode: but mercifully was dumb as well as deaf.

I felt distressed, clownlike, cruel.

But the girl liked it and gave a little snigger. I didn't like the snigger but I did like the girl and was grateful for her support; until I realized that of course the snigger was for me and the support for the gentleman.

'I am very sorry, sir,' I said. He looked up. I was partially forgiven.

'*Au revoir*, mademoiselle,' I said to the girl and I hoped so.

I passed on forward.

When I reached the front next the driver I gave the conductor a nod and did not attempt to interfere with the former. Thus passed a moment of hazard, for had I not, albeit inadvertently, placed my hand on the eyestreaked girl's thigh and touched, in error, her green-nippled breast? But now it was over.

The bus stopped and immediately I got out.

The bus moved on again.

I stood by the side of the road.

I wanted to wave to the girl and I did so, and to my surprise and delight she waved back. Safe enough now, anyhow, she must have thought; but was it? Was she? Was I?

Just then I remembered I had left all my papers safely in my portfolio on the rack above my seat. But perhaps it was as well?

# 26

On all sides were pleasantly shaped hills furnished to their summits with evergreen trees and bushes: Aleppo pines, maritime pines, umbrella pines, ilex, cork oaks, lentisques, pistacchios, coriander. The sky was pellucid bluish-green cerulean: it looked easy to fall into down there, up high, where the first swifts or swallows were wheeling and screaming.

I hate walking downhill because I subsequently have to walk up; I detest walking uphill even more.

I walked up.

A sun-smitten white limestone track, with red provençal earth straining through and staining the stones, wound out of sight through the glowing greenness. The warm air smelt heavily of resin and rosemary. I snuffled and panted, coughed and wheezed as is my custom. Soon I was away out of sight and all sound.

There was a conscious delicious silence: some seedpods were splitting with tiny explosions, scattering their progeny on the stony ground; there was a faint murmur of small intrepid insects:

I heard goatbells in the distance, and the lazy drone of some far-off plane. My feet rattled and slithered on the sharp, loose, shoe-cutting stones.

I went on and up.

I did not think. I did not think at all.

The clear air and warm sun, the spiny or smooth elucidated patterns of stalk and stem, symmetrical or contorted, the small movements of leaf or frond with their smaller sounds of rubbing and rustling in the lightest breeze, became part of me. I *was* those sounds and shapes and scents.

I moved only, and in moving, experienced; I went on and up and I did not think but lived.

I scarcely looked but I saw everything: I did not listen but I heard infinitely: I paid no attention but appreciated all things. I was participating, integrated; the hills and scrub my closest relations; my own limbs, my blood—their sap; my labouring lungs, my legs—their breathing leaves, their searching roots.

I went on and up unconsciously moving, most consciously knowing; this place, these places, were always my friends. They were bare and waterless, stony and forsaken, and if you broke your leg you could die there and stay there and no one would find you; but if you took them with you they were always with you, always friendly, their sun on the stones of some dark northern alleyway, their scent on the air of a suburban street in winter.

The track narrowed: it petered out.

There was no clear way onwards but only low pines and high undergrowth; juniper netted with *Smilax aspera*. Carobs pronged with terebinth, spiny coriaria with milky spurge, arbutus with bay, cistus with erica, woven and waving in a sweet-smelling tangle.

I had to pay attention, some attention, now. I picked my way this way and that as uncertain as a hen in a patch of tall nettles. Sometimes I tried to turn aside, making a wide detour and sometimes it was bare *garrigue* and I could proceed directly over the grey cracked stone.

I felt secret and safe.

When I got to the crest there was another crest and when I got to that one, another, surmounting it.

Several times it was so.

Eventually I reached an unovertopped top and looked around: in all directions green pine-covered hills, green valleys below them, outlined and varied in the clear bright light, never boring in profile or contour, sharply accented, un-echoing, still, luminous: to the south a band of scintillating sea.

Eastwards the Alps themselves, snowflecked, rockstreaked, far; hiding their summits in banks of menacing clouds. To the north the great escarpment and the gloomy entrance to a gorge.

On a ridge some four crests and five valleys away I saw a crumbling ochred village which I did not know at all: it had a squared church tower topped by a belfry from which as I looked I thought I heard drifting the sound of some bell strike the hour. The sight of the far-off village gave me the assurance of solitude; the distant sound of the bell a remote seclusion.

I was happy.

I began to talk to myself softly, then loudly.

I held double, multiple conversations: arguments.

I began to bellow nonsense and obscenities, insults to the High and Mighty, priesthoods, royalties, Gods: outrages to speech, words never spoken or printed, only thought. I was free under this sky—unshackled, unburdened, unbuttoned . . .

I screeched there as loudly as ever man did: I was a maniac, an aphrodisiac, a colombophile, a stool-pigeon. I was everything and nothing: I was *there*.

I began to sing part songs, madrigals, sextets. I played Bach's Fantasia and Fugue in C minor, first on my organ, subsequently on my clavichord: I repeated it on the harpsichord. I recited Rilke, broadcast Baudelaire, yawned Yeats.

All that I knew, which was a lot and nothing, tumbled out and drowned me—the half-digested vomit of my mind.

It was a relief and a purge, a bleeding and transfusion; I was drunk not having drunken, satiated not having swallowed.

I sang flamencos, doinas, fados, lasoos, laendler, sardanas, gopaks, ratchenitzas, frisses, saëtas, calypsos, horas.

I made love sprinting and hurdled on my back and front.

A frightened rock-thrush fled with a clatter of brilliant wing-feathers: he made me hungry. A passerine twittered and made me sad.

And then I saw, four-footed assurance and all on a rock, old Nick himself, bearded and peering: peering at me there with very grave displeasure:

'Go away out of that, you dirty old bastard, you can't have me yet,' I upbraided. And that rang his bell, for he ran away tinkling it, shaking high his horns as he pranced.

Ah, he had nothing on me: but the bird had sobered me badly. There was nothing I needed more now than a drink.

I started downhill as directly as I could, tearing my trousers and the skin beneath them on the hook-thorned sarsaparilla and wondering as usual would the blood-red berries purge or poison me if I ate them. I never bothered to find out so I shall never know. I have never dared to eat them and I never will.

I broke, with much difficulty because of its terrible toughness, a coriaria branch, and with it dragged down many a caterpillar's nest from the pinetrees. The embryo creatures writhed in a boiling unseemly mass and I trod and trod on them and my foot was slimy and I did not like it: but I did like the trees and I hope they liked me.

When I got to the valley the dry stream had water-polished stones from the thunder showers that filled it two or three times a year for a million or more. Two or three million days then, there it had churned: a thousand years altogether; not much but enough, it was terribly short.

The next ridge was limestone.

It was followed by sandstone which was followed by limestone.

For some hours thus I puffed geologically up and down.

The day grew advanced and my thirst grew with it.

Whenever I caught a glimpse of it, perched on the top of the ever penultimate ridge, the village never seemed to grow nearer: neither did it abscond; it simply remained. I decided that maybe it was over the frontier in Italy far to the east, and that some trick of the light or mirage dangled its image constantly before me. I had long lost count of the ups and the downs and was beginning to be unaware of the twin unpleasantness of climbing or descending and as to which was which, or the worst, or either. I was past beginning to get fed up with my long-cherished solitude and its privileged screeching between ceiling and floor. A long time had passed and my happiness was gone.

Instead of being free I was now hemmed in by the very same words and the selfsame bush.

I was reaching a pitch of frustration and annoyance which I felt would bedevil my day and wondering whether it would not be better if I tried to find my way back to the road, when I found myself looking down from the top of a huge grey ant-infested boulder at a cultivated alluvial valley, some small fields and terraces, scattered houses and a track.

I was delighted at these signs of human activity, having previously been overjoyed at their absence, and hurried down the hill through the maquis as quick as its twigs and thorns would let me. A very steep slope of slithering sandstone scree, some bushes of cistus and *lavandula stoechas*, a jump across a small neat newly-cleaned dry irrigation channel, a push through the reeds of *Arundo donax* and there I was.

No time, but my thirst felt certain it was noon or past it.

In a few hundred yards the whole atmosphere changed: the ground was level, young meadows were green, and pollarded willows grew where in summer the water from channels delighted their thirsty white roots.

The first habitation I came to was on my right, the bare stems of a huge old trained vine casting snakelike shadows on its pinkish peeling walls, soaked in and faded by the sun.

It had once, judging by the scarcely discernible letters here and there on its front, been some kind of shop or *bistro*. Maybe it was still? Across the door hung a heavy bead curtain tied to one side by a coarse unravelled piece of string. I went in.

'Messieursdames,' I said.

# 27

AFTER the bright sunlight it seemed almost pitch dark inside but I could make out several people there, dispersed around the dimlit room. Before me, behind what might have been a counter, behind her what appeared to be a row of bottles, I could just make out Madame; and as my eyes accustomed themselves to the dimness I could see she had a kind beaming face.

'Madame,' I bowed, 'good day to you. I am enormously thirsty.'

'*Bonjour, monsieur: mais oui, évidemment, c'est l'heure.*'

'A pastis, please.'

She poured it for me, and I slowly and lovingly clouded it with cool water from an earthenware jug. I had been doting on this moment for hours, so it seemed, and was not disappointed with its realization.

I poured in a little more water, took a delicious sip, rolled it round my mouth, savouring its texture and flavour of delightful association, then swallowed the glassful in three satisfying gulps.

I ordered another.

Then yet another.

I was enjoying it, I can tell you.

Around the walls were spaced several formerly white, cast-iron-legged, infinitely-wiped marble-topped tables; behind three of them, people.

I was trying to make them out.

There was a man, nondescript but self-important, with a kindly cruel face burnt with the sun. He was sharpening a sickle or it may have been an axe. He seemed to want to be ignored so I ignored him.

There was a girl, a child-girl of about ten or eleven: she was dressed in a pale cotton frock many summers washed and hung. Over it she wore several jerseys and pullovers, all shabby, some holey, some holes coinciding. She was pretty and shy and sat on the far side of the room to her possible father, the sickle-sharpener. She smiled at me and her smile was just like the eyestreaked girl's in the bus. It was so like hers that it pierced me, stringing that day in one stretch as a bodkin beans. I felt she must be her sister: she was an echo and a promise. I smiled back at her.

Seated at the table as far as possible distant from the other two there was a third, no, including Madame, a fourth personage; of indeterminate shape and uncertain size, clad in dark garments in the darkened room, he reminded me of unpleasant things which I could not recollect but feared I knew only too well.

He was leaning very blackly over the scarcely white table, his arms splayed awkwardly and unevenly across it, one of his shoulders higher than the other, his head lolling in a curious manner in the opposite direction, silently strumming some alfresco sonata, upon which he was furiously concentrating, with the tips of strong sensitive fingers, on the marble. Evidently he was drunk. Certainly he was involved in some world of his own and as I peered further, my eyes getting accustomed to the darkness, I could see he was dressed up in robes of some sort. Yes, he was a priest. I could see it now: or he thought he was anyhow. It was this that had caused me that unpleasant twinge in the first place, for I have had far too much of them in my youth, all my life, in my land.

I was revolted and interested, repelled and fascinated. Here, in any case, was a most unhappy man. I wanted to speak with him yet hated to do so. I wanted to probe, to ignore and to know him.

Meanwhile all I did was to call for another. Then I consumed it. And ordered another and consumed it. I wanted to get over my ambivalence somehow and the pastis I knew would soon see to that.

Drinking, I watched: and the silent sonata continued. He played with both hands; obviously he heard it; and as I watched I could almost hear it too.

Then I *did* hear it: he paused, lifted his hands, then began again. I could hear, I mean I could see it and hear it: he had begun the slow movement of the fourteenth, Opus twenty-seven—the *Moonlight*. It was, after all, easy enough to spot. The more I watched, the clearer it became, the slow chords in the left hand and the repeated line of melody steady and sure in the right. There was silence: a pause in the silence. Then, sure enough, he was off on the finale. It was strangely exciting; he began to sway as musicians do, his body tightening or relaxing with the music, his uplifted face now concentrating on his work; it was a fine performance and I shared it all with him.

93

It was over: in the continuing silence I found myself suddenly applauding, clapping my hands vigorously, and everyone looked at me astonished. I suddenly stopped in the middle of bringing my hands one against the other. I felt idiotic but the priest was consumed with a mixture of delight and apprehension, for he could not make out whether I was making fun of him or had, by some miracle, really understood the intensity of his effort. Pleasure and doubt swept alternately over his wine-misted face. I put him at his ease, the pastis helping.

'Sir, that was a fine performance. The *Moonlight*, wasn't it? I shared it all with you.'

I could not bring myself to call him Father, and in any case in France Monsieur was polite and sufficient.

He was so astonished that he could not speak; someone had burst in and shared his skull and his skill with him for a while; the pent-up emotions of an age of time in the silence of his outer world, in the tumultuous singing of his inner head, had at last an audience.

'How did you know? How? What? . . . Who are you, anyhow? A stranger, I'll be bound. *Who are you?*' he shouted, then gently, nostalgically, he went on. 'It must be thirty—no, forty years, since anyone heard me play that sonata. Who on earth are you? Where have you come from?'

I was disturbed by his sad vehemence and in turn could not answer.

I ordered another pastis.

I began to feel I did not know where I had come from and certainly not whither I was going. Nor, indeed, had I any idea where I was.

I swallowed the pastis.

'I do not know exactly. I was once in Ireland. My name is not interesting and would convey nothing to you. I do not know where I am going, nor do I know where I am. I only know that I am drinking here because I was thirsty and am now nervous, and because I myself and all my family have often found refuge in drink as you yourself evidently do too. I recognized the sonata during the slow movement: it was easy. Tell me, how is it that you are so drunk at this hour on a Tuesday? Why?'

'I do not think it is Tuesday and as to the hour I neither know nor wish to know of its existence. In fact I think your question is most impertinent, but since you recognize and admire my playing I shall presently try to answer you if you will spend some time with me and have patience. Meanwhile *you* answer *me*: What are you doing here at this early hour (for I see by the sun it is still at least morning), more especially if it is, as you aver, Tuesday, which I very much doubt? Don't you know very well that visitors are only welcome at week-ends? Don't you know very well that neither Madame nor myself wish to be interfered with, and that moreover neither of us have the will nor sufficient supplies to entertain during the week? Don't you know that?'

'I have never been here in my life and I do not even know where I have got to, so how could I possibly be informed of your likes and dislikes? It was by pure chance I stumbled in here and now I am going. Give me another pastis, Madame, and I'll be off. Where am I, anyhow?'

There was a general silence. The man stopped sharpening his sickle or whatever it was he had under the table. The girl gave a little giggle, nervous—melodious, though. Madame served the drink silently and brought over one for the priest.

No one answered my question.

'Don't go, no; do not go, sir, I beg you. I am sorry for sounding rude: you see, we are not at all used to strangers. They are, frankly, not encouraged. We live our own lives in these parts; maybe they are peculiar ones, but our deaths are normal—that is to say, final. Do not go, sir. Allow me to play you something else. What would you like?'

'Do you know the D minor? It is one of my favourites.'

'Indeed I do: well; well! I have been practising it lately at home. Listen!'

Everyone held their breath. He was a changed man. This time there was an audience. He was on the platform. The hall was crammed.

He swallowed his pastis with one gulp and drew himself up on the chair, adjusting the tails of his coat. He drew the chair up to the keyboard. There was the intense silence preceding a concert whilst all of us adjusted ourselves to listen, coughed quietly, and waited.

His hands struck the first soft chromatic notes; they flowed and they carried me with them. I listened entranced. I watched as his features, his eyes shut, reflected every shade of expression and timbre. How often had I listened to music with my eyes shut, or to the gramophone? Now I was seeing the performer, hearing nothing, yet all. Perhaps this was the way? Everything was conveyed, nothing missing or stolen.

At the end of the first movement he paused, pulled up his trousers, massaged his hands for a few moments as if washing them, once more drew himself up and then, his fingers momentarily poised, launched into the second with closed eyes and uplifted face.

The other movements followed, the fiery running finale carrying me before it and in it like a rushing flood.

Then it was over too and he opened his eyes and spontaneously everyone applauded.

He had succeeded in transmitting, as does an accomplished acrobat poised high on pole or wire in the darkened heights of a circus-tent picked out by a single spotlight, the tension, co-ordination, and art above all, essential to convey the whole living will of one person to those outside them.

We had *taken part*.

It was a long time before anyone spoke.

Then, very slowly at first, the man went on sharpening whatever he had been sharpening, the child began to wriggle, Madame began to rearrange her bottles and glasses and the priest gave a huge loud yawn.

'By Heaven I'm thirsty! What'll you have? This music exhausts me. Bring us both the same again, Madame, plenty of it. Here's luck!' he called over. 'Good health.'

'No luck or health to either of you,' said Madame, but not crossly. 'It's bad enough having Monsieur le Curé boozing away here every day of the week. I've spent years of my life in keeping it quiet or trying to. On Sundays of course he's at work as best he can, swigging away in his own place: and on Saturdays I sometimes persuade him there might be a couple of interesting confessions to be heard. But generally he manages to get the gist of them out of me first, for it's hard to tell him just enough to whet his appetite and not too much so that he feels it's not worth him hearing them in person: and then, Lord knows, there's not very much going on here anyhow with most of the young people working in town . . . But on Mondays he's out first thing for a cure and for the rest of the week it's always the same, one after another till nightfall and beyond it, asleep on the bench or the floor, for it's rarely we get him to his bed. But now if you, sir, foreigner or whatever you might be, come and encourage him in his music and his drinking, surely the gendarmes will hear of it and close us. And then it's good-bye! Good-bye to my one and only really constant customer. I do not wish to seem at all rude or unwelcoming, Monsieur, but I should be very grateful if you could manage to take yourself off on your business. Allow me to offer you a drink for the road as a token of my esteem!'

She poured me another.

'Madame,' said the priest, 'I have often told you not to worry. The bishops have long ago despaired of me, and the gendarmes never come down here for they've other fish to fry. Besides which, when I am in the way of offering up prayers, which I admit is not perhaps as often as it should be, I tell you that nine-tenths of them are offered on your behalf. You should hear them! They would cost you a fortune normally. You are perfectly safe with the authorities—on High!' He pointed vaguely at the fly-blown ceiling. 'Meanwhile this gentleman' (he waved his arm in my general direction). 'Meanwhile this gentleman has been sent to me by either God or the Devil himself. He came from the end of the road, from the west! You know as well as I do there's no means of coming here that way! . . . I insist: please welcome him: be glad he is here, Madame. Kindly serve us.'

We were served.

'Tell me, sir,' I said, 'do not think I am simply curious, for it is rather more, far more, than that. I am an itinerant worrier and wanderer: as I have told you I do not know where I have come from nor do I know where I am going. I myself often suffer, as do most men, from the terrible desire to escape: to escape anywhere out of life to somewhere which is yet not death, although even death tempts me at times. Sometimes I drink, at others I dream: more often the one assists the other. But why, tell me why, do you, a believer, wish to escape? Why do you drink? Why are you drunk?'

'Because it helps me to believe in belief. Because it helps me to disbelieve in disbelief.'

'It helps me to believe in life. It helps me to avoid it and yet keep it. For I love it and hate it.'

'And it helps me to believe in death, I mean life after death.'

'Ah! So it seems we have much in common. We share uncertainty and music. We share many things, but I do not believe in death. We shall end, but I do not believe in the end. It's a nuisance not even to know that if nothing else.'

'Listen. Come home with me to my house. It's a queer place but it's my home and in it we might discover and explore many things for the time being. Come and have a meal with me! Lunch or supper? Later we shall know which. In any case we'll eat it . . . Or it might be breakfast: not much use . . .'

'I'd love to and I surely will, sir.'

'I live,' he said, 'by the Body and Blood of Our Saviour Jesus Christ: and nothing else. Wait till you see!'

'What time is it, for heaven's sake, Madame?'

'About ten,' she said, 'judging by the sun.'

'What time do you have lunch, sir, if you don't mind me asking you?'

'When I am hungry and no longer thirsty; generally between noon and sunset.'

'Where do you live? Near the church?'

'Both . . . both. Near to and at some distance.'

'What's the name of your village?' I tried again.

They all looked at me, then at each other, their eyes winking and wondering. Then they gave four little short laughs: the girl, Madame, the priest and the man: soprano, alto, tenor and bass.

But they did not answer me.

'Well, anyhow, I shall go there later and find out: but why won't you answer me?'

Silence this time.

'We shall stoke up now and eat up later,' said the priest. 'Give us another round, Madame.'

But I was getting very hungry and the innumerable aperitifs had dreadfully whetted my appetite.

The man was still sharpening his something and forcibly reminded me of a butcher. I felt I could not wait.

'Could you possibly let me have something to eat *now?*'

'Now?' they all said querulously in unison.

'Yes, *now*. I am ravenous. NOW.' I was impatient with their nonsense.

'We eat at noon, but I suppose I could scrape together something or other if you really insist.'

'I do. Please. Immediately.' My mouth was watering; I was slavering unpleasantly. 'What can you give me?'

'*Eh bien* . . . let's see . . . An omelette fines herbes, a slice of ham (or you can have it in the omelette if you like), some of this morning's bread that Martine fetched (Didn't you go to the baker, Martine?) . . . an artichoke vinaigrette . . .'

'That'll do fine. Quickly, please, I'm famished . . .'

'Patience, Monsieur, and I shall set it before you.'

I had, all this while, been standing before the counter. Now I seated myself opposite the priest, delightfully anticipating. Whilst Madame retired to prepare my feast I got Martine to bring us more pastis, drinking them full to the brim with cool water, savouring them slowly.

The man continued sharpening, whetting his metal.

His Reverence was talking but I paid no attention for my mind was as stuffed as my stomach hoped to be later.

Finally I ate: with enormous relish: each texture and flavour making fervent excursions on my lips and my tongue, in my gullet and throat—the scratchy sharp bread, half-cooked creamy flocculent herb-laden omelette, silky smoked ham, plucked sweet acidity of artichoke-calyx, inexorably flowering to its gorgeous blue thistle. Between each mouthful I poured gulps of red wine: at the end of each much-relished item, a litre.

Then they were talking and I was dozing and the pattern of sun moved on the tiled floor.

99

# 28

'LET'S go now,' said the priest.

And so I went with him.

Whilst I had been dining the spring had come, like Li-Tai-Po's to his drunkard, overnight.

The birds were now singing; two redstarts, a chaffinch and a hen golden oriole, a cuckoo, the sustained musical warble interspersed with mimicry of a shrike, the monotonous trill of a Bonelli's warbler (slow and single-noted and contrapuntal to the cuckoo) and the poo-poo, sweet and far, of a turtle dove.

Being not at all hungry they made me very sad.

'Come along now,' said the cleric.

So I went.

The grass had sprouted further, fresh short blades were translucent in the sun: the fields were studded with countless flowers of *Anemone stellata*—magenta, rose, pale-red, purple, pink—all turning with the light.

There were strong bronze-green shoots on the vine and the pollarded willows sparkled catkins. Water was running merrily in the ditches, the swallows sweeping low for their flies.

The road was dusty. We walked as slowly along it as children returning from school, uncertain as to which was most reluctantly accomplished, to go or to come. We walked towards the perched un-named village on its steep high hill. We seemed slowly to approach.

Garrulous before, we were silent now. The priest had put on his biretta and his shadow before us looked like some fine knave of cards.

'You seem an educated man: I am glad to have met you and still more glad you accompany me now. You speak good French: where did you say you have come from?'

'From Ireland,' I said.

'Direct? Very interesting and curious; it accounts for a lot.'

'I have not come direct; not at all direct. I came from a bus, through the maquis,' I said.

'Please,' he answered, 'that's enough now. Let's leave it. We can discuss this all later if we must.'

We walked on in silence, the only sounds the persistent rustle of the watercourses and the early croak of an eager frog.

As we got closer to the village it appeared more and more beautiful, the now visible detail increasing its texture and charm.

'That's my house, there,' he said, raising his arm in a curving, drooping gesture that pointed in no particular direction whatever. But somehow I judged that he indicated an enormous many-storied old building wedged between others and perched on the edge of a sizeable cliff.

'I have another, my once official presbytery, next to the church-tower over there; part of it, indeed. But I do not care much for it or my housekeeper who smells of soap and incense, things I abominate.'

We turned up a cobbled mulepath which struggled up the hill and soon we were in a narrow sunless street scented of herbs, old wood, and munching domestic animals, sounding only of the munching and our own deadened feet. Another still narrower alley brought us before an enormous chestnut-wood carved door, some of its embellishments struck off or rotted, peppered with the neat holes of dry rot, standing firmly to attention awaiting its imminent end.

He fumbled in his voluminous faded black clothing and produced an enormous key whose complicated tongue he fitted in the serrated mouth of the lock, creaking and crunching as he turned it twice. The door opened with difficulty, unevenly groaning on its out-of-true hinges, small powdery showers of grub-eaten wood falling silently down its sweet-grained sides. Within it was dark and smelt coldly of slate.

'Come in and welcome, sir. Make yourself at home.'

There seemed nothing less likely.

We started to climb a flight of dirty stone stairs which disappeared before him and against which I could barely discern his toiling mounting figure. Any light there was filtered through cracks in the tightly closed shutters. On each landing was a door.

There were many landings, many doors. We went on; up and up; wheezing sniffling and snorting.

I had lost count of our ascent when he stopped abruptly and I nearly fell on top of him. My exaggerated effort still carrying me upwards, I clutched at his boots. They were just before my nose and I studied their heels and soles carefully: once well and often polished, they were now shabby, mudstained and truly down-at-heel. During the few seconds I lay there, my face resting uncomfortably on the gritty surface of the stair-tread, I could distinctly make out the two types of clay adhering to those boots; the pinkish-grey siliceous fine loam of the sandstone overlaid and re-overlaid by the sienna red-brown of the limestone's rich earth: on top of all tiny pieces of straw and specks of dried goat-dung he had only just acquired in the street down below.

Apologizing profusely, I scrambled to my feet. We were now before another heavy door at the head of the stairs, there being no landing. Another key was fumbled for and turned: the door groaned open and we shuffled into a dim room occupying the entire area beneath the roof.

He went to the shutters, opened them partially and hooked them that way: a stream of air flowed in; dust and moths danced in the narrow shaft of light.

# 29

THE room was huge and had little furniture: an iron bedstead, the bed unmade; beneath it an enamel chamber-pot filled to the brim; two or three old upholstered armchairs, their tapestry covers, lacerated by use, time or cats, hanging in hapless fringes to the floor; a table on which were the remnants of a meal and upon which, amongst the crumbs, crusts and peelings, two mice unconcernedly nibbled and pried whilst a mangy looking tabby sat near by on the floor and miaowed us a welcome or appeal.

There was an enormous open fireplace, the long dead remains of many a fire overflowing onto the floor-space around it, piles and piles of books, papers or manuscripts all around the walls, and at the far end a giant desk stacked with toppling heaps of similar objects, the smaller and narrower volumes often beneath, heavy tomes capping them like crazy cromlechs. As he closed the heavy door with a bang several of them plunged loudly to the floor, raising small clouds of dust as they landed.

He paid no attention whatsoever.

'Make yourself at home, sir,' he said once again, but I saw little prospect of doing so in this comfortless barrack echoing to our scrunching treads like a long deserted warehouse in an abandoned railway station.

'Make yourself at home!'

I lowered myself gingerly onto one of the chairs, brushing off some small mouldy potatoes, which rattled dully across the floor, as I did so: it creaked dreadfully as it took my full weight and I very much feared it was going to collapse.

It did so.

I came to the ground with a thud, raising a fresh cloud of dust. Both back legs, eaten with beetle, had disintegrated. Without turning round, for he was occupied with something near the table, my host murmured absentmindedly: 'Never mind; there are others. I am glad you like music, at any rate.'

I was so taken aback that I did not answer him but dusted as best I could the black dirt from my hands and my clothing and obediently seated myself, even more gingerly, my hands leaning upon my knees and thus conveying as much of my weight as I could through my legs to the floor, on another one which complained but held fast.

'I admire music, indeed I adore it, but I hear none now except in my head where forever it is playing: and when my head is occupied by other forces it plays elsewhere, in my heart, in my guts, in my legs,' went on his Reverence, ignoring this chair business, 'Sometimes I am lost in one sort of music, in one century, in one style: for weeks it may be Bach; for months it *is* Bach. I know all his keyboard works by heart, the preludes and fugues, the Goldberg Variations, the little Organ Book—*all, all*. My father taught them to me. He was an organist in the Ardèche and he left me all his scores, all his music. There they are!' He swept his arms outwards, embracing all the jumbled stacks which in some places reached the ceiling in symmetrical pillars and elsewhere lay scattered as the slates off a roof after storm.

'Sometimes I am with the early ones, the first singers, the masters, believing and kindly, human and divine. Sometimes it is Jannequin, Costelay, Palestrina, Orlando di Lasso, Luca Marenzio, Dufay, Okegem or your English Purcell, Byrd or Irish Dowland: or further away still with the Minnesingers and Troubadours, their harps and their hymns, singing before all was corrupted by my Church and the world force-fed with guilt subsequently lived up to. But they never succeeded in ruining music as they wished, they never stopped its singing and its songs; and I still listen to Missa Papae Marcelli with tremendous pleasure when I can get a performance together; or Vittoria or King John the Fourth of Portugal—do you know him?'

Without waiting for my answer he disappeared through an arch at the back of the room where the roof sloped down towards the floor, where he still went on talking. I could see him in the shadows and caught the glint of glass, but I could neither hear what he was saying nor make out what he was at. There was the squeak of a wooden tap turning, as I thought, and then sure enough the gushing of liquid went on for some time and he reappeared carrying with both hands a wicker-cased demi-john of wine which he plumped down with a grunt on the floor next my chair.

He went and came again with two large elegant crystal-stemmed glasses which he set on a stool, filling both to the brim with some difficulty but no spilling, by tipping the demi-john carefully on its side.

'Drink up,' he said, lowering his glassful with one swallow. 'Or it might be the lutenists or mediaeval guitarists, especially the Spanish ones, that accompany me, plaintively plucking their jewelled stars from the darkened years they have survived, the silences between each note as exciting and taut as the rising or falling cadence itself, so that I hold my breath wondering which way it will turn or relax at the inevitable crossways before it, to solution. For weeks I am lost there wandering with them, itinerant, eating little, drinking a lot, a purseful of coins thrown down to reward me, or hounded out of town by soldiers and their dogs, over the mountains to the plains, to the Landes, northwards to the Low Countries or enlisted in the Crusades. I have lived a long time with them. I have travelled very far in their time and in their place.'

He paused, golluped another glassful, poured me one also, and went on:

'There's nothing like good wine, now, nurtured and matured in the right and proper way—a comfort to life and a short cut to death: plenty of it, both ways. And what about Mahler? An abused fellow; slobbered over by Germans who hacked him and Heine to silence in their maniac mentalities—How could we ever do without them? The Germans, I mean. The answer is we couldn't, I tell you: we couldn't. They are part of us, a vile part, a sure part, an essential part. Must we amputate ourselves? Hobble half-legged? Maybe they'll do it for us? Maybe they've done it for us already and we are poisoned already throughin and without? But we have *Kindertotenlieder*, *The Song of the Earth* and the Ninth and many other things. Why don't you answer me? *Are you deaf?*'

He was shouting at me now: ranting.

'No indeed, far from it, mercifully.'

He ignored me.

'As for Mozart, I live years with him. Why are you so ignorant?'

'I am not.'

'Or Schubert? The Octet? *Winterreise?* Were you ever an organ-grinder or a dog?'

He was shouting again.

He ignored me.

He refilled the glasses.

'And of all, and of all—the last Beethoven quartets—the final wonder surely? The *Heiliger Dankgesang* addressed mercifully to no friend or acquaintance of my bishop or his Pope, what do you think of them? How closely can you listen? How truly can you play? Can you enter each instrument and, burrowing downwards, stumbling along each resounding string to its curled key, become part of this great mysterious chanting? Only an unbeliever could

105

so deeply believe, only one deaf so resplendently hear! Or take Berlioz: only he, the vituperant, could have explored and absorbed the Mass: only he, alive, knew death and despised it: only he, Berlioz, could have written his *Grande Messe des Morts* and walked with them forwards and over and back again; and set it down. Do you know it? Can you hear it? The Kyrie? Can you?'

He gave me no chance, ever, to answer him.

He went on and on.

'Ah! How I hate God, the God of love who is the God of hate; the merciful God without any mercy: I wish He was at an end. Here's to God's enemies!—To *their* God's enemies—May He damn them!'

He lifted his glass again and drained it: refilled it, drained it again: refilled it, drained it again.

*Da capo.*

'No. I don't care what you say' (I had said nothing for I had not had the chance) 'only music can speak in its riches universally. What's the printed word compared to issued sound? You can carry it always around with you. Who knows or wants to know Molière or Racine, Ronsard or Claudel, all by rote, quite by heart? It would kill you.'

'The printed word,' I said, 'is and can be issued sound. It can be read inside or uttered outside.'

He ignored me.

He drank glass after glass. He rambled on. He ignored me.

I kept quite far behind him but found that I too was now filled with this music he spoke of with such passion. So we played different tunes, separately encased, soundproofed, silent. It went on for hours and when I next heard him he was talking of Vivaldi and Alessandro Scarlatti, father of Domenico.

Suddenly there was a clang of churchbells.

It was the Angelus sounding.

He picked up a bottle, rushed to the window and flinging the shutters wide, threw it out with all his force.

'Curse that blasted Angelus!' he shrieked. 'Take that!' and he pitched another bottle in the general direction of the belfry clearly visible over a sea of old roofs and chimneys.

Of course it could not reach its target: never. It landed with a tinkling crash on the third roof from us and I realized that this must be a habit for the roofs were already well littered with broken glass.

He rushed back to the table, seized his biretta, a breviary and other books.

'I must go,' he said. 'Damn that Angelus, it's always interrupting me. I was enjoying that Aria, weren't you? It's exquisite. Don't go: wait for me; I'll be back, I won't be long. But I simply must go now for I have to keep my job.'

He banged the door behind him and clattered down the stairs in a flurry of dust and dirty dark cloth.

There I was.

I had scarcely spoken.

I filled up my glass and swallowed the good wine.

## 30

SHOULD I go or stay?

Unfortunately I was hungry again, and after lethargically studying the objects within my range of vision I got up and decided to explore. Perhaps there was food around somewhere.

I fixed the shutters wide open and in the released sunlight every step I took sent a little cloud of dust spurting from between the cracks of the boards.

There was music piled and scattered everywhere: miniature scores, full scores, single sheets (some manuscript) and huge green faded volumes of the standard classics—Beethoven sonatas, Haydn quartets, Handel's concerti grossi, some evidently recently used, others forsaken, black with grime, no longer to his taste or fashion—Viotti, Wieniawsky, Paganini, Tartini, Chabrier, Albeniz—discarded, skewed, trodden on, rejected.

In one corner there was a great ball of what looked like discarded much-used wire-netting, smothered with dust and festooned with cobwebs. I approached it cautiously and put out my hand to feel it: at my slightest touch there was a releasing tension, a small twang; the dust fell or spurted away and I saw there thick copper wires, thinner ones with them, silvery, slightly rusty. I shockingly realized I was fingering the degutted interior of a concert-grand piano. I saw in the middle of the bewildered ball a haphazard pile of disintegrated keys, white or black, ivory coated or ebony still, and behind it all, against the peeling wall, the heavy gilded piano-frame itself with its triangular shape and weight-saving circular holes—mouldering, grime-covered, spider-woven.

There was nothing left to this corpse but skeleton and entrails and they greatly disturbed me.

I decided to hurry up with my search for some sustenance and get out.

There was nothing else of interest in the room: no books, no pictures, no mirror: just the furniture, the piles of music, the chamber-pot, the glasses and wine, and on the table a large knife.

I decided to explore the appendage or loft at the back. I looked in but could see very little. There was a small tight-shuttered window giving no crack of light.

Just at that moment I heard a frantic clattering on the stairs growing increasingly loud as the person or persons (for they sounded many) ascended. There was a crash and the priest re-erupted, a larger than usual cloud of thick dust surrounding him like a nondescript cloak.

'Terrible news: frightful news!' he spluttered. 'We'll have to finish off Rablon at once; he has gone and got killed off his cart. Just as he was maturing so very nicely too! I sampled him one morning last week! Our work is cut out, my dear fellow, for he was a huge man, the largest in the whole parish and there's no room to decant him anywhere at all except into Mademoiselle Bayon's (which we are at), and the two of them never mixed well or got along together anyhow. No, there's nothing for it. We shall have to finish him off before morning even if we have to get help. But you'll help me, won't you? We shall do our best together first; I am sure I can count on you. This is terrible: even scandalous! It's so downright wasteful, and if there's one thing I object to it's waste. He was young and strong, hale and very hearty and I always make use of them first. And last too! I tell you they like it; young and old, men and women. We'll just have to polish him off! And at once!'

I stared at him: evidently he was out of his mind. Indeed that had been pretty well obvious long before. I had been worse than foolish to remain once he had gone; it had been a splendid chance to escape. Now I should have to humour him. I was, I must confess, most decidedly frightened and cast anxious glances at that knife.

Even as I did so he seemed to collect his wits and to my horror rushed over to the table, seized that very weapon and made straight for me in an apparent frenzy.

'Let's cut it open! Polish him off!' he roared.

I put my arms up and over my head in an involuntary gesture of surrender and abandon.

'I had tied it for the winter; come on, let's cut it open.' He dived past me into the darkened place beyond. I removed my arms; tremblingly I looked after him. He was sawing away madly at the rope that tied the shutter of the little window: it was a thick rope and it took him some time to get through.

At least, I thought, the knife was not for me.

Having severed the rope he pushed wildly at the shutter which, breaking finally free from its one intact hinge, fell clattering out into space to land far below with a splintering whack sometime later. There was suddenly revealed a most beautiful prospect far and wide over the green valley we had trudged along that morning; far small houses; willows, watercourses and ridge upon ridge of those hills first hazily green, then increasingly blue, to the distance.

He paid absolutely no attention to me.

He was standing with his back to the window, both arms outstretched as if he were preaching or welcoming his flock.

'Look,' he said, 'just look!'

So I looked.

It took some time for my eyes to transmit to my mind and they having done so, for my mind to comprehend, what they had told it they saw, such was the incongruous reality—indeed sur-reality—before me. The great long loft, the Roman tiles of its now unceilinged roof slanting downwards to the back wall, nothing between them and the heavy-boarded floor: there they were, line upon line, tier upon tier: *coffins*!

Some were arranged on the floor itself; some were on trestles at waist level; more on higher trestles above them at eye level; others perched still higher on a kind of rough scaffolding almost against the roof.

Some were freshly made of oak or olive, others of plain deal; some were stained, brown and old. All of them had their heads to the wall and their feet towards the light from the small opened window. On the foot-piece of each was chalked a name echoing that and those I subsequently made out on the tight-shut lids I could look down on, and each name was set out with its data like this:

CARCIN, Michel. né 12 avril 1879, décedé le (here was a blank) 19 . . .

BERTHOU, Suzanne. née le 4 juillet 1902, décedée le . . . 19 . . .

BOUYON, Raymond né le 17 juin 1929, mort le . . . 19 . . .

BENIA, Martine Joyeuse. née le 20 décembre 1936, morte le . . . 19 . . .

RABLON, Marcel, né le 28 octobre 1912, décedé (here his Reverence picked up a piece of chalk and completed the legend) le 14 juin 1955.

'Here he is, damn him, full to the very brim.'

It was only then that I noticed that every coffin was fitted with a wooden tap or bung in its near end, and that next each tap and further to the names I have set down were chalked other inscriptions, at first sight far more apocryphal:

chez Bourbourtelle 46

Le Virat 48

Les Moulières 54

Drac 47

chez Grive 52

Bellet 50 . . .

His Holiness kept his wine in the coffins eventually destined for his parishioners!

'You see? (Do you see?) Don't you understand? (Do you?)' he

said. 'I've done this for over thirty years now. I am not only the soi-disant spiritual guide and mentor of my flock but I also supply them on top and in addition to any last sacraments or that sort of thing, with their final fine resting places: and they pay for their last lodgings and burials by instalments! As soon as I've measured them up (with my own little cock-robin eye, of course) I get to work: at once, instanter, so I shall not be let down however soon they depart. Who can tell his appointed hour? And, my Lord, is it not just as well? Ha! Ha! Ha!' he laughed disturbingly. 'Of course, sometimes they grow fat or shrink up and then I have to change the provisions.

'One day I was endeavouring to draw off a *bonbonne* from a barrel of excellent Bellet I had at the time. I was thirsty from working on a fine oak plank for Maître Lacquet and between one thing and another—you know how it is—out gushed the wine into a coffin I had practically ready. By Jove, I tell you, it was an excellent job! Out it gushed into it, noisily, pushingly: not a drop leaked out though! Not a single bloody drop! I looked at the workmanship, at the clean close-fitting joints: there was not a drop nor a stain to be seen. I was able to scoop it out, all of it, and put it back through a tundish, at once and with small loss, right into the barrel. The coffin was beautifully stained and the wine-wet wood smelt splendid.

'So I said to myself, why waste all this grand elongated space with *empty* coffins when I've hardly room enough now for my sweet rotund barrels? (I was using up wood I had found around the house). So I filled them all up as you see and put bungs at their feet and made even better jobs than before of their lids (which took some doing, if I may say so) so that they were practically airtight. There they are!' said he, with a grandiose wave. 'I chalked each owner's or future occupier's name provisionally at the end (the engraver, I should like you to understand, only makes the brass plates immediately after death), and meanwhile the wood is most wonderfully seasoned, very often by the identical wine its future occupier consumed with relish all his life; so that they finally unite, steeped within and stained without, with their own life's aroma! . . .

'Some of the girls like white, of course, but I must confess that I do not; except perhaps at first communions for colour's sake; so I compromise with rosé from the Var. Mercifully these activities bring me a nice little income, almost enough to keep the coffins filled all the time. And that's why I do it.

'Yet no matter how I plan, the same thing always happens: quite unexpectedly a blossoming girl or heart-healthy man dies. Or if there's an ailing invalid and I drain off their coffin, having already anointed them, they live on and live on until I can no longer resist filling up the well-seasoned vessel once again: whereupon of course they die—generally unministered to. So you see how it is! Look, here's Rablon, a fine-bodied red from Le Luc. I haven't a stick of room for him anywhere except the breadbins for those over ninety; and I dare not risk filling one of those.

'So help me, lad. We've a good seventy litres still in there and it must be empty *and* dry by the very small morning without fail. Come along! Drink up! And let's have a loaf with it—Here!'

He shuffled over to the far end and opening one of the hermetically-fitting lids with difficulty and with the aid of the above-mentioned knife, took out a couple of remarkably fresh Richelieu loaves, their crusts still audibly crackly as he squeezed them. He broke off a morsel.

'I live, as you see, as I told you. Bread and Wine. The Body and Blood of —— except for the odd meal at Madame's or the marvellous occasions when my niece comes from town, alas far too infrequent, when we have a good finely-arranged, carefully-purchased cooked-by-her blow-out to relieve my gastronomic monotony.'

He took down from the top of one of the trestle-raised boxes a five-litre earthenware jug with a spout to it and very carefully turning the tap adjacent to the spot where Rablon's feet would soon be, let the first spurt of settled wine fall bloodlike on the encrusted floor: he repeated this operation and then began to fill the jug slowly and affectionately. He poured two glassfuls: it was of glorious colour and splendid body. He took a mouthful, rolled it lovingly against his palate, behind his cheeks and to the roots of his tongue, then thoughtfully swallowed it, his eyes closed.

'It's a dreadful shame to rush this but alas—Hé—we've no choice. Here's to poor Rablon, long may he rest!'

He drained his glass.

This was the procedure we followed: we ate a lump of bread—took a mouthful of wine—savoured it—swallowed it—drained the glass.

This continued for hours.

'You have told me a lot, I must say. May I ask you some questions, though, now?'

'By all means: fire ahead,' he nodded, rolling another mouthful.

'May I ask why it was that you apparently destroyed your piano? Unless I am mistaken, that over there is the remains of a Pleyel concert grand?'

'Wood,' he said.

'Wood?'

'Wood for my work and wood for my warmth. We've nearly come to an end of it now and I must honestly confess I don't know what I'll do.' He gave a deep sigh. 'I could not get the ivory off those keys and it smelt awful, though they made good kindling: except for the black notes, completely incombustible: that's why I had to leave them. I have used nearly all the wood to hand. There were four floors and their joists below this one: *twice* so, *twice* there. Now, just beneath where we are sitting there's a drop of over eighty-five feet to the roof-vaulting of the cellar below! I used every bit of that flooring for my work; for the comfort of my flock.

'It was hard to know where to start. I was foolish enough once, on my hands and knees on the fourth floor, to cut away all the planks round the door first; and as I had had a few jars at Madame's that afternoon I had a tricky time tightroping it back. Now those joists are all gone too and I should not be surprised if the whole house fell down one day, with nothing to strut it: though of course my neighbours' are sound enough, I suppose, and in any case it's all the same to me as you may imagine.

'I call the room that was formerly below us the Bishop's room; for in the old days the visiting bishop, who used to come by mule or sedan chair, was accustomed to sleeping the night in that fine four-postered mahogany bed—now planked or burned. One night, the two of us in our cups and forgetting the work I had done there, I went and opened the door wide saying, "This way, your Eminence". He ambled towards the old room and was just going to step into space when I seized him by the back of his oily-necked coat and wrenched him to safety on the flat of his back, sprawling on the landing. I fear he took it very badly, calling for an explanation which was very hard to give. And when I held out the candle in the flickering darkness, showing him the pit into which he had so nearly plunged, he turned, gave me a quizzical glance and made the sign of the cross over me. It was at least a mercy he had drink taken himself.

'In the morning he let it be known that he regarded the matter very seriously indeed and would have to report to his superiors on the matter and that, at the very least, he would see to it that I spent the rest of my life here, where I was and still am, to expiate my extraordinary indiscipline and tantamount to murderous neglect.

'He also ordered me to have the floors and furniture replaced at my own expense. But of course I couldn't. And many years later, when the new bishop came (the old one being dead), and I showed him round telling him how dry-rot and storms had almost destroyed the entire church-house over the years I had served there, he took pity on me, even knowing my record, no doubt, from their files, and replaced the whole lot out of central funds.

'So I left them a while, for a year or so anyhow; then I got out my saw, set, tried and sharpened it and put it to its old use. That's how I've still got material for my work: but there's not much of it left.

'Maybe the new bishop will visit me? The quite new young one! They say he's very progressive and liberal and I am still a poor parish priest. Perhaps he'll come and visit me and we could risk repeating the business. . . . I could tell him the floors had been eaten by cockroaches and rats, couldn't I?'

'I suppose so,' I mumbled, gulping the wine.

By this time (it was deep night long since) we were both well on the way to even greater unreality than we had previously enjoyed since my coming. Strange thoughts, wild ideas, kept milling in my head; whilst he himself was launched again on music.

But I could not apprehend him, giving illustrations I could no longer follow although he seemed very thrilled with them himself.

'Isn't that a wonderful passage?' he would exclaim. 'What splendid and subtle modulations! Only *he* could have thought of them! We had an old organ here once and I used to play those very canons on it until one day the mice ate a hole in its bellows and then the rats built a nest in the swell: I used the rest of the leather for boots that cold winter. Some day they'll repair it.

'It was sweet, clear, eighteenth century: with additions of course. The *very* instrument, I tell you, if you liked Gabrieli and the Venetians.'

He was silent at last: staring, red-faced.

I could feel and see the music coursing through him.

I thought I even recognized the piece as it moved beneath the surface of his skin, sparkled in his half-closed eyes, twitched at the corners of his mouth, lifted one hair-lined nostril then another. It was the final fanfare welcoming the Doge and his Courtiers to St. Mark's square on that sunny morning: I could hear the crowd's ovation!

'Bravo!' he shouted. 'Bravissimo—Wasn't it? Wasn't it?—*Bis! —Bis!—Bis!*——'

I was once again startled and I finished the full glass in my hand.

This business was infectious: my own head began to tune: then all the written notes fell out in a turbulent roaring heap, drenching me, drowning me, burying me. I began to hum and shout, whistle, conduct and stamp my feet. There was, there could not be, an end to this—ever! Our music was on the largest scale— Brahms and Sibelius symphonies, Walton's *Belshazzar's Feast*, *Symphonie Funèbre et Triomphale*, *La Grande Messe des Morts*, Bach's fugues FORTISSIMO! I was in musical delirium; he was in it too: rival barkers blaring in a monstrous fairground, our booths flaming with flares and great sounds—whirling; separate; in unison; continuous. . . .

We drank more and more: poor Rablon ran low, an ebbed-tide of redness scarce level with his bung-hole. We baled him now with a large silver ladle; we sampled him as soup; we sipped him with coffee-spoons; we sucked him with straws; squeezed him with a sponge. He was finished.

It was late night now, the small unillumined hours when death's sordid sickle swishes close enough to scare: when you feel its fluttered air on your overheated cheeks and your surfeited lips and your eyes behind their cowering brittle lashes.

Then soft songs occurred, age-old, reassuring; songs that had sounded so long that the past and the future, birth and death, were the same even road of humanity, of love. Lutes, zithers, recorders, viols, gently admonished with their sweet lover's singing, and we whispered and walked softly to hear ourselves severally.

But the organ interrupted with pedal-notes of fortune; the organ again; all organs; all organs trodden on!

And that one far away in the Thomaskirche in Leipzig. . . .

And everything fell together in confusion, sweeping and swirling in the potholes and the gorges of our rock-hewn cauldroned minds; in infinite multitudes; in octuors; in sextets; in quatuors; in duos: evenly. Debussy with Verlaine, Duparc with Baudelaire, Schumann with Heine, Wolf with Moerike, Britten with Blake, and Rilke all alone . . . singing . . . singing.

And His Holiness, His Eminence, His Grace, His Majesty, His Reverence—ranting and jigging, stamping from the very last of his fine five floors the greatest of his dust-fevered clouds; spilling wine, conserving more, slobbering and swallowing it . . .

Rablon run out and we ourselves with him.

Rablon run out but the thumping continuing.

Rablon run out but the trombones braying.

Rablon run out but the timpani thundering.

There was light in the sky . . .


# 31

IT was the causeway and the iron bridge over the waking waiting mullet, head to jowl, cheek to tail. The shindy of our passing could be heard miles away: from Sutton to Santry, from Swords to the Asylum, if the wind blew only rightly.

And there *were* the sand-dunes and Portrane's red-brick, brittle and too clear in the ever-paling sun.

304D.

I did not like it nor its location.

There were orchards rippling by in quincunxes.

Jam orchards.

I wanted to go back from where I had come from.

I wanted to be off from where I had got to.

I wanted to sleep until at least Rush, Lusk or Skerries.

I wanted to lay Rablon in his last wine-wet ditch.

*I wanted to go to sleep.*

And so I did.

# 32

THAT was the day he was bunched at last: so many and varied had been the alarums and excursions, such a strain and tearing between affection and avoidance.

I always wanted to hurry off to him, to drop everything, down tools and join him in delirium, at the same time hoping I should miss that last good-bye—it would be too painful: but too painful also to escape.

It was a fine day in August, a rarity in those parts; a Friday, I think.

I was working in the drawing loft at the time on cross-sections of part of the bilge-keel of a new Clan liner shortly to be laid down on Number Five slip. They wanted them for moulding early next week. The afternoon shift had just started; I had heard the siren. We were all on overtime; it was essential to get them launched in good time to be sunk!

I was just thinking I would go out for a breather when Hector, the foreman-wine-glass-collector from Inchmackie said, 'You're wanted on the telephone.'

I knew at once what it was, of course: Maggie again. Maggie as always alarmed and isolated away up in Cowall. But how was I to get up there at this hour?

'Yes, Maggie?' I said.

'He's really very bad, sir. Woeful bad this time, sir, and Doctor Shearwater says you are to come up at once. He's been asking for you since morning. He's crying out for you now.'

She paused: there was silence. Between and behind the faint buzzing of the line I thought I could hear my uncle's far-away mechanized voice raised in demented appeal.

'Come quickly, sir, quickly.'

'I'll do my best, Maggie, my very, very best: certainly I will. But how can I cross now? At this hour? You know yourself the afternoon boat's been taken off and there's none now until the morning mail.'

'Maybe you could take a train to Whistlefield or Arrochar; or a car from across the water from Dunoon or Kirn or somewhere. I don't really know, sir. But please come soon, sir. Soon; at once.'

'I'll do my very best, Maggie. Tell Uncle not to worry and give him my love. See you later.'

I put down the receiver.

It was always the same.

Now I should have to go to Hector and beg him to let me off, losing possibly my overtime. Tell him that Uncle Melchi was very bad again.

At least he knew I was not making it up for *I* knew he had been listening to the whole conversation in the nearby works exchange, his left hand holding the hand-mike, his right one caressing Jeannie the telephonist at the most conveniently accessible worthwhile spot on her sonsie anatomy; for he was gone on her entirely and I cannot say I blamed him.

Yet it was foolish and upsetting and I wanted to get that bilge-section out of the way and be off for the week-end up the Laws or to Lamlash: now I supposed I should be back, hangover and all, over Sunday as well.

Far away in the corner I saw Hector come in as clear as a puppet under the brilliant shadowless strip-lighting: I paused, waiting for him to come slowly nearer.

'Hector, it's my old uncle again: you know how it is! I'm afraid I shall have to go up to him; they say he's bunched properly this time. Can you give me compassionate or will you have to dock?'

'Well now, that's too bad, me lad; we'll see, we'll have to see. But you know they're screeching for those bilge-secs. Can ye no come in the morning and finish them? Or Sunday? I'll be here anyhow.'

'That depends how I find things up the loch; but I'll let you know. You know it's not my fault, don't you? I don't wish it so. It's nothing but a nuisance, at this hour especially.'

'All right: go along!'

So I went off down the steep stairs into the yard with its clamour, machine-gun riveting, hissing arc-welding and a whining electric transporter-crane agitating and irritating a huge prefabricated sternpiece hanging menacingly, twirling slowly above me, as I cut across to the main gate towards MacKay's at Gourock.

I would go there and plan what I would do whilst I sat at an upstairs window and contemplated the lie of the land, very literally before me, drinking strong tea, eating scones and oatcake.

I took a tram.

It was indeed a rarely splendid afternoon, all the hills of Cowall and beyond mirrored in the streaked stillness of the cool sunlit firth; two liners, three tankers and a couple of new for trials dozing at their cables at the Tail o' the Bank waiting for the tide. So still that I could hear the valve steam roaring from the pipe of the furthest away.

The sky was static, pellucid, fluffy-clouded—very pale blue and cream; the shadows dark and sleeping over mountain and lochan. I could clearly hear the rapid small-diametered paddlewheels of the *Lucy Ashton* rapping the water away near Craigendoran. Should I go there, over towards Ben Lomond's sunlit reflection and risk a train for Whistlefield or maybe an evening cruise up to Tarbet from Balloch? That might give me a golden opportunity to stoke up so as not to be too handicapped later with Uncle Melchi when I reached him: but of course I would likely overplay my hand and never reach him at all: yet I always liked a sail in the poor old *Prince John* if she was running. Yes, a good idea on the whole.

Or I could fetch over to Dunoon or Kirn and get the Strachur bus by Loch Eck and walk over the hills by Ben Bheula: rather too much of a toil though, I thought, in spite of some possible fun in Dunoon where they said there was a big fine Fair for the Paisley weeks.

The matter was decided when I realized the time and saw, puff-bellowing badly-stoked coal-smoke, one of the North British boats heading across from Helensburgh; very likely one of the last evening regulars. I think it was *Marmion*, her vermilion funnel with white band and black top catching the now westering sun from down water.

I paid my bill and hurried off to the pier just in time to scramble on board her as they cast off.

Across to Craigendoran then, slipping the northern edge of the river where it shallowed and narrowed, and sandbanks, then mud-flats, took the place of the cold plunging rocks: from one pier to the next, holidaymakers strolling, open-shirted, sweet-sucking—to where the Glasgow train was snorting and snuffing its super-heater a few paces only from the gangplank.

I did not want the train or the gangplank either, yet nonetheless crossed the deep dripping pit between paddle-box and pier to the booking office, behind whose verdigrised bars a sad-looking Scot peered uncertainly at the excursionists from his tethered self.

Ah, he knew very little for certain, situated as he was: but he did think that if I got maybe as far as Alexandria or Dumbarton I'd very possibly get a train or bus to Balloch where Yes, more than likely, there was an evening cruise to Tarbet or even beyond; but of course I'd be quicker direct up to Arrochar or Whistlefield from the junction, if the train stopped there at all or up above either he couldn't say; but what with week-end-eve and early-enough-still, likely enough, sooner or later, I'd find convenient connections to wherever it might be I was contemplating going: if she stopped.

Armed with this accurate outline of possibilities, I decided on walking or at least on climbing, as little as I could. I would risk

Whistlefield and the chance of Johnny's boat to the Lochhead or anyhow old MacNeilish to row me to Carrick, Stucki Beagh or near it; east or west shore to their choice.

So I walked over between the sad paintless level-crossing gates and along the road to the pointless junction where sure enough in half an hour's time, so they maintained, there would be a train up North for Crianlarich and beyond, stopping at all stations and at Whistlefield by request only; which would be seen to.

I bought an *Echo* and walked to the nearest pub to peruse it, sipping some good Islay: but I paid no attention to the whiskey or the news for I thought all that time of dear Uncle Melchi; of how he was, how much I loved him, how he would be; and of how and what state we would both be in when I joined him; by whatever devious route.

How he loved falling ill in inconvenient, inaccessible places, 'Inverdonich' of all of them the end of the track; no light but too much water, with the falls thundering away night and day directly from the cliffs into the creeping glassy sea on both sides of the house; miles from the village by boat and the road enough to smash all the springs of his old Model-T every month when he recklessly skimmed its bouldery outcrops. Luckily the telephone (and very soon his turbine) would change much of that.

I ordered another double. I drank it.

I got up with my *Echo* and wandered to the station where soon the toffee-coloured carriage, reminding me too closely of 304D where I really sat, enclosed my senses and accepted my body, box within close-fitting box.

I was in two minds in two different trains but the NB tank had a different puff, poppet-valves, superheat, compound as well.

Back by the land near the seas' piers then: Helensburgh, Rosneath, Rhu, Shandon: along the still shore of the Gareloch, its seaweedy strands growing oranger further from seawater, its ranks of laid-up ships much depleted, swinging together gently as the tide turned. I had rather, far, have been out on the water but in fact was instead on the rails (though I had much liefer run on these than the others there outside) to Garelochhead, mirror-still also, supper smoke rising in parallel columns from the multi-fluted chimneys of its fretwork-gabled storm-solid erstwhile Victorian lodging-houses, and the climb, puff and grunt, to that Lord-knows-Why station on the saddle, its location superb, buildings suburban, one foot in wild woods, the other in Gorbals.

I managed to get out.

The second train rattled on down out of the box of the first; down easily, combing and nicking the rail-joints unevenly scattered on the constant curves; down, down along the otherwise untouched unknown hills to Arrochar and its blasted torpedoes.

I asked the station-boy if he knew whether Johnny was below; I asked him if he knew whether MacNeilish was out or below or if a bus was soon passing for Inverary: to all of which he affirmed and re-stated he was a stranger there himself: which I wasn't.

I gave him the *Echo* for his lack of help and walked out under the advertised iron railway-bridge along the Arrochar road for some yards, then took the track (or lack of it) downwards and westwards towards the erstwhile landing place, its fine-shingled strand and slippery stone jetty.

After a short while I sat down on a soft, mossy, still-wet glacial boulder to look at the view, contemplate myself, and consider my plans.

# 33

FIRST: the place: the present.

It was still stiller: it was loudly silent: laden.

Laden with the past and the slow flood tide oozing solidly, uncompromisingly, from Kintyre and the ocean beyond into the palms of the Clyde and its long-gloved many-fingered hands: cool, solid, some herring, many mackerel, weaving stinging jellyfish, saithe, lythe, milkpollock and goldies.

Behind me, as I knew so well but could not now see, the Gareloch there, half-remote, half-urban; carcass-ridden from Tomnan-Gamhna in the slump of ships; from the silent wind-whispering dried-calyxed bell-heather, loud still with multitudes of unkempt bees, the southerly ribbon of sunstreaked river, Greenock and Gourock and their thousands unemployed.

More northerly, Ben Lomond, satisfied, summery, pondering over its island-spattered sweet brown waters with their powanfish and houseboats, hikers and lovers, and debased caterwauling of its bonnie-banks song; the high road to liberty, the low to the gallows, the two of them imprisoned then in Carlisle gaol, whilst I was shackled now in my own idiot skull, free but deathbound, with old Melchi between us.

Up to the north Vorlich and Loch Sloy; many tearing midge-laden burns edged with mitigating bog-myrtle, dazzling after early frosts; grass of Parnassus, purple cross-leaved saxifrage, bog-asphodel, creeping willow; furtive whistling ouzels, snowbunt-ings, curlews, ptarmigan, hares: no one treads there now but the trains and obligatory grouse-shooters obeying the social injunc-tion of the twelfth.

But I had trodden there often, my legs stained to the knees with bogwater, my mongrel terrier quick to seize the half-fledged birds, brindled or black, lurking in the heather, equally tender.

Before me—my upraised cartilaged knees on which I leant my lowered spiky elbows, they holding my opposingly-splayed would-be-symmetrical hands, in turn cupping my badly shaved itchy chin—before me the satisfying meeting of the two wide lochs, Goil and Long, at the tip of the tumblingly indentated humpety rock-strewn Bowling Green with the white-floated lily-lochan in it.

Both arms still: my own and the silent-moving waters: all things echoed, mirrored upside down; better on your head than your heavy heels; better the waters than your heavy-laden heart.

The sunlight struck as it pleased, diagonally from the west, revealing red rowans, concealing great cliffs.

But no boat: not a single white reflecting V of a wake on the darkening mirror; not a house nor a croft but at Carrick and that half-hidden by the curve of the hill.

I had better hurry on and I did so.

I scampered down and the midges followed me, recruiting their gangs as they congressed in the succulent forest of my sweat-moist scalp. I followed the burn, alder and bush-birch tickling and brushing me and ended at last on the small flat-stoned strand.

To my surprise, Johnny's clinker was beached there, its long painter many times half-hitched to an old rusty ring. As the tide rose, so by degrees it would float; and I felt very sure too that Johnny would with it.

I walked to the peninsulared end of the jetty, popping the air-floats on the varied sea-plants, crushing or unseating incautious limpets, scattering small yellow periwinkles whose musical plop in the rising water was now irrevocable; though by high tide they would be back, laboriously scaling the sea-forest cliffs of their own home-rocks where the hermit-crabs lurked, their pincers at the ready for just such tasty wanderers, to the same secure haven between crack and barnacle, their hungry tongues weaving in the fresh flush of the renewing sea.

There I sat down on a cushion of soaking iodized algae, wetting the seat of my office-trousers thoroughly, to wait, to cheat the midges, to try once more to think.

I am not good at waiting: the salt damp cooled me, the midges soon found me, risking the few yards of creeping water for their meal. Dusk was still a good hour off, but I needed to move.

The boat was just beginning to rise by the stern from the shingle; small imprisoned sandhoppers, gleefully released, scudded half-sideways in search of still smaller ones to devour beneath its lifting keel. The very gentle motion of the rising tide lapped its counter, loosening and cradling its bow on the cool small stones to an almost inaudible crunching, each infinitesimal moon-wanted ripple advancing a shrimp's whisker more, turning the light grey-green of each mica-glittering pebble to a darker hue with its ever-creeping wetness.

I got up, pulling the seawatered serge from my saltwatered buttocks; itching thereabouts.

I listened and I searched: there was silence and no sight: so I loosened the painter.

I took a leaf out of my diary, a clean one further on, which I found was my birthday's thus prematurely entered, and wrote on it:

Dear Johnny,

I am in a fearful hurry. The Captain's very bad. You'll find her at Carrick or maybe further. Forgive me your trouble.

D.G.

P.S. Let me know what I owe you.—D.G.

I put the note under a small flat stone on a flat rock above h.w.m. on the land end of the jetty.

Then I took away the stone, threw it into the sea where it plopped like a falling risen trout, and replaced it by two half-crowns, replacing them in turn by another similar stone and a pound note under my own one, replacing the two coins with my left hand in my at that time hole-less right trouser pocket: quite a feat.

Whereupon I carefully extracted my note once again and scratched out the P.S. as thoroughly as I could.

I put it back.

After which I took it out again and carefully folding the blue-lined rather flimsy paper so as to make a crease, tore off the P.S. entirely. Crumpling it up, I threw the tiny morsel on the water; it drifted slowly but steadily away from the sea and Kintyre up the shortly-splitting loch.

I walked down to the bow of the boat: with my right hand on the stem-post and my left on the starboard gunnel I heaved twice, three times, and more. The boat moved, crunching stone against wood, groaning, squeaking, unwillingly willing: she moved until seven-eighths waterborne, one-eighth shore-tethered.

Then I gave a great shove, leaping cunningly aboard her upon one knee as she launched, balanced on the teak curve of the vee of the bows entried meeting.

I scrambled over some assorted ropes, stumbled over the mast-holed forethwart and plumped down proudly amidships. I lit a cigarette and reached for the oars. They were not there; nor the rowlocks either.

Oarless and rowlockless, thus I was adrift.

# 34

I LOOKED back and could see some fifty yards away on the forsaken shore the padlocked boathouse I had never thought of. Even as I looked it moved further from me. We were moving slowly landwards up the solemn-sounding loch.

There were some loose foot-boards and I picked one up but on second thoughts threw it down again. Not much use trying to reach shore against the tide, then possibly being unable to break open that padlock: better far to make certain I took the right loch's mouth, westward not eastward, Goil and not Long.

I went up to the bow again and having selected the apparently most viable of the planks began to paddle myself, four to starboard, two to port (for the tide was running well) across towards the dark-shadowed western hillside.

Vigorously I plied my inefficient blade: crabwise I crossed the massed rising water: and well before the solid general drift had carried us murmuring to the unmarked boundary of the two new waters, and in spite of the far stronger tide running up Long, I was in the soundless sidestream rounding the flat-rocked promontory with its dozing oystercatchers, scarlet beak under black-and-white feather, each having eaten their fishy fill at the full-out ebb that long-gone afternoon ago.

Some varied waders piped now and then most plaintively at the nostalgic water covering their bill-guzzled feeding grounds—not to be newly uncovered until morning and the echo of the jangling milk-train from the hill.

So, on the still flow, no ripple but the web-footed wake of a swimming gull or a diving cormorant cutting as a diamond the smooth patina of molten-cold plate glass, I floated upwards and northward towards night and my aimed destination; silently, with slight lapping only in my ear: silently but with great clamour, in my heart.

This strained silence, the total lack of human evidence, neither house nor plantation, felling nor fooling, so near to the struggling Clydeside shipyards and the furies of factory and pub, drove me in and outwards, a piston plunging; building pressure, blowing it: knowing nothing, knowing it.

Soon, if I kept on with the drift at my elbow, far away I should see Carrick Castle and its pier: its Manse, Fraser's, and Macwhirter's, the grocer's: and its aimless white road from nowhere to nowhere on which Angus MacDougall loved to rev his motorcycle, (boat-borne there, orphaned and childless), accelerating off in a flurry of dust to the ends of the earth fully two furlongs distant away.

And sure enough I did, but was meanwhile regaled by the thump and sneeze of the up Glasgow mail, the last of the day, climbing desperately on the taut heathered mountainside, its shrill whistle-for-nothing carried birdlike, soft and sweet as a turnstone's as it rounded the bank to the summit I had come from, disappearing into silence over the lip of the hill: not stopping; forgotten instantly.

I was now round the curve of the ever-buoyant loch, shut off too, the pale light dwindling slowly to dusk as it does there in summer.

It was warm enough: I drifted further.

I was tired though, so lay down for a while sprawled in the sternsheets, my feet in the bait-fouled bilgewater, cockle- and mussel-gut vieing for supremacy, looking up at the cut-card profiles of the well-known summits of the crumpled mountains, allowing myself luxuriously and knowingly to drift in the simply-checked direction of the way I wished to go.

How was Melchi now, I wondered? Almost within powerful earshot: certainly on a still day you could hear from his window that elusive train-whistle which had just tapped my own drum. Yes, if there was an east wind and a gentle one at that, you could clearly hear but not believe it: there, from or at his window.

Melchi, old chap, I'll soon be with you. Before night, before light, I shall kiss your scratchy dear old russet face; in any case before the following new darkness: or yours——

Why in heaven's name does no boat pass? Generally at the week-end yachts or motor-cruisers, sailers or steam, fetch up in the evening, anchor for the night, glow white in the rare morning sun. They should be coming soon: I could hail one; it could tow

127

me and I would cast off later and make straight for the boat-steps, open the gate and be off up the rose-scented garden to greet you.

But the silence prevails absolutely; only the faint sucking sound of the tide in the chinks of the tumbled plunging shore-rocks, of the mobile still mass of the rising flowing waters.

I took to the board again, paddling ourselves further forward (for you were with me) round another rocky spit; the seaweed hanging in sad dangling tresses from tide-mark refloated and mumblingly popping very softly on the creeping mirror of the flood.

I could hear simultaneously and separately in unison the milliard sighs of small hustling crabs, sand-eels, sea-slugs, whelks and all bivalves, delighted to be back in their food-bearing element, safe from their enemies the cruel-beaked birds and voracious shore-rats; to eat and not be eaten.

Many million squeaks, separately unheard: numberless delights amounting to a whisper: incalculable whispers amounting to a small murmur: innumerable murmurs amounting to a small sigh.

The dusk made the silence still deeper and slowly we were nearing, now part of the flow, places I knew well in the deepening night.

The current would carry us to Carrick now; it was only a matter of waiting and watching to paddle to the pier when the right moment offered.

I dangled my hand in the ice-cold water, staring over-board at our shadowed reflection slightly distorted by the licking lap of the minimal ripples on the boat's overlapping side, and wondered who I was down there and whether I was the same as the one outlined against the pale night-burgeoning sky? I saw an early star winking from the water below me and then, down darkly beyond it, in the middle of the dense greenish-black reflection of my own —*our* own hat and skulls—the silent twisting of a conger-eel lit by the summer phosphorescence pursuing its undulating scavenging way along and amongst the deep-seated boulders long ago tumbled from the overhanging hills when the whole earth writhed in its labour.

I coughed, so I moved. Small musical water-suckings coursed along the listing side of the salt-smelling clinkers of the hull.

I looked up: a fistful of stars were scattered. I looked down: there were the same stars and through and beyond and below them, more fishy creatures, greenlit and twining.

Suddenly I saw, startlingly as starlings in a winter's sky, co-ordinated in their whirling, unanimously patterned, a whole gorgeous shoal of pollock or mackerel, twisting greenflaring rockets, sparking this way and that right under the boat: in its ripple-rimmed shadow: in another utter silence: in the sky of the sea through the sea of the sky: leaving wakes of new stars.

With the flat of my hand I slapped the hard meniscus: on all sides, bursting from the slapping-point, to all sides, fleeing from the tiny impact, fish by reaction and stars by refraction fled and danced radially from my impertinence.

With the curve of my hand I ladled a handful and brought it to my mouth: between the slits of my fingers glinted the firmament and creatures swam glowing in the hollow of my palm. Out of my mouth I spat planets with plankton and my sea-salt wet teeth dribbled stars.

With the tips of my fingers I played a sea-tune on the sky: the key-board of the running flood sparkled to my touch. I tickled Andromeda and the spiral nebulae in the sky-borne sea . . . almost fell overboard.

So I stopped.

By now I could see the first freshly-lit oil-lamps, orange in the small seemingly-snug houses by the pier. I judged it time to make an effort shorewards and soon ground to the landing, grating on the strand.

I tied the long painter to a ring near the boatslip and walked up, stumbling over loud jettisoned cans and other refuse, to the sandy road and the small stuffy hotel where I was greeted politely by the landlord and one or two people I had known by odd meetings, often only on water, long ago.

I ordered a drink and whilst savouring it, realized and stated I was ravenously hungry; the landlord's wife thereupon very kindly offering to let me have a split mackerel rolled in oatmeal and grilled.

Whilst waiting for this feast in slavering anticipation, held in check by successive glasses of Glenlivet and other stills, I inquired if anyone here had a motor-boat or outboard that could run me up and across to Inverdonich and Melchi immediately. But nobody had, the only one available having gone off with a party to a Ceildhe at Ardentinny and not expected back until all hours likely.

My best tack would be to take the old road (now a new one) northwards as far as Cor-na-monachan or Speans and ask or take one of the Douglas boats there straight across, not much more than a mile, to Melchi's. The keys of the boathouse, so they told me, were on a hook two handsbreadths to the right of the door-lintel under the eave.

Having eaten the glorious spectrum of a mackerel washed down with some more of the best turned browner still with pure peaty burnwater in ample quantity, I set out in fine fettle from the faintly lit village, now ready for bed, along the stone-strewn track through the still-starched blackness of the woods.

I stumbled along more asleep than awake, more awake than alive.

By the time I had reached the clearing at Cor-na-monachan the first indistinct signs of the approaching dawn were haunting the north-east, on towards Ben Ime and its cushions of *Silene acaulis*; and it was as cold as it often is at that blighted hour. Before there was any light I was almost opposite old Melchi's and there, sure enough, bright in the bow-window as usual, as if set to guide us back on a dark night from a party over this side or southwards, was the big duplex lamp, no doubt to welcome and encourage me to him; I who had delayed far too long to his calling.

At that hour I was afraid, mortally afraid of mortality: for it was the dying hour, the weakest lonely hour for the struggling spirit in the worn body, the slow-pumping, low-pumping snuffing of the long-journeyed heart.

I drove myself on half eager, most reluctant: I wished I could leap the loch: I was glad I should have to scull it.

No one was awake at Speans. Why on earth should they be? It was almost too late now for the Inverdonich lamp, quenched as it was by the stalking sun in the wings of the mountains; but instead I could see a thin plume of pale smoke feathering from the kitchen chimney and I knew that Maggie must be keeping vigil, boiling up a kettle for tea or hot-bottle.

Unfortunately with the light came a sharp and mounting breeze, the loch now fluttering small white horses right across my course; the very thing I wanted least.

I went down to the tripping-lines and drew in the light dinghy reluctantly tugging southwards on its painter, its smart immaculate mastic varnish and white rope fenders gleaming in the increasing light.

I went to the boat-house, found the keys as instructed, and brought back the best pair of oars I could find. Then I pushed off, turned and drew painfully and bouncingly out on the steep sharp waves, my back to Melchi, my face to Ben Bheula and the dark pines waving on Witches Point.

Looking forward, I looked back: looking back, I *saw* back.

# 35

OF course it was old Uncle Melchi whom I saw most patently: of course it was he; on this water, on other waters, my back to his sundimmed light, to his bow-windowed sweet-sour soon-impending death. Pulling hard on oars is a very boring business. . . .

The time of that Trio at the Douglas's: I had practised very hard but half of it escaped me: not the notes, nor the fingers, but my knowledge; and simple Haydn needed knowledge. Poor Lily and her 'cello; not much to do but done assiduously, every grunt judged correctly.

There was to be a performance—(why a *performance*? My grandmother used to say of her old pug-dog Jock at evening, before he came in for the night, 'Has he performed?')—there was, anyhow, to be a performance that September evening about nine over at Pier House; and possibly another later in the month in the village Hall or in Helensburgh; I don't know. Why was there that urgency, or why did he insist?

131

It was rather late, in any case; after steamer time, soon after dark; and a bitter wind swept down from Drymnsynie and its yellowing larches, chopping the loch into angry sizzling waves. Not high but furious, they meant terrible leeway crossing on the ebb, at that time flowing fast. Even if it *was* a long way round, we should surely have taken out the T: failing that the sweet one from Mittenwald or even the Guarnerius: but Melchi had insisted on the sea and the Strad. And down we had to stumble with it, with him, out of the warm lamplit supper-room and the crotcheted cocks' heads on the freshly boiled eggs, straight onto the terribly slippery precariously-uneven stones of the loch-lashed jetty to the vague heaving whiteness of the old green-gunneled four-oar, Melchi plunging wildly into the sternsheets with the fiddle-case held high above his head lest he slipped and got a ducking.

Percy and I took the forethwart, George and Barney the midships; both with old Knox's square-cut leather-bound featherers balanced in the tholes.

We pushed off at once and knew at once we should not have done so. We took five pulls and were doubly certain of it. The sea was one foaming ferment, rampaging, demented, great white crests rolling away from us, their long trains of foam hissing like angry ganders.

'Come along, lads! Pull! Pull!' shouted Melchi above the bedlam of the waters unleashed, holding his fiddlecase aloft as a puppy above its mess, by the scruff of its choice leather neck.

Soon that very same twin-wicked lamp was dancing at all angles, drunk and disorderly in our slanting bubble-riddled wake. Heading due west, we were making south-west at a pinch: we pulled very hard and by mid-loch we began to ship it at each microcosmic roll; loads of it, solid now, blueblack as ink.

Holding his miserable fiddle aloft at his left arm's length, Melchi began to bail madly with his right, at first foolishly flinging it to windwards from whence it clattered back like hail, then more wisely throwing it to be seized by the scudding wind and carried out of sight in the darkness before it touched water. Yet he hardly kept pace with our certain sure flooding.

'Pull, boys!' he croaked, 'pull, boys! Why can't you?—or

you'll ruin my fiddle and that'll be the end of me. Pull there! Pull there to the lee of the Witches and we'll edge up and make it nicely. Pull, blast you! Pull! . . .'

Then, with an extra heavy swing of the cast bronze bailer he launched it, water and all, into the confused roaring depths of the all-foaming sea.

By no whit daunted he took off his Harris-tweed deerstalker and catching it by its two flaps, dipping it as a cook might skim a fine fresh broth, continued at a still greater, more frenzied pace to empty the sea into the sea as it filled us; it slowly gaining.

'Don't mind me, mind the Strad,' he shouted. 'If I should go over keep it strong and safe. High, mast high!' (we had no mast). 'If it's wet at all, take it to Hill's—he'll sort it properly—he's got the right glue; the good right glue—he sorted it—that time—that time——' (all this bellowed in slight lulls in the storm)—'He sorted it that time I came down too heavily—too heavily on the double stopping at the opening—of the last movement of the Brahms—or it may have been—yes it *was*—the Chaconne—when it sprang—sprang like a bloody whip—whipping top from my fooling fingers to—to the rug—save it—never mind me!'—and he stood up, the idiot!

'Sit down at once,' we all chorused imploringly. 'Down, Uncle, down for God's sake'—as if to a dog. And down he went, pole-axed, this time to the boat-bottom, on the water-swilled teak-and-mahogany trellis-patterned sternboard, still holding his fiddle on high. He groaned and cursed, smacked in his lumbago.

It had taken him a long exhausting time to exhort us thus and given us a desperate time at our oars; in the agony of its passing the time had passed with it and now—Yes, the water was coming aboard less, far less: you could hear it now individually, by gout and wavetop, spilling and trickling: we were really in the lee.

'Where's me pipe?' said Melchi, as if nothing at all had been happening. 'I'm damned if I haven't forgotten it. I'll borrow one of Bob's though they're really always foul. Pull away, boys, we've made it!'

And so we had: and did: just.

The Trio went surprisingly well, Melchi relishing his own and his fiddle's survival (though it turned out he had brought along one of young Keenan's jobs in fact) with constant mephisto-phelian raising of his big bushy eyebrows in the slow movement and luscious intakes of breath through his hairy-nostrilled nose throughout.

We should have tackled the *Heiliger Dankgesang* quartet that night if ever; no moment could have been more propitious, with a viola there too and Barney with his fiddle. But we didn't and now we never shall; and Melchi, I think, regarded the mere sug-gestion as an indirect criticism of our hazardous voyage; for who but he had been captain?

We played Trios all night and rowed back in a calm dripping dawn.

I wished it was calm now.

Even then as I was thinking of this moment in the dinghy (or in the train), the wind died also; the present or the then wind died; the teased sea jumped foolishly up and down for no reason for some moments and fell still.

# 36

I PULLED easily and steadily for the shore. In ten minutes I was gliding along next that large geologically inexplicable brown rock near the garden gate.

I jumped out, painter in hand, clove-hitched it round the 'in' tripping line post, hurried up the steps, opened the squeaking-hinged tall wooden gate, and stood on cool grass in the rose garden sweet with the scent of Caroline Testout, La France, General MacArthur, Betty Uprichard and the old hybrid teas.

The smoke was vertical from the chimney once again, rising on the newly-still air.

Everything and all things were still again except the sparrows with their ceaseless, futile, seasonless chatter: and my heart.

I panted up the hill towards the door.

The house, too, seemed silent.

I opened the outer door quietly, then the glazed inner one to the music room: it smelt the same as usual; of Ronuk, brass cakestands and very old sou'westers.

I opened the far door and went along the passage and hearing sounds, stood still.

Uncle Melchi was calling; deliriously, wildly, incoherently. I was horrified. And then out of the incoherence all too clearly, vehemently ringing—

'Tell that bloody nephew of mine he's late again as usual. *Tell him he's too late!'*

I dashed forward, burst open his bedroom door.

It *was* too late.

Melchi lay dead, red in the face, in his narrow bed. I bent and kissed his stubbly cheek, the warmth of his life still lingering in its emptiness.

'I'm so sorry, Uncle Melchi, do you hear me? I'm so sorry, do you hear?'

But he did not hear; he could not. Never more.

The sun was up.

He was bunched at last.

The speckle-sparkled sea shot lightning dances on the shabby ceiling.

Maggie at once began drawing irrevocably the thick faded green plush curtains.

I wanted to tear them open again and shout:

'Do you hear me, Uncle Melchi . . .

'I'm so sorry . . .

'Do you hear?'

# 37

BURN's or Laird's: animals or flowers: *Tiger, Viper, Vulture, Puma: Lily, Rowan, Rose, Maple.*

Later on they were all Lairds anyhow. Lairds this and Lairds that: they started with *Lairdsburn (ex-Louth, ex-Patriotic)*, and were of no real account.

But at that time—so-ago—they were animals or flowers,

fiercely competing: *Tiger* with *Lily*, *Viper* with *Rowan*, *Vulture* with *Rose*, *Puma* with *Maple*: black funnel with red and white and blacker smoking top.

In any case I had now had the misfortune to wake up: neither of us need ask, I think, where.

To my right there again was the grey extreme sea and its scatter of islands—Shinnich, St. Patricks, Church and the other ones—with their herring gulls' fine large warm rough brown eggs comfy on the angular black rocks; splotched and speckled, fertile, addled or rat-nibbled.

In my upright still seat I tore forwards and rushed backwards; forwards to the buffer-stop, backwards to the *Tiger's* grip or the *Rowan's* safe shelter . . .

It was always a migration.

It was always a great comfort, excitement, decision, upheaval, reassurance.

It was all things simultaneously. The dog, terrier- or lap-, tremblingly unwell, snivelling at the spluttering sizzly siren, its whistle always blocked by condensation, starting like a fart, proceeding to a comb-and-paper hum, only finally clearing its brassy gullet for a lacerating loud hoot.

There we were: Mrs. N. and her family, my mother and myself, my father fuming on the quayside, his farewell admonitions repeatedly drowned by the nasal intonation of a shawlie as steeped in J.J. as himself, singing interminably *The Girl from the Country Clare*, puffing at his putrid Kapp and Peterson, uncleaned but straight-grained; put carefully aside for him by that nice man at the top of Grafton Street, said my mother.

They warped out the *Tiger* or *Rowan* (or *Vulture* or *Puma* or *Lily* or *Rose*) with a fine thick piano-wire of a hawser stretched across the ebbing silent Liffey towards the rickety four-storeyed tile-lined pub at the corner of the cobbles opposite the tar-distillation enclosure of the gasworks, the said hawser being first fetched across to its hook and/or bollard by a mud-coloured row-boat with red waterline and a white number, the part property of the Dublin Port and Docks Board at that time.

As it lifted from the river-bed the hawser in its turn fetched deliquescent morsels of machinery, vegetation, fish, stones, bones, canisters and bad herrings, leaping appallingly too taut, shaking terribly, vertically only, shedding its mud and above-mentioned inventory with reverential plash back into that famous still water, whilst the forward old Clark Chapman windlass wheezed and spat and did its job valiantly, dragging the twelve-hundred ton hull across the river by the nose until the slow current caught it and we faced the open sea.

Then the snug-doors across muddy Northwall Street flew temporarily open, their inmates, glasses in hand, breaking the grind of their diurnal swallowing to observe the hebdomadal sailing: the siren cleared and churned again, the seagulls swirling for pure form's sake—for a siren's a siren: and so we set sail.

Down along past the last pawnsign and the few old cockle-boats, and Roche's codboats, and the Great Southern and Western coal-sidings with their old puffing red-leaded coal-cranes bending over Savage's *Fields*: *Broomfield* for the coal-shutes of Garston, *Gorsefield* for Whitehaven, *Briarfield* for Ardrossan and *Oatfield* for Llandulas—all light, never to return in that condition; passed the Extension hailing-station to port, Ringsend church steeple, canal-locks and trawler *Father O' Flynn* with fridayfish to starboard, and the first fresh whiff of the open buoyed bay. Rossbeg and Burford as usual in their places; mournful Poolbeg, humming Kingstown and Baily's buzzing bee the eternal triangle of these patchy shifting waters, shot by a soft sun, striped by a soft breeze; with Kish at his guns out further.

Silently and surely ships move in narrow waters; South Wall reeling like thin black thread, promenaders promenading, fishermen fishing, lovers covertly loving, out we go between black and red to seaside suburbia, high and dry at low tide, decidedly deluded at the flood; out then, north-east ourselves, inside one bank, outside another, near enough now to see and to read the buoy's own nameletters, normally a speck, painted feet high on the pile of heaving steelwork, their robot-lights flashing foolishly in the still glinting sun; on past the picnic places and the afternoon-tea houses, Drumleck, Ceanchor, Mahaffy's and the rest, all of us settling down nicely I can tell you, the dog howling its guts out

137

in the 'tweendecks up a great cowl like a slaughterhouse ghost, endlessly hysterical, so that I long to dump him overboard, kindly smart whiskers, damp black nose, and all; Mrs. N. retired, parasol folded with her, down in her four-berth with Ken; her daughters to follow shortly, after Lambay.

We were rounding the Baily close inshore, the displacement of the *Tiger's* bulk shifting the waters adjacent to us, sucking at the salty seaweeds in the cracks of the rock, throwing a wash-wave into the seal's cave, cool and wet and lightly barnacled when you've scrambled down to it; cool and wet, breath-visible, pink-sanded, when you've scrambled down to it on the warmest summer's day: now simply abeam, abaft the beam, astern, left behind far astern, out of sight, remembered. Remembered with the whole soiled sunny bay settling for the night below the westering sun; *now* in the cooler greenshot shadows by the bare east cliffs, guillemot, chough and puffin all nesting, fulmars to follow them years later; *now* in the opening sea, slightly heaving, pulsing slowly. To the islands on our far course; all the islands and those same rocks; all the islands with their fluffing nestlings and murdering rats, picnics and seapinks and seals, turnstones and sea-pies and bar-tailed godwits; all the islands and the reefs and the rocks beyond them far, sketched against the dimming north-western paleness—Carlingford, Mourne, Sanda and Pladda; and summerholidays, summerholidays . . .

Ah! Those delicious formalined fillets, exquisite chemical ketchup, cold soggy crust-rid toast, jellied marmalade, tongue-tanning tea—all swallowed kneeling bare-kneed on the crumby upholstery, sniffing the laced-back once-brown plush curtains, peering through the round polished porthole smelling of Brasso and very old oil at the heaving grey foam-raked slow rollers tumbling in from the thin line of coast, each unavailing to stir the proud *Vulture*, thousand-tonned, twelve-knotted; cattle-stuffed with stores for the lairings at Girvan; down near the dog.

My mother was embroidering her formidable hat, a desperate wild jungle of ill-spent cross stitches; but *Vulture* never stirred.

I went on eating the soggy bread-and-fillets; but *Vulture* never stirred.

Her side bilges, littered still with refuse from the sailing—orange peel, toffee wraps, cartons and newspaper—took the broadside sea, loosing all her soiling; but *Vulture* never stirred.

To bed in a bunk, my mother insisting to the starched stewardess she should open up the porthole to freeze us both well; through which aperture I stuck my head, knocking my skull on its anvil hardness, out into the great sibilant aprons of the rejected waves, our ship's path through the gushing sea straight down below striking the odd thread of beady phosphorescence from the pink boot-topping in the dark green watery gap between steel and saucy hissing froth. Into bed-bunk, tightly tucked, thistle, rose and shamrock scraping my chin from the strong special-weave linen sheet, the Blackwood and Gordon triple-expansions' beat far more reassuring than my own windy heart, an odd auxiliary pump or generator flying furiously in the face of their even solid sound, young bucko priests on the deckhead up above walking off their tea, waiting for their ease, hoping for a quiet night troubled by no dreams of the buxom girls in the smoky singing steerage.

Heart, heart . . . Thump, thump . . . Heart, heart . . . Thump, thump . . . revolutions even; steam expanding; shake, gentle shake. Hillocky, hillocky . . . bell-wishing, bell-wishing—going away and returning back. And I for the morning and still Clyde waters, Cumbrae and riveters and summer summerholidays . . . summer summerholidays . . . summer summerholidays.

# 38

BUT when I awoke it was raining as usual.

I could sense it and hear it and feel it before I ever opened my heavy-hanging eyes.

And I was not any longer in the *Vulture* or the *Tiger* or the *Puma* or *Lily* or *Rose* or *Rowan* or *Maple*.

No. The old engines had stopped.

The old engines had stopped and someone was shaking me.

Maggie was shaking me (Damn her! Damn her!)
Maggie was shaking me; the old engines had stopped.
It was raining as usual.

It was raining as usual; a continuous remorseless curtain falling
from the half-drowned sky into the wholly-drowned loch; on the
streaming steaming dropdappled windowpanes; hissing and tap-
ping on tins, puddles, grass and deep water.

Yes, the old engines had stopped.

But which? Whose?

The *Vulturelilytigerose* was drifting, but . . .

What on earth had stopped? Why the silent slack water? Why
the slack silent water lapping indifferently, continuously?

Why was I waiting? Where and why was I waiting and for
whom?

The old engines had stopped.

Why, oh why? Do you hear me? Do you hear me?

'The Cap'n must be put down, sir. Wake up, sir. The Cap'n
must be put down; you must go for the Minister, sir. The Cap'n
must be put down.'

And so I was back. Here it all was! Inverdonich, Uncle Melchi
. . . Everything!

I reluctantly remembered it all. I abortively rejected the whole
sickening thing. I threw it out into the outside, the light there, the
outside.

But it stayed.

'Sir, *please*,' the God's curse went on. 'What will you have for
your breakfast? For the Cap'n must be put down this day and you
must go for the Minister for the Cap'n . . .' My God! She was at it
again, '. . . must be put down today and you must . . . What'll you
have for your breakfast?'

'Bring me the bottle, Maggie. The Captain's own bottle.'

'. . . but the Cap'n must be put down this day, you must go for
the Minister to put down the Cap'n . . .' she simply could not stop.

'Bring me the bottle!' I shrieked, sitting up. 'At once!'

So she brought it.

I slugged a gulletful from the dirty-grey peppermint-smelling
toothglass, chasing it with a throttleful of carbolic-addled water.

This then I several times nauseatingly repeated.

Whereupon I got up, placing my still-socked feet in my very cold sock-polished shoes, and then these latter, with very much difficulty through the interminable legs of my still sea-damp Sunday serge trousers, eventually onto the Turkey-carpeted hay-feverish floor exactly under that copper-shaded twin-wicked duplex strung from the now flyless ceiling by its heavy brass chains . . .

Ah! To Hell!

Just look at the very day before us!

'Put down': Yes. We always said 'put down' when the extra large sinewy leg of mutton my grandmother repeatedly and mistakenly ordered from the fleshers grew maggoty and luminous in the warm July night threatening thunder that so rarely ever came: then it had to be 'put down'. But down generally in the rosebed à la Winwoode Reed, nourishing Caroline Testout, The General or Betty Uprichard for us all; for their sweet pearly-dropped summer scent. Or, when the accumulation of blacklead bottles, meat paste pots, Brand's Essence jars, Ronuk tins, passé button-boots and other phernalia grew gargantuan, overflowing the wee back ashpit, down too they must go, 'put down' the loch to the deep-darkened congers.

I stood up and snapped up the dark buckram blind, its wooden-tipped cord striking viciously the rain-streaming glass—enough and more than enough, I should have thought (but it was always so and never did) to break, at least crack it.

I dragged on the rest of my gross recalcitrant garments, bristling with nipping buttons, biased drag, inner hurting ruffles and rumple and crease.

And I shouted then:

'Maggie, bring me some breakfast: hot porridge with cream and Demerara sugar and boiled eggs and hot buttered toast. Quickly!'

'Yes, sir. At once, sir. What about the putting down, sir? It'll be hard on him, won't it?'

'I shall see to it, Maggie. Where's Mawk?'

Mawk was my late uncle's dog. He had been called Mawk for

some involved but none too subtle pawky Scots reason and was a very disturbing animal.

He came in barking loudly and smelling as usual, for he was much overfed. He was delighted to see me and snapped playfully at my nipples or thereabouts; for he was very large. We had once been good friends before those grey bristly slobber-drenched hairs round his mouth were so coloured.

I ate away at the sweet squelchy porridge and wondered how I could ever manage this day and how on earth I should begin it.

I decided to make a start by walking to the village. I was afraid of more wind, north wind, and had had enough of rowing.

I should have to visit those two unchristian creatures, neither of them worthy of their miserable jobs, to wit: to keep the already split particles of whatever was then left of the Scots churches for ever sundered. My grandmother, to be fair to them and very unfair to me, had always insisted we should ruin Sunday by attending both their services, however resplendent the sparkling day.

Now, at any rate, it was teeming: and somehow I wished it should continue, this being no time for fair-breeding skies.

Melchi, although officially seriously disapproved of by both ministers, was none the less in fact their fairly close friend; for he found them both victims of great-constrained society and loved to tease them wholly in their self-imposed stocks, viciously enough too. For he hated cant and these two swam in it.

Had he not once made a pass at Maclaren's pretty daughter, long ago now, before the kneeling and scrubbing of the endless stone manse-floors had scumbled then scuttled her beauty? For he knew a fine girl when he saw one, did Melchi.

Had they not once kissed by the big brown fly-feeding trout-pool, under the free-flowering horse-chestnuts by the Donich, when Maclaren, God help us, himself poaching with a jacked spinner on forbidden water, had come too abruptly upon them in flagrant delight-o? The twin matters were settled out of court all right—just; fury and fish-scales flying all around.

And about the same tale they had had with old Neil and his daughter too—I tell you they somehow begat wonders—only this time all done by tears over some Mendelssohn or other, was it? . . . or the Bach Chaconne or . . . No, the G string; of course it was the Air on the G string that did it. Mrs. Neil almost in tears and the girl much reduced, well seduced, in this key, so that she hardly felt his hand up her leg afterwards.

But in any case he had been intimate with both as well as many theological arguments; for Melchi had once studied for the Church, until, well on in his Second Year Divinity, he spied some other girl and thought more of his fiddle.

Well perhaps I could do it like the wedding, toss for the honour and then ask the other? Yet I had to admit I had much rather Maclaren's graveyard there near the tidal river-mouth where the Evinrude ran mad one fine day, firing on the very first pull, the string far too long, falling over the seats, smashing the nose of the old white clinker slap and splinter against its retaining wall, pitching the two of us—Melchi in his mac and deerstalker, I in my school cap and chapped inner legs—deep into the brown rippling water full of grilse.

It was early enough now but soon all the neighbours, distant and crossloch and up Drymnsyniewards, would be afloat, paddling along on the raindropping multi-ringed water; commiserating with death; seeking out survivors to console them.

In any case there would be rows, for they all loved Melchi and hated me; and I loved him and disapproved of them. And of course—I hadn't thought of that—both ministers would think that *they* should have been sent for, not I; sent for prompter to 'ease him', 'see him over', 'on his way'. As if they could!

Yes, I must be off: he must be put down quickly before they all got at him.

'Mawk!' I called. 'Come along, good dog, and we'll go.'

I dragged on a stuck-together oilskin and a plastered sou'wester and thus stiffly apparelled made for the front door. Mawk gave a great retching bark, splayed his front paws playfully on the crimson hall-carpet and started to bound madly back and forth over and on it, to and from the foot of the curly cast-iron stairs, his claws tearing, like calico rending, its worn surface pile.

'Maggie,' I throttlingly shouted, 'we're off.'

'Tell me, sir,' said the erstwhile jewel, 'what's for lunch? The Cap'n had in one of Hector's sea-trout and he was to have had it today. Of course, he only messed them around, you know, sir; but he liked the pink flesh of them. Oh dear, he loved sea-trout, sir. Red-herring he used to call them when he took them in his net; never put them back. Did you see him this morning, sir? He looks well, I am sure. I always thought he'd make a lovely corpse, sir, and, dear God, so he does.'

'Very well, I'll have the trout. No, I have not yet seen him this morning. I am going to have a look round now by the village and fix with a minister (which, I do not know) for him to put down Uncle Melchi tomorrow, if that is possible.

I picked up a walking-stick (no one in Inverdonich ever went out for a walk without one; it was simply unthinkable) from the old blue faience umbrella-stand in the corner of the dun-papered hall and started to cross the music room. My heavy shoes seemed to torture the well-polished floor so that it cried, calling out, 'Do you hear me? Do you hear me?'

I fled from it out through the double porch; its fly-rods long uncast; hurricane-lamps rusting; old ottomans tumbled with tangled triple deep-sea lines, leathery-dry mussel-bait still fixed on their big cruel hooks; down the two soaked concrete steps to the schisty, geologically amorphous gravel from the small strand, and across onto the sopping lawn which had squelched so warmly once between my bare toes; delicious after summer sun, after curtaining showers. There the musty ex-A.S.C. bell-tent, hoisted on its printers-blue pole, was often pitched when the house was overfull, and we smoked rolled brown-paper, coughing our chests into multi-coloured stars in the reeking damp; no night bird but the curlew, nor sound but the stream to the Kepplethwaite's tank, to interrupt.

The great round rosebed, grave of many an overhampered ham, the above-mentioned mutton and tens of thousands of mackerel from our over-productive net, still flaunted its heavy-scented full-paunchy flowers as Mawk scampered snuffling around it, hot on the cold trail of some rabbit or domestic cat; dark green tracings on the moisture-tipped laden cut lawn.

Beautiful: exceedingly beautiful: multi-hued strange: dear Melchi the devil for budding and grafting and a greater one still for acquiring the buds: a bunch of the latest rose from a friend, a sprig from a trusting nurseryman, the outcasts and debris from the Glasgow or Edinburgh stagings; all the latest hybrids, far sooner than most, were grist to his fast-spinning mill. From a flagging stalk of the latest Macready or Dixon he would extract, surgeonwise, the growing kernel; and in a year or two the very dearest newest flamed next the latterly fashionable; a wonderful apricot flushed salmon pink on a deep dark velvety red on a harvest-moon yellow: no man in the kingdom was up to his tricks.

Strange: exceeding strange: because being, as has been hinted, at times overfond of good wine and whiskey, he occasionally managed mighty miscegenations, grafting the leaf-buds of one on the stock of another, so that in all nature or disparate artificiality never was suchlike seen nor yet heard of.

Thus, here and there amongst glowing polyantha in late August, pears hung ripening and wasp-worried; whilst cherries had been known amidst Lancaster and York. Moss roses hung from American pillars and Irish Peach rivalled with Soleil d'Or; Standards sprouted Roulettis, figs damn near thistles, until the whole assembly had rather the air of a very old Herbal or very new chintz than a regular round rosebed, thus as it stood, as I looked at it now through the damp sad air, a tumble of reddening rowanberries dominating it all, heavy-weighted with the oily-keyed rain; dripping, dripping, dripping.

'Mawk,' I said, stirring myself with difficulty from my fast-sprouting sodden soaked roots. 'Good dog! Come along!'

He made a great bound at me through the air like a wide-flapping huge hooked skate, his brindled fur as ugly as those fishes' skins as he struck and straddled me, knocking me helpless on the green slimy path, all affection, his great hot tongue banding my face with ribbons of dogspittle until I struggled from his morbid embraces to my feet.

'Down, Mawk, down, Mawk, for God's sake, down,' I implored him.

He got up from his springing posture and walked off ahead up the path past the beds where my grandmother used to make us weed by weight; five pounds of groundsel, two of chickweed, three of shepherd's purse or ten of mixed composites and crucifers being passed as a sad summer's afternoon work—but no soil, mind you, no soil at all adhering to their quite unbroken roots—on up past the acres of Scottish London Pride to the cockerel and donkey pens for eating or burden.

Out, at last, onto the sandystoned road.

Out, at last, past the always-frightening neighbour-children, dotty (so they said) and daunting (certainly)—but in any case barefoot on their mouldering coconut doormats—to the groves of macrocarpa, sweet-smelling as usual, sweetly rainsick, pineous; nostalgic to the feel of our feet on their fallen sprigs; water up our sleeves from their growing ones.

Down the first dip, Mawk zig-zagging, leg-lifting, sex-wheezing, factual—a real slice of dogged doggie life—all scents hovering on the droplets of the oozing air: red and white paint, duck's feathers, pendent Leycesteria, verdigrised nameplates, no hawkers no tradesmen, damp Plymouth Rocks, Johnny Archie's cows, alder boughs, bogmyrtle, ink.

What on earth was I going to say, though?

Neil's was too soon, Maclaren's not far.

Should I leave it all to inspiration where none was likely to spring, or work out some sort of scheme or score in advance?


# 39

Too late! There I was outside the high black wooden door in the grey granite wall, staring at a small plant of rusty-backed glaucous-fronted Ceterarch growing in it, and the solemn brass plate, highly-polished, raindrop-sullied, of the Minister of the Established Church of Scotland.

There was nothing I could do but turn the uncomfortably graspable spiral-patterned wrought-iron ring of its handle, push it open, enter the dark green-black alley of immensely tall rain-splashing Euonymous, and make for the holy front door.

I saw Mrs. Neil distorted behind the badly-glazed though ever-cleaned panes of her drawing-room window, but the daughter in her green house-beret (for dusting) came to the door.

'Good day, May. How are you? Is your father at home?'

'Ah, D., and how are *you*? I didn't know you were up the loch again. Yes, Father's in; reading his verses, I think. He'll be quit soon. How's dear Captain Melchi?'

'He died early this morning,' I was consciously curt.

'Mercy on us, how terrible! . . . Terrible! . . . Mother! Mother! Dear Captain Melchi is very ill!'

She came nipping along.

'Dear, dear. How *very* sad. Is he bad?'

'He's dead,' I said.

'Oh dear, oh dear! How dreadful! This is a very great shock. Only the other day last year he was playing that beautiful, beautiful music to me after tea; I forget what it was; it was so beautiful. I must fetch Neil. Neil! Neil!' she churned off calling, and he came.

'Melchizidek,' (I had the misfortune to be called that same name too, amongst others), 'this is indeed grave and dreadful news, but how is it that *I* was not informed? Eh? How is it that *I* was denied the sad pleasure and true duty of comforting him from the scriptures at his last end? It is most pointedly out of order that neither you yourself, nor Margaret either (though you can hardly blame her, poor thing, for I believe she is of the Roman persuasion), called me immediately when it became evident that his life was drawing to a close.'

'I cannot agree with you,' I answered, 'for I do not think that my uncle would have wished his death to have been accompanied, being such a great one for playing solo. Also I only arrived during the night, a few hours ago; just after his death, for which I bitterly regret I was late. Do you hear me?'

'Tsuk, tsuk, Melchizidek boy!' (How I wished he would not call me that). 'I am thinking of your uncle's precious spirit and immortal soul, lost and passed on without its due comforts, *not* of his dear, poor—er—body, no doubt resting now as it has not so rested long since. He has, I know, suffered and paid dearly for his possibly forgivable—er, peccadilloes and desires—his, er weaknesses, let us call them. Poor Melchizidek (how indeed he relished the biblical name). Poor—er—the *two* of you indeed!'

I decided there and then to make a clean—er—breast of it (this business was infectious)—er—take the bull by the—er—horns, without necessarily committing myself eitherways.

'Oh yes. I know all that very well! But you see I am in a quandary now: he is dead and we cannot alas revive him, do you hear me? My uncle was always very fond of you, Mr. Neil, and he often expressed the wish—that is to say he was very good friends with Mr. Maclaren too, you know—and Mrs. Maclaren—and fishing, you know, and so on.'

'Oh quite, quite. Yes, a tolerant man, an over-tolerant man one might perhaps indeed say; or too kind. Yes, let us say too kind.' (He mooed the too's.) 'In his own way, if you follow what I mean. Do you hear me? But after all to us fell the joy of marrying him did it not? It seems a long time ago now. You were away in Foreign Parts, young man: but it was *we* who had the great honour and joy of uniting him, lawfully and before God, with Hetty that summer in our own dear, very dear, church there, if you remember. Do you hear me? And that being the case, the irrefutable case,' he tapped his black waistcoated paunch with his sliding silver Koh-i-noor pencil case, 'the full accomplishment of his then living wishes as expressed to me personally—do you hear me?—it seems to me—do you hear me?—that no man can come . . .' he was now almost shouting his palsied peroration.

But I was on edge, on the splitting spinning edge, and I interrupted him:

'Yes, I saw the film of it backwards: the one the Douglasses took; and I never saw it forwards; nor do I want to.'

'I *beg* your pardon, Melchizidek. I can scarcely believe my ears. Do you mean to tell me that you dare speak so lightly at this solemn juncture of your dear late uncle's marriage? You must not—do you hear me?—under any circumstances, at this grave hour for us all. He was a very fine, a *very* fine, if not wholly religious, man. Do you hear me?'

This terrible repetition, this infinite slobbering of shibboleths was unnerving me.

'I am not speaking lightly. I am not speaking at all: and any words I may utter are not necessarily addressed to you. But who will put him down? Who will Cockrobin him? You or Maclaren, eh?'

'Sir, I consider it my duty to point out to you that if he in the fullness of his life confided the consecration of his Earthly Union —er—here—on Earth——' (he was gutting me.) 'Ahem—to *me*; then it seems at least justifiable that We of the Church of Scotland itself should admit him to His last Rest—here on Earth and in the Great Eternity of the Bosom of HIS MAKER. . . .'

He spoke with all the capitals, never missing or failing to emphasize one of them and I could no longer tolerate his bumbling morality. The whole thing disgusted me and I cried out loudly:

'Who will bury him? You or Maclaren? My uncle would have wished you both, yet rather neither. Can you not lean a little towards each other, co-operate Christianwise for once, just to put him down?'

'I—er——' (he was stumbling a little: at last he was stumbling) '—I should have to think it over; have to think it over . . .' and then, with a great new wave of self-righteousness: 'But these Free men! Give them but an inch and they snatch an ell—although one has to admit, no doubt, that Maclaren is a Minister of sorts before God.' (He was using his capitals again, lifting up his eyes, breathing like a pug dog, profoundly with his diaphragm at least.) 'Think of the Swan!'

I thought of the swan: a bad business: we should never hear the end of it.

In fact, Maclaren had had his arm smashed like a twig by one of the great cob's threshing wings as it fought off his flailing oar. My mother had gone on for a decade about it, and the Lord knows how many liars or Ledas had claimed to have heard its ultimate deathsong.

'Swan or no swan (and my uncle liked them best stuffed with samphire and roasted on a spit) I believe he would have liked you to lean, to relent, to unbend and for once to behave like what

149

might be called a Christian. But I should have known better. I shall go and see Maclaren who may be less frightful in his wrathful self-certainty—but I doubt it. Good-day. I shall expect you.'

So I left.

# 40

W E went on down the road towards the village, more like the bed of a stream now than a track, its underlying strata of wrenched living rock showing here and there like the ribs of a lost starving dog, a dozen rivulets running together to a gurgling muddy runnel in its centre. Leftwards the high wet walls of lochside gardens were broken here and there by blechnum or pennywort, whilst up to my right the numerous burns of the rock-stepped hill gushed torrents of spray short-circuited from the clouds clinging there opaquely a handstretch above.

I passed the fleshers: chops and sausages, collops and kidneys. Passed the lodging—serviettes, dentures, laurels and cockle-edged casements: passed Miss Jefferson's sawdusty shop: passed the pier and its pierhead store-sheds and urinals, to the rock and postcard peppermints of Haggle's post office itself—wet clothes, wet news, wet Woodbines, wet minerals with glass marbles clutched in their narrow throttled throats—round and along then by the shallow headwaters where flounders, dabs, plaice and the very odd halibut or brill lay ready to evade in a streak of scattered sand our meniscus-distorted spear as we glided silently, oars resting, not dripping, the sunrippled surface chasing itself on the tide-rippled sand down below, *past, at last past*, that cutstone rain-tight lacey-ridge-tiled house of Neil's-own-God to the (brown this time) low wooden door in its longer lower wall.

To the other.

The path led straight across a huge sea-salted meadow of coarse grass edged by large ugly lumps of grey-blotched white quartz which might have been collected assiduously by some great hideous dog, related perhaps to Mawk who was slobbering beside me, through a thick rigid holly hedge whose berries had blown off like bullets, stinging terribly, in the great winter storm that laid all the larchwoods, to the bleak pale limewashed manse, silent near its river.

I knuckle-knocked on the now knockerless paintless once-front door and a faint echo whispered back at me from the stone-flagged passage beyond. Katie the daughter, once-a-while beautiful enough to set your heart thumping, came to answer; her eternal deck-brush in one hand, galvanized pail in the other.

'Ah good morning, D; I no knew you were down. How are you? Excuse me.' She put brush and pail to one side, wiping her thick calloused hands on her thin threadbare skirt.

'Fine, thanks,' said I. 'My poor uncle's awa',' dropping thus into her metre.

'Do ye mean gone awa'? Dead, do ye mean? That's fearful news indeed and my father's out now at his business, if ye know what I mean.'

I knew what she meant well enough: poaching as usual, very likely with that same spinner too.

'I'd wish to see him, Katie.'

'He'll be home any minute now. I can tell you that for certain. I suppose you'll wish to speak to him of the downing. Dear, deary me!' she said with a sadness exceeding the words, and a sigh like a last flutter of rain towards nightfall.

'Yes so. That's it.'

Mawk was squatting on the overgrown clipped grass shivering and slobbering in his unpleasantest manner, his sexual organs stimulated by some masochistic misery of downpour or cold or some sniff or scent from the dark interior passages of the manse. This much embarrassed Katie, and I pitied her embarrassment now fast spreading to myself. She was so much neglected by her father's unceasing attention.

Thus we continued to stand miserably, she in the draughty doorspace, I on the deluged doorstep, asking time's end, which only approached when I saw over the further hedge the curtseying curving rod-tip of the minister's weapon as his gum-booted cultivated-manly strides raised and lowered his fishing-and-praying shoulders in exaggerated fashion.

So shortly he scrunched on the round sea-gravel and I was thinking of his pitiful socks, in there, inside his rain-sodden leaking waders; and the loneliness of his toes in there; and his toenails, now battered protection only, once so admired—pig-to-market—by his dear old doting mother.

He was boastfully forlorn.

'Good-day, young man. I did not know you had joined us at all. Pray, why have we this honour? How is your uncle? He was not very well, so I heard.'

'He died last night.'

'Well, indeed? Very sad and sudden, no doubt. But shall we say hardly surprising in view of how he lived? He would take life neither seriously nor easily. But truly I am sorry to hear of him leaving us. Yes, truly sorry. . . .'

He paused: water dripped from his hat: we were standing in the rain.

'I came to . . .'

'Ah yes? His downing? . . . Very sad certainly.'

'I came to ask you . . .'

'Come in. Come in.'

So in we went by the echoing stoneflagged everscrubbed passage to his bare cold study where a high horsehair chair was drawn up to his American-clothed desk upon which sat in very great gloom a neat heavy pile of once black now green theological treatises and a moth-eaten tortoiseshell cat called Tissy who spat us a welcome after his own bad taste, leaving worse in my mouth.

Mawk, who had followed us in, now growled.

'Please put that dog out. He is not comely.'

Comely, my arse, I thought. What about Katie? Katie was comely, I thought, but I said:

'Out you go, Mawk, old chap. Good dog,' which I did not think.

And I thought, you're a nasty piece of uncomely un-Christian half-mouldering rubbish; your moustache is mucousy; but I said:

'I am here about my uncle. Let us consider him, please. He was very fond of you, as I daresay you know, and of your churchyard by the big pool, as you no doubt knew, too . . .'

'Exactly so, exactly so. Let us speak no evil of the lately dead, my lad.'

Oh the soapy-mouthed hypocrite, I thought; but I said:

'I have absolutely no intention or desire to do so, for I dearly loved my uncle and would ask you to cut out your slithering innuendoes. He gave me to understand as his last wishes . . .'

'I understood you did not arrive quite in time: or was I misinformed?'

Maggie, the old bitch, on the telephone; not a doubt.

Ignoring him I went on:

'In the past frequently, and recently even more often, my uncle told me how he would like to be buried in your . . .'

'Ah, so he . . .'

'*But*,' I pursued, raising my voice to a clanging mechanical level of insistence, 'he wished first to have a service said over him, God only knows why, by his other old friend and your supposed colleague, Mr. Neil.' I was shrieking now.

He puffed himself up like some fungus from a damp crypt, expanding his skin until the hairs stood scattered only on his head and upper lip.

'Oh indeed! So you think I should play second fiddle, do you, to that worldly plump gentleman smelling there, almost, of incense and braided all over with ribbons! What next will you expect of me? What else do you propose I should stoop to?'

'I expect less than nothing. I know you are too vain by far ever to stoop. But I see now, as I always have seen in my dim-sighted despair, that as long as wretched people like you dare to hold over us poor humans threats or promises of an after life that is an insult to all tenderness, they will always have to walk in your administered fear. If there is a God, any God, you and your kind are his murderers; you miserable threateners and farcical bribers! I asked you only to attend to my own uncle's wishes, for he is not here to insist himself and would never have done so if he was. I find both of you miserable and callous; so-called shepherds of the human soul spitting at each other like your moth-eaten cat there!'

Tissy spat again.

I got up.

'I'll tell you, Mr. Maclaren, what I am going to do. I am going to carry through my uncle's wishes. I am going now to fetch his box for him. I shall go today and fetch it and tomorrow or the next day I shall bring him up in his boat. And I shall expect you, and him you call worldly and plump, over at the loch-head, both of you to accompany him—incense or no incense, cross or no cross, Christian or pagan or whatever you may be. Be there, because he wished it. Be there, I shall expect you. Good-day.'

# 41

WE went back to the pier and its piermaster, Ian.

'The Captain is dead,' I said, 'please fetch a box for him from wherever it is you get them; good plain quality but no trimmings. Have it here by morning.'

'Oh dear Lord, I am so sorry to hear it. You know we all loved him, we ordinary folk.'

'So did I, Ian, you know that too. Can you get him a coffin? I am going to have trouble at his downing anyhow with the ministers quarrelling over him like vultures already.'

'Oh don't say that. They've no right at all to; he was friends with both of them, good friends too; though maybe not of their God's. Yes of course: I'll fetch him one today or in the early morning, certainly. I'll bring it straight down in the *Arrow*. It seems to me, sir, he had better be ferried to his downing; the road is so terrible after all this rain it would be hard for the old hearse and horse and he would surely get a dreadful bumping. Well of course he wouldn't feel it; but still it would be upsetting somehow. I'll tell you what. I could fetch him in the *Arrow*, too, sir.'

'No, Ian. I'd like to row him. All his life he has been used to the tick-click of old Farrer's featherers in those teak thole-pins. We shall carry him in his box in his fine old clinker unless it's too wild a morning, and land him at your jetty, and there you shall meet him. See to it, man. See to it for me.'

I made off again along the dog-ribbed road and went home.

I opened the upper gate.

I went down the geological gravel path, igneous alternating with squelching alluvial. Everything dripped and I joined in the dripping. I was part of the drops, of eroding and oozing; sharp sand in my shoes and my heart a cold lake; soft mud in my shoes and my centre a swamp.

I opened the door of the inner oilskinned passage and cried out: 'Maggie,' with irritation and spleen.

She appeared instantaneously from the kitchen, guiltily indignant, her hands dappled with fragments of finely chopped parsley.

'I was just about making your sauce, sir.'

'What sauce, Maggie? What *kind* of sauce, Maggie?'

I was unreasonable, persistent, relentless.

'Parsley for the sea-trout, sir; the Cap'n's pink sea-trout. The bluebottles were at him.'

'Flit them and give me my dinner.'

So I dined.

Afterwards I sat on in the dining-room. The sun, astonishingly, had come out, soothingly reflecting a pattern of skating crystals on the cracked ceiling, the copper lamp, and the inlaid bookcase with its viols, harps, columbines and curios.

I went over and opened it, its hinges of good quality brass throwing a fine powder of dry-rot on its polished frontal curve.

Inside it was chock-full: prints and books and loose folios and scraps of paper useless and useful, worthless or valuable; all formerly treasured. The affected Gavarni set of Musicians, mildewed, mouse-eared: Turner's varied Liberi—Studiorum, Fluviorum—Pluviorum? Days and nights of things for the looking and things for not looking at at all, but for hearing always: scores of all music clutched in their B and H pages: music held dead, ears now unopened, notes unreleased, now unreleasable the way he would have wanted them, the values of each cadence re-cast into its twitching mould: velvet framed faded images of long lost, long loved teachers: Sevchik, Leschetizky, Joachim, Brahms: bow cases and bows, resin cases and resin . . . music overflowing; but I pushed it all back . . .

I took down from its peg an old floppy round-sewn hat, put it on and went out.

The loch was simmering with its turmoil of life: newly injected tide-life with its millions: holothurians coming, plankton going, trilobites and zoölites gone: the basic saline of the sea itself running in our bloodstreams, feeding us with oceans ages back in the rock-strata clock of time, flowing and weaving, breathing, vascular.

Down beneath the waters, great stillness.

Great stillness down there long ago.

Ages ago up there on the hillside: the train: Whistlefield: sitting on that boulder.

But *now* there was Melchi.

The seawater had risen to its landward limit: the saltwater had encroached its furthest on the sweet fresh: stones long dried of its saltiness were wet.

When it stood still at the moonchange, at the overriding pause of the great intake of held breath of the spinning earth and its boozed-up satellites there was a wonderful stretched and tentative balance; and although I knew it could not last, that very temporariness, self-evident and closely inevitable, by a paradoxical twist lent it a permanence greater than any mountain on a map.

I clung to that temporary permanence.

If you overturned one of the larger stones on the upper levels of the remaining foreshore, under it you would find a multitude of indeterminate creatures, some crustaceans, others almost insects, leaping up and down in confused parabolas not knowing whether to retreat towards the immediate salt-ridden land or advance to the all-swallowing sea: simply leaping: up and down only. Here and in such places there dwelt a perpetually living belt of the most terribly certain uncertainty: to crawl towards the advancing sea meant death, to scrabble to the towering land, oblivion. All they could hope for was an odd whiff now and then of the antidote with the poison: between the Devil—ha! ha!—and the deep sea indeed. They were the pitiful ones, and I was much one of them.

Maybe I wanted to be one of them, there dwelling? Thus dwelling? I bent and dragged over a fat grey slab. There they were! Up and down they leapt.

156

I scooped and took some in my moist frightened hands: some of them stuck to my sweat, others fed from it.

I bent once again and grabbing them together, pressed them living and leaping up into my mouth. They tickled the roof of my palate and I ate them: some tasted of dust, others of bone: some were slightly moist, others utterly dry.

There in my stomach, the most pitiful and lost of creation's creations, on the narrow margin, somnambulant funambulists, they held me at the tension, at the turn: at the tide's held breath, at the sea's greatest rise, at the earth's lowest lot, at the spinning sun-and-moon-enemies' embracing . . .

Melchi was missing; I was very, very sad.

Melchi was missing and he had to be put down.

So in the end I got up (if I had not really been standing all the time) and went up the uneven steps through the gate with the once so perfectly known slam, past the place where the ever fermenting seaweed heap was formerly hot as breakfast porridge to my barefeet from the cold sea, again onto the pampered rain-soaked grass, back to the lopsided house itself.

I rang the bell and Maggie came running.

'Oh, I'm sorry, Maggie, I forgot I had a key.'

She gave me a queer look, a worried look, and I cannot say I blamed her: for there was no key and we knew it very well. Melchi had lost it in the Crinnan Canal years ago when out on one of his skites and had never had another one made. From then on his door had never been locked, scarcely ever closed.

'I am sorry, Maggie. I am silly. I am rather over-wrought. You see, the Ministers were like vultures over the Captain . . . picking what's left of his poor flesh like vultures . . . I don't know. By the way, how *is* the Captain?'

'Lord, Sir, my God, sir . . . He's . . . you know it very well . . . I mean, he's dead, sir.'

'I know that, idiot! But how is he faring now that he is dead? Can I not inquire after him? Are the bluebottles still at him? Do they bother him? . . . naturally not. But are they *at* him, Maggie? That's what I want to know.'

'No, sir. Oh my God, sir, you frightened me, I can tell you. No, sir, I flitted him—them, I mean. That is to say there was only one. Oh dear.'

'I shall go then to see him.'

Melchi lay, as often I had seen him, waking in the middle of some scarcely darkening summer's night in the bell tent far up north near Lochinver or Kylesku or Durness or Tongue, or on some other silent strand or remote phalarope-haunted lochan or shore, like the effigy of an early bishop on his tomb.

In tent or tomb I felt I was with him and I turned my head then or now, the dry bracken rustling through the rubber-scented groundsheet. In the aquarium light of the tent or the tomb he heard me also, turning also towards me.

'Hello, D.,' he said, without moving a hairsbreadth in or on his tomb or bed, me in mine. 'Are you not sleeping well, old chap? I haven't slept at all so far. I've been rambling, old chap, rambling . . . *Je ne tiens pas à te faire un savant de la Musique, mais seulement un amoureux de la Musique; ce qui est bien plus important* . . . Do you follow what I say? Who said that, I wonder? Did any one say it? Do you hear me? Do you hear me?'

'Yes . . . why, yes . . . I think so. "*Un amoureux de la Musique*" . . . Yes, you have made me that . . . Yes, indeed you have done that. But tell me, why don't you sleep now?'

'I do not know. I don't know and I don't mind. I am not a sleeper, for there is too much to think about. Do you hear me?'

'I am sorry; so sorry,' I mumbled.

He continued to lie there unmoving; I, too, where and who I was.

There are some places that you know go on without you, always and easily without you; with you or with others: other places only live when you are there to experience them, know them, make them in your mind and being.

The loch had stopped without Melchi.

It lapped no longer now; nor did the Mayburn roar in spate, nor the bluish smoke rise vertically from McEacharn's chimney, held in the still air.

Everything had stopped without Melchi.

I left his room.

I went next door and lay down on the sofa.

There I got wrongly ready for the next day, the day after, the following one after that and all subsequent mornings.

His game was up but mine, by God, was not.

And when I awoke it was raining as usual: and still, still: with not a leaf moving or murmuring against the drops.

I went to the telephone and rang them both up.

Both said they would come, both they and I hating it all and each other.

# 42

THEY had him battened down and we carried him.

The boat was moored at the uneven jetty: the tide was equivocal half.

In great danger of slipping and dropping him and with much suppressed cursing on account of the reverent company, we lowered him, between the whole lot of us and with the aid of a rope, lengthways along the thwarts he had so many times warmed with his eager old bottom: a cold cheap mock-brasshandled upstart coffin where the living man had sat.

I pushed off: four living and one dead: at the last moment boarded with a leap by the dog Mawk, wheezing and snuffling up and under us in the bilge to the sternsheets and back again to the bow, the last thing I wanted, his behaviour afloat being even worse than his antics ashore.

Now to arrange ourselves, animals all.

The two crowblack clergy arrogated uncomfortably to themselves immediately the Mawk-moistened broadseat at the tiller. There they sat juxtaposed; furious in the cox-place.

Who was to row?

The four of us fumbled, squashing ourselves down between coffin and gunnel, oars stuck out beyond their leather fulcrums, their inboard ends scraping the fresh varnished side of the now central box. We took small wasteful unbalanced chopping strokes and progressed miserably in the water-gurgling silence.

Meanwhile Mawk, an uninspiring figurehead, perched himself in the bows, ready to attack with all his might and wrath any coloured mooring-buoys that hove within his hazy eyesight's muddied range. This he invariably did, had been encouraged to do so by Melchi for the fun of it, with a great show of ferocity, sometimes falling overboard in his eagerness to be at them, drenching all passengers when subsequently hauled in.

I was far too despondent to care what happened next and I looked back (for I had the bow pull) over the coffin and the backs of my fellow oarsmen to where Neil and Maclaren sat glowering and downcast, a perfect example of Christian co-operation, in the stern.

I was far too despondent to care, do you hear me?

I was far too despondent and pulled grudgingly in silence.

We had gone about half-way when I was disturbed by a series of whimpering snivels from Mawk in his perch at the bow.

But I paid no attention.

Then he burst into hysterical barking and I knew he had now seen a buoy. He became more and more frenzied, I with him; so I suddenly spun round sideways and seizing him by the collar screeched:

'Down, Mawk! Down, blast you! God's curse on you for a filthy male bitch of a dog anyhow!'

I do not know how it happened and now I never shall, but my 'Down Mawk' fired him with new fury and he gave a great lunge dragging me with him well over the side of the boat, the same listing heavily.

I tried to lock my feet, first in the stretcher and then in the seat, Fletcher before me turning and grabbing me also.

However it was we were all grabbing each other and I was grabbing Mawk and he was three-quarters out of the boat throttlingly growling and foaming at the mouth and in the confusion the coffin abruptly shifted and before you could say knife had toppled into the water.

Thereupon I let go Mawk and made a great grab at the mock brass handle, in so doing loosening my foothold and kicking Fletcher in the face so that he let go too. The two Ministers, who should have known better, also leant forward, half rising from their seat and the next moment everyone was struggling in the sea.

I held very tight to that mock brass handle fully expecting him to float but to my great consternation far from floating he began to plunge downwards as inexorably as a rock. I held him very tightly and I sank down with him and in an instant we were in the green half-light, bubbles rising from us, time growing concentrate, ears and eyes stinging and spinning, and the mind telling tales like the one about the cormorant who was a wool merchant and hired bat and bramble as crew for his wool-ship and of how the ship had sunk so that ever since . . . ever ever since . . . the cormorant has been diving trying to retrieve it . . . the bat, yes the bat . . . has been hiding from sheer shame . . . in the darkest damp caves . . . and the bramble, yes the bramble . . . stealing wool . . . from sheep's backs . . . to pay back . . . to pay back . . . to pay back his debt . . .

The water sang louder; the green grew much darker: and I thought then, at last: 'By the Lord, Neil and Maclaren, old boys, you've been diddled all right and cheated of your services.'

'Good old Mawk! Good old dog, after all!' I shouted.

And my mouth promptly filled.


# 43

HE was at the Tartini again and I could not go to sleep: over and over again that double-stopping passage with the same note always out of tune: with the same note not quite in time.

He was walking up and down continuously, taking a deep snuffling breath before he attacked each passage, venting it out noisily after the strain had passed, parenthetically humming to himself beforehand or afterwards snatched phrases already played or still to come.

Meanwhile the rain continued its irregular patter on the single dormer-window's thin roof and when a gusty wind blew, rattled on the panes themselves, blowing great slopping drifts off the kerria and pernettya bushes up the hill onto the outhouse slating down below. Malcolm's little burn was roaring in spate, blocking and filling no doubt the small cement dam that guided off the water to our tank with its glinting schist-pebbles and their ground-down white sand, so that instead of overflowing it would be empty in the morning and the lavatory cistern, whose ballcock was stuck anyhow, would be empty too; so the flush would not work.

I hated that because it meant going to the 'mens' outside earth-closet perched over the putrefying ashpit, damp cold and draughty from below when it was wet, noisome with bluebottles when the fitful sun shone. And smelly always.

I could not go to sleep and Melchi went on practising.

He was on Bach now, the E major concerto with its vigorous entry, humming and shouting in the pauses the missing orchestral accompaniment, stamping out the time with his foot in the silences; counting out loud; counting as he sang; stamping as he played.

I could not go to sleep.

I could not go to sleep so I groped for the matches on the horse-hair chair beside me, striking one to light the guttered candle in its white, flushed-pink, enamel candlestick. It only gave a feeble glow: warm yellow, though, and comforting.

There wasn't much I could do: scarcely bright enough to read. I was bored anyhow by the fat Arthur Mee that granny or Mrs. N. had given me, though the pictures were all right; the pictures, yes, were lovely. I had finished Chippy Bobby and had it all by heart.

I started to repeat it.

Then Sheila stirred over in her bed, there right close under the shadowed ceiling where it sloped down and turned into the wall under the eaves. She gave a little snort in her sleep, moving her head forward away from me and the candle, and I saw her long hair move on her pillow like some small furry animal dragging itself along. What a funny girl! She always slept like that, falling off immediately; and always I had trouble rousing her in the morning when the gong went for porridge and salt: an egg for the older ones, porridge for us: strawberry for the older ones, goosegog for us: Demerara sugar for Hugh himself only.

She was queer all right; but then she was a girl and I didn't like girls much anyway. Of course there was the Mellin girl: she was fun. She was great fun sometimes with her tricks in the water and much gayer than Sheila was anyhow; but a bit of a bully, always making me swim far further out than I wanted to *in* that icy cold loch when I'd much sooner spend hours *on* it in a boat, rowing or sailing or drifting with the tide.

Sheila was a sulky one; she didn't say much.

When we were together she hardly spoke at all, except sometimes when we were far off up the hill deep in the hazel woods or bracken; and then it was fairies or ribbons or other kind of girl talk.

She was stupid too; very stupid, I thought. An ass; a dunce; a silly stupid fool!

But look how she played! All those Heller studies, pages of them; perfect. As easy as wink too, reading them at sight when I couldn't manage them at all, though I loved that one where you crossed your hands over. I had learnt that from her like a parrot; knew where and when to put my fingers down anyway and how to put them down too: that was easy as pie; even if they bore no relationship in my mind to those crotchets and quavers with their slurs and their staves. And now, blow it all, she was working at the *Cuckoo*. How I'd love to play the *Cuckoo*!

Da-da-da DA, da-da-da DA
da-da-da DA, da-da-da DA
Da-da-da DA DA tweedlyda DEE . . .

It sounded all so easy in my head. I knew it all exactly and how, too, you emphasised the Cuck-oo part, hopping with your right hand like that: and even further on when the tune was repeated higher up. Ah, I should have been able to play it *easily, easily*. But I couldn't and Sheila could. No expression, of course!—all just run out like a pocketful of glass marbles, all quite even and as dull as tapioca made with skim-milk—but the right notes and as fast as anything. Damn her! She was always practising away like Melchi, with a clock on the piano before her to tell her when her two hours were up. But Melchi could play, by Jove—sometimes. At

163

least I had heard him do so: at least he used to be able to and perhaps he could still . . .

The wind huffed violently: the rain rattled and splattered outside: my candle guttered and wobbled, throwing great dancing shadows of our twin cotton bathing-dresses, hung hopefully on a string near the window to dry, on the varied sloping ceiling and my old plaid dressing-gown stitched up from a partly once moth-eaten rug on its hook on the back of the door.

I might as well put it out before the wind did. So I snuffed it, licking my finger and thumb first, enjoying the small resistant hiss of the flame to its extinction.

But I still could not sleep and Melchi was still at it.

He was playing now in snatches and pauses, filling in the parts for himself with his humming and thumping—some ensemble work maybe, a trio or quartet.

'That's it,' I could hear him say clearly. 'That's the way. That's better,' and he gave a loud musical sneeze and a cough in a chromatic downward scale in D minor and started on the Bach double, following it straight on, stopping and snuffling and stamping as before.

And, oh my dear God, I was thereupon catapulted to a much later day, flung out of my childhood bed forward to a moment from which it may be I had only fallen in.

I do not know how that awful moment came about (for it was an awful moment) . . . I do not know how . . . but I know very well if I could only have undone it . . . if I could only still undo it . . . do you hear me?

# 44

WASN'T your Uncle Melchi a pupil of Joachim's once? And of Sevchik? Wasn't he a great fiddler in his day? And teacher too? Most of the front desk of the orchestra there were his pupils, weren't they?—Yes, indeed he was, indeed they are. He doesn't do much now but once upon a time he used to.

Well, wouldn't it be a great idea, if he would consider it, to ask him to play something for us, with us, for the fiftieth anniversary concert? Eh? A simple concerto or something? Wouldn't it? Do you think he'd take it on? It would be rather fun, wouldn't it?

Well I asked him, but Oh No, he said, he couldn't make a solo appearance any more. Perhaps some kind of an ensemble? Yes, possibly, but not a solo. He was too old, not used to the platform now, you know . . . that was all long ago.

We thought of several things but all in their turn were discarded: too difficult, too long, never liked the work, mawkish. So we ended up where I thought we might have done anyhow by suggesting his old favourite, the work he'd been through again and again and again all his life long, up and down, from boyhood to middle age, in peacetime settled, in wars on the move, in the old days in Prague and the new ones near the cold sea. But now, alas, he was really getting on . . . Yes, getting on . . . but he thought . . . yes, he would really be delighted to try that if they would have him.

So a rehearsal was arranged and one of his very best old pupils came to play second with him and Sir Norman was there at the piano and he was very flattered.

He had a glass of Glenlivet and he felt very well and it went very well too.

They tried the glorious slow movement first, *molto adagio*, and except for his intonation which was at times a little shaky, excusable at his age, for the rheumatisms of Scotland were always at his fingers, all was nearly perfect. There were a few mild suggestions made over the speeds at which the outer movements should be taken but there could be little doubt that he was able for it and that his rather personal, perhaps too personal, approach and interpretation would have a flavour which would add distinction to the jubilee concert in view.

So he went off home in high delight and called in to see me on the way and thanked me:

'It's great! Enlivening, I tell you, for an old fellow like me. And, mind you, a good half of the front desks of the fiddles'll be all my own pupils . . . Think of that! It's great for an old fellow like me to be wanted again, even a little: and Doris plays second beautifully, just as I taught her in the old days myself; the very same *feeling* for the great work too. Her intonation may not be quite perfect all the time and of course her bowing's become a bit ragged I know. She will not keep her elbow down. But I'll play with her certainly. Indeed it's good of them to ask me.'

And I poured two fingers of Bushmill's for him—the best of both worlds he used to call it—not too raw Irish, not too sweet Scotch.

They had several more rehearsals, Sir Norman presiding, and Uncle Melchi's fine fettle grew finer and finer. Not so, alas, his playing: not so his intonation: not so his bowing or his breath. These, contrariwise, grew wilder and wider—the slow movement a long-drawn-out sentimentalized reverie, now haltingly dragged, now fumbled over distantly: the fast ones an impossible gallop, tripping and stumbling over the tricky-enough runs, falling down completely into breathless *non sequitur.*

Melchi was exultant. Sir Norman and Doris, embarrassed at first, terrified subsequently, and quite unable, no matter how they tried, to fit in with or follow his physical and emotional fancies.

They had a few more rehearsals.

The more they played, the more elated became Melchi; and the more elated he became the more eccentric and capricious his vagaries; the greater his continued interference with the score; the more frequent his libations.

By this time Sir Norman was in a panic, Doris in an outraged sulk.

Having persuaded the old man to take on the task it seemed to him downright impossible now to ask him to give it up. He had hoped, on a first hearing, that a few careful rehearsals, a few tactful promptings would guide the whole thing into the pleasantest of paths and that the old pupil of Sevchik, Joachim and Johannes Brahms (whose classes in harmony he had indeed twice attended) would be a noble partner, if not a virtuoso, for the fiftieth anniversary, for his musical offspring Doris Shea . . . Youth and Age and the world between . . . Ahem!

But alas no such thing occurred: once old Uncle Melchi had

the bit between his teeth, the bow between his fingers, the fiddle-body gripped beneath his stubbly dimpled chin, there was simply no stopping him; no possible deflection.

'Doris. Joachim always insisted and I in my turn insist that you start that passage (bar 180 or whatever it was) on the *up* bow, like this . . .'

'Sir Norman, a marked *rallentando* there please, a marked *rallentando* there. Professor Sevchik always insisted. It is consequent and logical as well as pleasing to the ear and that passage following should be taken like this: ONE and two, and THREE and four . . . ONE and two, and THREE and four . . .'

He stamped his foot, counting vehemently, spitting just a little, the saliva collecting in foamy flecks in the corner of his mouth.

'But that's really impossible Captain, for if we start off at that tempo what happens when we come in again later?'

'Fiddlesticks! Of course it's not impossible. Let's try it and you'll see. Doris! You've forgotten what I've told you over and over and over again. Hold the bow well up! Elbow down! Elbow! . . . That's it . . . and ONE and two, and THREE and four . . .'

Finally, very finally and very shortly, there came the first orchestra rehearsal in the sunless afternoon.

Sir Norman was in a frightful state: apart from anything else, what would the orchestra think?

What would they do? What would his leader, an explosive expensive choleric and very vain Italian say? Already he had had to dissuade him from insisting on taking the *violino primo* part himself by pointing out what a great honour it was to have the old man, this pupil of the great and illustrious dead, to play for and with them.

And what would Doris say, and what would *she* do? She was pretty and she knew it and she rather fancied herself as a soloist as well. She had ordered, so she had told him, a special new frock for the occasion, plain of course, marvellously cut no doubt; but she had a nice figure and it would not hang around her in folds: and a small tiara-affair like the one that young International Celebrity wears, you know, to show off her hair . . .

Uncle Melchi was late, they were all being kept waiting. The Clarinet gave his A and retired: the orchestra tuned and re-tuned, each player, out for himself, going over those difficult passages urgently, *pianissimo*, in a whisper.

Just as a terrible wave of impatience was sweeping like cold fever over the entire company, audibly evident in their instrumental bickerings, the green baize door at the stage-side opened and in came old Melchi, his fiddle-case under his arm, as pleased with himself as Punch. He raised his hat extravagantly, made a low and gallant sweep with it.

'My dear friends, Sir Norman, how delightful it is to be back—to be back in harness with all of you again—— Dear me!' and after a pleased sigh and a pause, 'I beg your pardon. Have I been keeping you waiting? This infernal—ugh—traffic. I'm so sorry.'

He quickly got his elaborate case unbuckled and his bow and his fiddle out, stuffing a handful of highly coloured spotted silk handkerchiefs between it and his chin.

Someone once again gave the note and he tuned up in a leisurely fashion, humming to himself as usual, calling or crying out relevant or irrelevant harmonies; snatches too of the parts to be performed.

'Very well, Sir Norman, are you ready? Doris, my girl?'

Sir Norman was quailing.

It was quite clear now that over and above any other factor Melchi had had far too much of his favourite DWD at the corner and probably a peg or two further along that back street towards the hall. However, it was too late to turn back: better disaster now before the whole orchestra than ruin later before a huge public.

Sir Norman tapped his desk.

Melchi sang out clearly and gaily the first few bars of the Partita in D minor . . . at least the same key.

'My little dog loves that,' he announced quite loudly to no one in particular, 'he always howls with delight—you should hear him—Ahoooo*wow*—ahoooh*wow*—*wow*.'

'Captain,' said Sir Norman stiffly, 'your attention please. We are already late and must now begin the rehearsal.'

'Oh don't let me keep you, Sir Norman. Come along, Doris dear. Attention to the desk . . . Eyes on the baton, my love!' and he pointed over his shoulder at Sir Norman rather naughtily with his bow.

Sir Norman tapped again.

Semi-silence reigned.


Sir Norman raised his baton and on its downstroke in came the orchestra with precision: but when his entry came Uncle Melchi missed it and when he realized what he had done struck in as best he could—as the orchestra, taking their cue from the conductor, ground to an infuriated standstill—with the opening phrases of that same dog-loved Partita. Then he grinned sheepishly, very nearly laughing out aloud, at the orchestra's faces molten with anger and impatience.

'Again please!' snapped Sir Norman, beside himself now: and once again they started.

This time Melchi was there all right: he came in all right, at the right place too; then he took or rather tried to take command. In any case the tempo began to drag, then to speed up, speed up far too much, Sir Norman doing his best to keep his players with him, somehow or another to co-ordinate the orchestra and Uncle Melchi's playing. As for Doris, she was forgotten in the struggle and fearful turmoil. Melchi free-lanced away, shouting out occasionally like a Rumanian gipsy, and by dint and by hook the movement at last clattered to its terrible end.

There were tears of frustration and anger in the second fiddle's eyes. Doris did not like it at all; and who would? As for the orchestra they were flabbergasted, exchanging sour looks, raised eyebrows, injured grimaces and, the few more charitable or humorous among them, winks and leers.

'Ragged lot of strings you've got, I must say,' said Melchi fairly quietly but not quietly enough. 'Didn't go too badly all the same if they'd only kept the beat. Surprisingly ragged lot. . . . Oh well!'

Some of them had heard him, the leader amongst others.

There were no winks now.

'Let's get on with the slow movement, I'm thirsty and famished,' said Melchi. 'Come along.'

Sir Norman tapped again, faintly, desperately, looking round with anguish at the sea of upturned faces, trying to smile, trying to cry, trying to convey by whatever contortions of his physiognomy and goatee beard he could manage that all might yet be well, that he quite understood, that of course we all quite understood.

So the slow movement began with its soft plucked accompaniment and Melchi came in leaning on his bow, trembling with his deep longing and desire and love for every single note. In it he immersed himself: he immersed himself so far, so very, very far, that he carried himself in himself back to the long days of lonely practice, to the sound of this rain and this waterfall, to his own bedroom with the balcony where he walked up and down in his slippers and dressing-gown, laying his Gold Flake, too smoky in his eyes, on the edge of the black marble mantelpiece as he passed it, there to be forgotten. He loved and lost himself in those touchingly wonderful cadences, surely the most glorious outpouring of lyrical melody ever written. Yes, he lost himself; and Sir Norman lost him too; and Doris as well; and the orchestra totally.

They did the best they could; they were very sad now. It was hard to be angry any more with the fine old man, his eyes tight shut, his face transfigured by his feeling as he played there to himself, an occasional chord of accompaniment only or a few notes fitted by the second fiddle, enraptured and enwrapped in that soaring melody.

And so at last they ended, they all ended; vaguely, apprehensively, together.

It took some little while for Melchi to come back and when at last he did so, there was dead silence, there were glum faces. He slowly opened his eyes as if he had been dreaming—those old green brown-spotted eyes with their great bushy eyebrows above them. Then, with an effort, he collected his proud scattered wits.

'Thank you so much, Sir Norman. That went beautifully, didn't it? Thank you, my dear friends . . .' He paused, the lights and shadows of consciousness playing and flickering on his face.

'Now we might as well get on with the rough and tumble, eh, old chap?'

Heaven preserve us, rough and tumble it was: everyone sawing away, some together, others separately, Sir Norman throwing up his hands, Miniaco, the Italian leader, holding on doggedly in mid-current, Doris putting in an unavailing oar here and there as best she could. It was a bit gay this time. It was grotesque and a bit gay all right. The noise was tremendous.

Melchi led over the hurdles, all the pack after him galloping and grinding. There were increasing and ever increasing crises *fortissimo* as the fearful end drew near. Cacophonous peak succeeded discordant valley and as the conventional, if musically questionable, final *rallentando* mercifully approached it was evident that Melchi, unable to stay the pace he had originally set, was in fact now some way behind.

The orchestra ceased, but he, Melchi, went on; the last five notes, clear and loud, unfortunately stridulent, badly flat, being played by him only.

It was over. At last it was over.

Bar the sequel, of course.


Melchi was delighted.

'Splendid,' he said. 'We took it a bit fast, I think, didn't we? A little more work on that tomorrow and then I don't think we need worry, need we? Splendid. Well, Sir Norman, I must admit I am a bit fagged: not used to this kind of thing any more, you know. Think I'll slip out now for a little refreshment, I've a long way to go home. Good night all, and thank you . . . thank you!'

The next afternoon (in my time as a painter) I was busy on a very large canvas I had been struggling with for months when they came and said Sir Norman was on the telephone and would I come at once?

'I am afraid I have terrible news, D.,' he said. 'Your uncle can't do it.'

'Do what?' I said. 'He told me the rehearsals were going splendidly yesterday.'

'Alas, no, oh no—in fact it's impossible, simply impossible. It's not his fault: he's too old, he's too rusty. We should never have asked him; never. But I wonder could you help me? Could you . . . could you . . . somehow . . . stop it?'

'What? Stop it? Stop the concert, do you mean? How can I? What can *I* do? What can *I* say? You should have seen to that. It's too late now. You'll just have to go through with it. He can't be that bad . . .'

'I tell you it's completely impossible. He just cannot manage it; and anyway, both the orchestra and Doris have refused to play with him, quite flatly. It's either him or they. It's awful!'

'It certainly is awful. But can't you do something?'

'What can I do? You could see him and tell him . . . suggest that after all . . .' And then I thought, My God, you yourself half suggested it. You were proud of the old fellow, *your* uncle, *Brahms's* pupil (how thrillingly he had once told me, I being excited about some modern work, the Bloch, I think, at the time—of how *he* had been present at the first performance of Brahms's Fourth Symphony *conducted by the composer*) . . . Yes, partly my own vanity, my own vicarious joy. But how I should have loved too, to have applauded him triumphant . . .

'What shall I tell him then? What on earth can I tell him? That he's no good?'

'Tell him anything you like, absolutely anything. Only for Heaven's sake stop him. Miniaco says he'll take his place. Very good of him indeed at such short notice' (I was angry with myself and furious with Sir Norman). 'The programmes are printed and advertised and . . . Well . . . I fear I just don't know. I am half crazy with it all. See what you can do. Please . . . for my sake. It's our fiftieth anniversary, you know, and I'll be ruined if you don't do something . . .'

'To hell with your ruin anyhow. What do I care?'

But I did care. I cared very much. I cared all round. And I realized there would be an appalling scene if the performance took place and Melchi was there being booed and being hissed, for that audience, and especially that kind of festival audience, was not likely to be fobbed off . . . No, it was indeed awful.

172

'I'll think about it,' I said lamely. 'I'll see what can be done. I'll try . . .'

'It is as much for his sake as for ours you know, D. Oh, I don't know how to thank you. I couldn't sleep all night.'

I hung up.

I was almost numb with terror.

What could I do? It was three in the afternoon and final rehearsal was called for that evening at seven. It was winter and the first hints of the coming night were already apparent in the golden light on the leafless beech trees outside my studio window. I went and had a good large whiskey; then another.

I got out the old Darracq, always a devil to start in cold weather, especially, for some inscrutable reason, in the afternoon. Melchi lived miles away and time was running out.

Oh God, what on earth was I to say? What was it I *could* say? I thought I had better leave it to the moment, the awful approaching moment, and depend then on my wits, on his mood.

I drove off. It was still afternoon.

When I got to his house by the cold winter's afternoon sea to my consternation no one was in. It was locked up. No fire in the grate. All the downstairs windows were shut and bolted. I could not get in. I had not bargained for this.

Oh well, he couldn't be very far. He would be back soon. I should just have to wait.

But to wait under such circumstances was dreadful; not to be stood in my condition, so I thought.

But I tried it.

Then I went along to Morrow's and had a few: a J.J. neat and a few watered.

And back again.

And waited again.

It began to grow dark. I would *have* to find Melchi, but first, I thought, I had better leave a note of some sort where he could not possibly miss it. But I found I had no paper, nor anything to write with, for in my confusion I had left my wallet, pen and everything else behind me in the pockets of my old painting coat.

I looked around then and saw that one of the bedroom windows upstairs was open just where the lean-to roof of the large hall-door porch met the wall below it. I judged I could probably scramble up and with some difficulty, scratching myself badly and tearing my clothes on the half-dead rambler-roses on the way, got up onto the slippery lichen-slimy slates. I was just putting my leg through the window into the room when there was a loud hail from the nearby road.

'What are you doing up there? Come down out of that and let me see you.'

A policeman, one I did not know, a young officious new one, was shouting at me.

'I am visiting my uncle,' I called back.

'Come down at once and explain yourself,' he cried.

I went on in through the window, down the stairs, snatched a piece of paper and a pencil from his desk in the dining-room, scribbled on it *The Concert's off: D.*, and left it in the middle of the table on the old faded olive-green cloth. Then I went to the front door, opened it and went out, nearly colliding with the guard who was standing at the alert, apprehensively looking up, baton drawn in hand.

'Who are you? What are you doing in an unoccupied house?'

'It's not unoccupied. I wanted to see my uncle on urgent business and when I got here he and his wife were out; so I climbed up there to leave a note on his table for him when he got back. I am his nephew.'

'I see. If you say he is your uncle I suppose you may be right. But can you prove that to me? There have been a lot of daylight snatch housebreakings around here these times and they're all quick talkers like yourself, with easy ready tongues. We can't trust anyone. Show me something to prove who you are. What's your name?'

I put my hand in my pocket to take out my wallet, forgetting that I had left it at home.

'I am afraid I left my wallet in my other coat at home, but anyone will tell you. I am well known in Baldoyle.'

'A good talker certainly. This is not Baldoyle. Is that your car out there?'

'Yes.'

'Got your driving licence?'

'I tell you I left everything at home.'

'In that case I'm afraid you'll have to step along to the barracks with me. I'm sorry to trouble you, but (he put his baton back in its round black leather case) I'll have to ask you to come along.'

'But look here, sergeant . . . it's most urgent I should see my uncle. It's very important business about a concert in Dublin.'

'About what? Never mind the concert, no matter where it is. Come along now please, come along.'

So I had to go with him.


Of course they knew me at the barracks and I hurried back frenzied with anxiety, and when I got back Uncle Melchi was there and as soon as he saw me through the window he came rushing to the door and let me in. His wife was there too.

'What's this, D? The concert off? What on earth's happened?'

'Your uncle's very worried, D. It's all very sudden.'

'Why is it cancelled? What has happened?'

'It's not exactly cancelled, Uncle Melchi, but you see . . . You see . . .'

'What is it then?'

'Well, you see . . . the fact is they . . . it's very difficult, but you see, Sir Norman, you see . . . they think . . .'

'What do they think?'

I looked hard at his dear old eyes; his sad now solemn face with its bushy brows, his cheekbones brindled with half-shaved hair.

I looked hard into his dear old eyes, muttering and mumbling. As I looked I could see them filming over. I could see grief and old age there in their speckled depths. I could see tears coming, welling up, flooding, the bright pupils narrowing, the curtain of dark wretchedness and bitter disappointment creeping.

'I see,' he said at last very faintly, lowering his lids. 'I'm no good any more. I'm not good enough for them; is that it?'

'Well you see they think . . . they think you're a bit out of practice . . . you see . . . another time . . .'

'There'll never be another time, D; never, never. That was my last chance, that was my last time. Now it's gone.'

'You should not have allowed it. It's scandalous,' said his wife. 'You should have told Sir Norman to go through with it.'

'But you see . . . he said they couldn't. He said they would not play.'

'You'd better go. This is terrible. You'd better go. He had his old tails out all ready. I had brushed them carefully . . . you'd better go.'

D minor: oh God, oh D minor.


# 45

I wAs back in that bed in D minor in my childhood and I could not go to sleep.

The candle was out and Melchi was still practising: the young D minor: the fresh tearing counterpoint, the sorrowful and joyous outpouring—all by himself then, all by himself later . . . but, mercifully merging, I was now up the hill towards Lochanbridge a few days earlier. . . .

It was one of those very rare days when the sun really shone. The sky was brilliant. Dark cobalt cloud-shadows skimmed and slid over the ochred grassy mountains and I don't know whether it was simply the contrast or the perpetually rain-washed clarity of the atmosphere, but the sun seemed hot, boiling hot; and we all wished we had brought our bathing togs with us.

The small fresh seeds of cocksfoot and fiorin, darnel and fescue, stuck to our hot damp legs, itching us as we traipsed wearily along the meadow from Lettermay; and when we came to the woods and the grey and moss-green bridge over the salmon-pool I said:

'Oh do let's bathe!'

'We've no togs,' said Sheila.

'Never mind,' said Barney. 'No one'll see us here.'

So we all stripped and plunged into the deep, orange-brown water. I was last and Sheila stood naked on a huge granite lichen-varied boulder, her arms above her head, her pigtails down her back, the sifted sunlight playing on her pale smooth skin, her shoulder blades tensed, taut rounded buttocks, there, before she dived.

I thought she looked lovely, not knowing exactly why, her slim figure so different to us boys with our troublesome mickeys sticking out in front where she had none.

She sprang in and her body gleamed under the water, brown and white bubbles frothing and curdling around her.

When she came to the surface she was smiling up saying it was lovely and to come on in too, which I did. And then I in my turn looked up at her standing there spluttering from the cold, shivering and shining, the drops clinging and running on her smoothness, chasing each other, racing each other, on her belly, down her legs. Funny though, the rest of her was much the same as us only smoother and rounder. I supposed when she was older she would have bigger bubs like the Mellin girl, trembling when she laughed, hidden and secret between her ever-folded arms with their tips so big from the ice-cold sea when she waded ashore in her black cotton bathing dress. They were quite small now, only just beginning, but their tips were quite big from the cold water too. . . .

I still could not sleep, I was feeling cold also. The rain spattered and lashed and dripped and Melchi was at it, repeating, repeating.

I still could not sleep, I felt lonely and cold and I began to shiver: and after a while longer, the rain and Melchi carrying me down further, I found I was getting out of bed, standing on the lino, still colder.

In two steps I was across to Sheila.

I gently lifted her blankets, felt a waft of warmth puffing up to me and slipped in under the clothes beside her.

She had her back turned to me and I snuggled down next to her.

I snuggled right down close to her, bending my body's Z to fit thus her body's curve, both of us that instant warm within our womb.

177

I snuggled right down and she stirred a little.

I snuggled close to her and was wonderfully comforted: as close as I could I crept, my bowels stirring within me.

And before I could properly feel or compute thereon, for a little while anyhow, I fell asleep.

It was the night after the funeral.

It was the night after the affair of the Concerto.

It was that night, when I was a child, when Melchi was practising, that I fell asleep, warm, in Sheila's small bed.

# 46

'BACK up?' Not yet.

If there was a hurry for the bus, there was none now for me.

On the contrary there was time enough—plenty of 'time enough'.

I unwillingly got out, staggering and flopping amidst the pullulating mass of upright party-coloured objects on the pavement that were people passing: people passing hither, people passing thither; shouting, jostling, greeting, abusing, cajoling; hurrying to catch their buses, to keep or miss their meetings, hasten home to their families, escape from their wives, join or flee their mistresses; end or begin, truncate or continue, the week, the day or this very new hour.

And I, having lost now all sense of direction—all direction, as a corollary, of sense—not knowing where I now (or then) was, whither I was now or then going or where I had come from: knowing only that sooner now or later then I must and should find myself—now (and then at that moment) decided to commit myself wholly and at once to that variously diverging, continuously gurgitated, vortex, whirlpool, mill-race of people and allow them to carry me wheresoever they were severally or all together bound.

At first, like a fallen oak-apple caught in a corner in an eddy by a rock in some rushing mountain stream, I stopped fairly (but only fairly) where I fell; aside from but not by any means un-affected by the roaring mainstream's tumbling current. Buffeted by the passers, dodgem amongst hurtling dodgems, now crush-ingly this way now violently that, I stuffed my hands deep in my torn trousers' pockets, held my arms rigid to my wheezy aching sides to prevent them being straggled out, helpless flailing booms of folded flesh on bone, catching precariously between passing uprights, snapped off, snaffled, or crushed in the mêlée.

Even so doing, I was greatly in their way and they were abomin-ably in mine, if I had had one . . . But Yes, now I had, if not a way, why then at least a means to a way; for did I not want eagerly to be carried off with them to be deposited like driftwood some-where near or far and shore-thrown verify my land fall?

Yet all that happened and continued to happen was an at once repetitively detailed and multitudinously anonymous can-noning. I was bumped and bandied between hard and soft, old and young, male and female, gruff and gay, until my outside teeth chattered in my skull and my inside skull rattled on my neck.

Someone pushed past me with a folded wet umbrella under their left arm, spokes facing me forwards, catching in my shirt, filleting my tie, tearing a button off one and the other in shreds so that its inner white lining flapped tapishly in my face. A large brown parcel of rattling joggled crockery crushed me in turn on my sandwiched other side; I threw my whole weight against it and if hurting in so doing my very squeezed-boxed ribs felt a satisfactory cracking not confined to them alone, whilst to my spiny left a duck-billed bird or fantail, borne aloft by a hurrier on his shoulder in a woven wicker cage, flapped its moulted feathers, rejected bird seed and ejected droppings on my face, and a sodden sack of hard knobbly potatoes scored my formerly right ear on my now left-twisting side. This sackman pushed me over, I nearly falling in the process, up against the resilient life-warmed bosom of a red-and-white-spotted lady who had seen better days, who in her bouncing turn transferred me to a more delicious breast which sidestepped, so I stumbled, scotching my already scrambled face on a splintery willow-hamper containing small animals who squeaked as well as stank; and this in its turn receding, I was transferred further to the perfumes of an upper-middle-class lower-type tart, wiping my now bleeding face on her artificial silver-fox stole as it passed; which was soothing.

Her scent lingered with me but not for very long, superseded as it was by a fine blast of garlic, in turn displaced by a bundle of clove-scented carnations, in their turn taken up by some dead fuzz of dirty sad hair, by coffee and warm artificial strung-pearls on a pale young neck, real ones on a scraggy, carrots and chrysanthemums, cauliflowers and caraway—lopsided and lingering I sniffed and drank them all—and petrol fumes, and diesel smoke and hot breathed wine.

I was spun there and spangled with their varied nasal visions, the roadway's wet lights wisping and streaking as a slow old photographic plate: shop fronts and cafés, spring-autumn park, suffocated sky, and the slip-slop clip-clop squelchy shuffle of innumerable leather-shod or rubber-soled feet. Nail varnish and peppermints, asphalt and armpits clashed in my nostrils. Still I bobbed there and bounced there hoping for my journeyway, seeking for some issue, overtrodden by all manner of passers: shoe-shod and gumbooted, high heels and mountain nails, soft crêpe and moccasins, ballet-types and riding-boots, fallow feet, skates!

. . . After an interminable further period of this insulting submission I managed to decipher amidst the addled turbulence of my pea-drummed head a terribly urgent desire at all cost to stay there no longer. Simultaneously, further along the pavement somewhere newly arrived buses now disgorging their hordes, I removed my arms from my sides, my hands from their pockets' refuge, and immediately, undeciding but decided for me, was swept into the menacing stampede backwards and would have fallen trampled if I could, but that my back was kept pressed hard against the warm brother-back of someone gone before me in the pressured onrush, so that I paddled frenziedly thus forward, backwards, kicking out madly to keep upright or afloat with my feet, looking up the while into the full shining face of a presently beautiful girl behind whose head as I moved or was moved the canopies and palimpsests of shops and *bistros* slipped illuminated or shadowed by the criss-cross figures of the lava-flowing crowd.

She did not notice me at first but subsequently looked down at me (for I was half down anyhow), laughed out loud showing far too many stainless-steel teeth, closed her mouth again mercifully to its former heartening smile, and said:

'You'd better look out quick. Pull yourself together or you'll pretty soon be trampled underfoot.'

So with a sudden twisting jerk there I was the right way foremost, front once again to front, marching along in the mob.

In and on with them I went, carried off the pavement onto the wide road, across the road's large uneven sets clinking like giant dominoes and suddenly, to my feet's unprepared horror, beyond the top step of an ill-known steep stairs in darkness, down—leg rattling, bone-straining—from the high level of the new, near the 'bus, to the narrower secret streets of the old town below.

Here, wheeled traffic being less, the escapers took freely to the roadway; and there spread out I found I was hurrying along now quite independently so that each and every one of them—right, left, before and if necessary behind—might be examined, if not at my leisure, for how could I have leisure when hastening to a post-conceived meeting, at least by quick glances, Compur-shuttered in all directions, severally.

If not all identical, they at first, viewed from my battered twin ill-focused lenses, appeared to me so; saving only the difference between trousers and skirts; even that not always holding however, some girls wearing plaid-slacks, two Scotsmen, villainously incongruous apparitions that they were, kilts.

As we so passed, still flowing well, down a dimly-lit street of high old Italianate, pink-façaded, sea-green-shuttered houses rising on each side several storeys above man-lighting, vanishing then into soft human darkness, the crowd, at first gradually, later more rapidly, began to cease to be one.

Some turned up, some turned down the narrower alleyways landwards or seawards; others disappeared into swallowing doorways, pattering away sadly up dark echoing passages, pale public-stair's lights discouraging them homewards, feebly coldly glimmering when they pushed their public-switches.

In such a manner, thus, there fled leaked and melted what had once been a mob (*nothing*, but not lonely) until a few individuals (*everything and* lonely) proceeded, yards apart in space, miles apart in mind, hundreds now in heart, everyone but myself to their separate and peculiar known destinations.

And so I, knowing no goal, nothing certain terminally forthcoming, decided to follow the last one to their F or M door.

Lagging behind deliberately until all were well before me I counted them carefully and now they were seven: 4 F and 3 M; their legs and appended feet moving with the maximum speed concomitant with not running; feverishly hurrying to arrive at their leisures, their lives or their meals, however pleasant or unpleasant, adequate or inadequate, galvanic or sedative these things might be; at the end of their passages, at the bottom of their trajectories, at the beginning of their night, in this their town.

Of the four F's, two were stockinged, one barelegged, one trousered; all three M's were in overall blue. All were not old; some of them were young.

Silent as it was now, all footfalls sounded; two clicking high-heels, barelegged sensibly sponge-shoed, trousered sloppily sandalled; us four—two smacking leather, one springing rubber, one silent rope.

The first to evade me was a high-heeler, in through a latch-keyed door beside a bright shop up to lighted shutter-slats, there to her encounter with soft words, softer deeds or soup. Then the rope-soler passed under a seaward archway, his silhouette sinking, rising a little, falling further, down steep cobbled steps to his kneebacks, his taut waist, his squared shoulders, the back of his peaked canvas cap, out of sight. Two veered off next up the hill, calf-pushed to our left, their mounting bodies thrust upward unevenly as they climbed into unknown and unknowing dimness —my companion leather sole and his barelegged soft-shod improbably possible bride.

Thus there were left one heelclicker, three trousered: one questionably, one spuriously, and myself.

The pace then quickened perceptibly, each of us now afraid not only of ourselves but of each other, even though probably all (except I alone) well knew where they were, walked the same walk each and every working evening, and knew that walk's aim and very end.

And so we proceeded.

The street narrowed further and was even more deserted; everyone being busy at their every-evening meal.

And so we proceeded until the remaining high-heeler, coming to a corner some way ahead on my right, almost collided with a dark figure under the non-light of no lamp-post. A few hurried words too far and soft to hear reversed her progress and the pair now sailed, sauntering towards us, gazing at each other's faces whilst we looked at them only as they passed through the former link of our tenuous ephemeral association, leaving unexpressed and even un-thought vague desires and inclinations in their wake.

And so we proceeded, rubber-sole, trousered-sandal and be-leathered I; and the street began to twist its way gently between still older houses, lying light and mendacious shadow.

And so we proceeded until, this time on my remaining left, further still ahead, rubber-soler in his turn coming to his corner, easily avoided collision, not collusion, with a very bright figure under the candent halo of a tip-top flaring municipal candelabra gas-lamp. A few hurried words—will you? Won't you?—once again, and arm-in-arm, uplifted mask summing downcanted face, they also passed back between the last two of us, casting in their turn a handful of uneven plopping pebbles in the lacklustre stillness.

And so we proceeded, trousered-sandal and myself.

And I followed her.

What else could I do? What else should I have done?

Was the suggestion not explicit?

And if not explicit, tell me what it was?

I followed her, being here at the end of my crowd-carried journey, almost now deserted. I was a spent rocket, stiff stick and soggy cardboard falling, if I was not very careful, through undetermined space to thud and splinter on the hard wet sod.

# 47

So I hurried on seven steps behind her; and now, being not distracted, she was all my eyeful.

Semi-silently, her feet small, forward pouting, her *écossaise* bum prettily waggling beneath a sleek scarlet jacket like a soldier's, she walked as if she held an exploring pernickety poodle on the end of a pigskin leash.

I was forwards-, she was rearwards-conscious . . .

A nice girl, a pretty piece, with her ashy-blonde horse-tail dangling down her scarlet back; I had no intentions towards her erotic nor yet social. I simply had to follow her to get to an end; to find some egress from my present *non sum*; to come at long last to the ultimate buffer-stop; to find my way back.

And so she proceeded, and so I thus followed her—and this one went a long way, a far way, so it seemed, compared to all the others—though the difference was more likely between following and being carried.

We came out at last through the end of the ever-darkening, ever-narrowing street, I always seven paces behind her, she always hoping for my waylaying, (each time we passed a light-rimmed group of anxiously signalling girls she looked round, deceived at my impeachable persistence), onto a vast square, its towered public clock winking its warm yellow disk whilst a great peppered sea of feet-worn story-patterned black-and-white cobbles reflected the brazen effulgence of a thousand day-night-lighting tubes suspended on wires high up in the affronted privacy of the sky.

In its broad expanse one or two creatures still moved towards the corners, ants in a newly-swept room; and she, sandal-trouser, set out crossing it diagonally, I following, unrelated, isolated, right out in the middle where the market-stalls peopled and crowded it at dawn, soundless now but for the night wind in the banyans in the rimming public gardens and our syncopated feet.

The matter was become serious now and she kept on looking round nervously, I following always seven steps behind, slowing when she also slowed, quickening as she furtively speeded.

She ran a few steps and so did I.

Stood still: I stood still also.

Then she took to her heels and flew fast right-handed to the safety-first line of never near enough buildings, in through a doorless shadowy-mouthed portico, far along a squeak-tiled earaching hall, up, up—patter patter, thump thump—a stuffy wooden stairs, I after her, breathing stertorously; no light.

She pressed a switch and there she was taking out a key, fumbling at a lock in a high brown double-panelled door with brass fittings.

She turned and she was beautiful.

'What are you doing following me? How dare you! Go away!'

'I don't know how I dare. I am following you to get to the end . . . to the end of my present road . . . to the end of wherever I must turn and go back . . . to the end of my looked-for yet unknown present tether. And, so it seems, I've got there, haven't I? I *am* going away. Don't you worry; I am going back.'

'You're a queer fish I must say. Are you quite well? Are you mad do you think? Why did you not go with one of those girls along the street? Eh?'

'Because that was not what I wanted; not what I want now either . . . I don't think so anyhow. Perhaps I do want company? Perhaps I want comfort? I really couldn't tell you. But I do know what I want now to be certain of above all things. Where have I got to? Where am I? Can you tell me please?'

'Yes, certainly, if that's all you want. Number 57, corner of the rue Halévy—Place du Palais de Justice.'

'Yes, but what town? What's its name for Heaven's sake?'

'What's its *name*? Surely at least you know that? *Everyone* knows that. You shouldn't be let out if you don't even know what town you're in, much less whereabouts you are in it. Who are you? What are you up to? Where have you come from?'

'I am afraid I do not really know.'

'Where do you want to get to?'

'I fear I am not really certain. Indeed I may never be certain. . . . No, never. Perhaps I never really knew? Eventually I want to go back to where I started from; but alas, I am not even at all sure where or when that was . . . *"Perhaps I was a virgin of many divers origin"* . . . Did you ever hear that song? I knew an old wanderer who used to sing it beautifully to his own setting and all he wanted in exchange was tea or, preferably, so he said, something else to imbibe. He was in the habit, I might say, of imbibing a little too freely at times . . . Oh yes, I was forgetting: please excuse my vagueness . . . It's all my own work, as the saying goes . . .'

'Well I can't ask you in if that's what you're aiming at: my father's inside'—she pointed with the key—'and I don't even know if I would if I could . . . but I think . . . Yes, I would: but I can't for my father's inside.' She gestured again. 'Why are you so queer? Don't know where you are, you say: expect me to believe that? Really I advise you to go back to one of those girls there. You look as if you needed one. It might really do you good. I tell you what, ask for Dédé: she's the one for you: she'll settle you and your hash. Have you any money?'

'Yes, some—but of course never ever enough. That is to say that if I knew what I wanted it for I could say I never had enough —even at times, I suppose foolishly, too much. But as in fact I am invariably uncertain what I should spend it on, demands running counter to necessities or experiences and these two to bare sullen facts and the facts to deeds, including drinking not to mention eating, and other essential but totally unnecessary so-called luxuries such as love and music, it is quite irrational for me flatly to aver at this or at any other moment that under the circumstances, given my needs, which are boundless, and comparing them with my known or unguessed desiderata, which are . . .'

'Oh for God's sake shut up! You utterly depress me. Are you an automaton, sleepwalker or zombie or what? Wake up! Stir yourself! Have you or have you not enough money for a good f . . . ?'

'I think I *am* awake although I am not entirely sure, looking at you there with your beautifully shaped and moulded heads, bodies and legs: do you know that game? It's great f . . .'

'That's enough of that now. I have told you before, I cannot bring you in. My father's inside,' she gestured with the key. 'Here!' she took a few steps down towards me, the light behind

186

her casting her eloquent shadow on the sordid badly-swept steps near my varied-levelled feet, her figure approaching and descending on me simultaneously, for the first time towards me, inviting breasts foremost, pivoting waist, smooth stomach and rounded thighs under them, nearer, nearer still—I took two steps downwards and backwards.

'Here is some money for you' (I took a large folded note in my half-folded hand). 'Do what you like with it. Only take my tip, Dédé's the girl for you. She'll bring you back to earth. She'll knock the nonsense out of you. She'll soon sober you up. She knows what's what . . .'

'Good-bye then, and thank you.'

I held out my hand.

'Well of all the fantastic . . . Aren't you even going to ask me my name?'

'What is your name? N. or M.? . . .'

'What the hell are you blathering about? It's Yvette.'

'Impossible! I know an Yvette and you are not her.'

'I should bloody well think so . . . certainly not. Where did you know her?'

'In the country; not far from here I should say. I believe she used to work here. So she said anyhow.'

'What at?'

'Oh the street, the street: one of the girls: one of *them*.'

'Wait a minute . . . I believe I did know her. Tall and dark . . .'

'That's her: black and white and read all over: and big nipples . . .'

'I beg your pardon. I wouldn't be supposed to know that. But up till recently that girl was around here somewhere. At the Café Normande or thereabouts. Well, you should go and look her up: it would do you good. I was at that game once upon a time myself but now I have—a father. Good night.'

'Good night.'

She was gone, the door closed behind her.

I had come to the buffer-stop . . . the turning . . . the terminus.

# 48

I STOOD there then on the fourteenth step, the banknote in my hand where I had taken it, and I turned and sat down on the twelfth. The light, having finished its mechanically-determined illumination, extinguished itself.

*Tant pis.*

Very well. The door was shut, the light was out: so I should sit for a while now at least.

Wanly cadaverous, a reflected glimmer seeped from some-where to my present gloom, *ritornello* perhaps from those tubes in the square.

What should I do? Now at this turning?

Where exactly was I?

Ah, but I knew that lacked fact now very precisely. Let me then recite it:

I was sitting with my weight and buttocks on the twelfth step, my feet on the fourteenth, down from the door-landing fifth floor of the building at the corner of the rue Halévy and the Place du Palais de Justice in the City of —— *but she had not told me . . .* In my left hand was a five thousand franc note . . . *but she had not told me, espèce de putain . . .* in my right . . . there was nothing in my right: Oh Yes there was: there was the top of my right knee-cap, cupped under it. But that, I suppose, was probably fortuitous and did not count anyway . . . *but she had not told me the name of the place, the miserable female arch-shite . . .* but wasn't the money in my left hand just as much fortuitous though? Wasn't it? And that did count . . . *but she had not told me, she would not tell me, mistress and monstress of crapulous perversity that she was . . .* but at least in this position . . . *she would not tell me . . .* seated as I was . . . *the bitch . . .* I suppose that the fact that my right hand was placed . . . *well she had given me the money at least . . .* on my right knee . . . *I would have to be grateful I suppose for small mercies . . .* was normal and ergo . . . *all right, all right, it didn't matter . . .* and ergo . . . *what the hell, she was a bitch anyhow . . .* and ergo perhaps scarcely altogether fortuitous . . . *let's leave it, bitch or no bitch . . .* It would have been quite another matter if I had been walking . . . *bitch all the same* . . . walking, I mean, with my right kneecap clasped with my right hand or for that matter, even more so, my left hand . . . *bitch* . . . and very difficult to manage too . . . But the overriding fact was: *SHE HAD NOT TOLD ME THE NAME OF THIS TOWN AND I DID NOT KNOW IT*, but . . . I did know where I was in *a* town, in this one, and I was sick of searching and would search no further . . . *BITCH! BITCH! B I T C H ALL THE SAME!*

I was sitting here and now on this described step, this particular step: that must be enough: that must be the turning.

My job now was to re-constitute myself, somehow to go forwards, to go back; somehow to live, inevitably to die . . .

In this dark pause, as in waking dragged from sleep in the small and fearful hours of insidious twisted night, the act and fact of living grew overladen with significance, terrifying at once in its importance and lack of it, dreadful with implications, utterly lacking them; prelude, postlude; no note sounding at all . . .

There I was at the top of those stairs waiting to go down again; if I ever went down; if I did not eternally evade the business of descent; stay up there; go still further up; find another less shut door; occupy an attic; cross across a roof; descend thence by sheer force of gravity to the brightly lit street, to the tube-infested square—Or the light might go on suddenly (What else could it do, being electric?) . . . Someone else might come; someone else might come *up*; several other people might come *up*; someone from higher up might come down; several other people from higher up might come down . . . or . . . or the light might simply go on; for someone might press it; press the switch just to see . . . just to see . . . if their cat or their milk bottle or their newspaper or their mat was or was not still there; or now there; or gone away; or been taken away . . . from outside their door . . . Or to see if it still worked at all and the current still flowed in the mains . . . or to look at the time by their wrist- or pocket-watch, having no matches, their own light being cut off at the meter for failure of payment of account . . . to look at their wrist-watch or pocket-watch which no longer ticked (Did mine?—Tick, tick—Yes it did) . . . and these people, alone or together, ascending or descending, in groups with their pets or alone with their thoughts, might meet me here: or rather, as I had no intention whatsoever of yet moving, encounter me there; beg my pardon; beg permission to be allowed to pass (Permit me, sir!); and I might or might not let them, entirely according to the condition of my fancy at that moment or *their* condition, sex, age, apparent financial status, manners, nationality, politics or what have you or what I should have then erupting in my own conceit *if and when they came.* And these same people or this same person coming up or going down, might or might not dislike, adore or ignore me; detest, molest or be indifferent; most likely of all indifferent.

BUT I WOULD NOT LET THEM.

I would on no account let them.

I would and I could simply and very surely and tremendously efficiently trip them up; put out my foot at the mechanically correct instant so that they would go headlong or at least risk going headlong forward, since gravity ordered it, to perdition or something like it down the sordid unswept stairs, cracking their nuts, their arms or their legs on the edge of the seventh or eighth step below, where the used pink pistol-caps of some now sleeping cowboy nestled with the dust in the corner next the wall; or alternatively, and even more outrageously from their sweet sensible well-thought-out viewpoint, which would serve them then for nothing, infest their silken stockings (if they were females) entwisting and obstructionising my Afton-stained hard-bitten fingernails in the secret upper reaches of their half-guinead hose.

The stairs was a great place for waylaying fairly or foully, a great place for encounters . . . and so I would encounter, yes, by God, I would encounter . . . these possibly pertinent side-steppers, down-steppers, steppers-up . . . and never, never go down, never ever go down, not by my own will or on my own legs anyhow . . . until they came.

Handpitched, yes: frogmarched, with no choice: on a stretcher? Why certainly! Leaning on a loving arm? With the best will in this world: unconscious in a coma—I would thus have no say. But by my own wish and will, lowering my leathered feet step by step, my hand on the possibly splintery bannisters?—NEVER! Unless . . . unless of course no one ever came up; unless of course no one ever came down. But If I waited long enough (Hah hah! there could be no doubt about this) . . . sooner . . . sooner or later . . . or . . . OR . . . If the door, that door, the one there over my left shoulder and a little way up to the right . . .

Supposing it opened again! She might look out and see me and call me in like a lost dog or cat—*Minou! Minou!* (Father or no Father)—and give me a bone or a sweet saucer of milk and take me up upon her silky satiny lap where I should and would purr and purr and purr *ad infinitum*—until the whole thing became a hoax or a flat feeble farce (which would not be terribly purring-time long) . . . that is to say if I was or if I had been a cat which mercifully or alas I was not . . .

Or might I not die there by luck or mischance, by great grace or the uttermost outrage, my blood ceasing its battering surge, forsaking the fluted brain, abandoning its effort to penetrate the futile and febrile extremities of my antennaed limbs which throbbed so and throbbed so . . . ?

Stop the business; stop the business decently and quietly. . . . According to the precepts of the law, of course . . . according to and cognizant of the precepts of the law; of our own elected Truth.

Or . . . but by God (*Holy Father, splutter on us all! Encrust us with thy fanciful murderous Mercy! Scar us with thy fortunate Flames!*) . . . the house up above, down below or on either four sides of us might straightways take fire and the *pompiers* would come with their hoses and ladders and helmets and heroes and thus end the lifelock! . . . But much the most likely, I knew it in my heart and I had it in my head, I would sit there a while, a good long, a terribly long while; there, on the fence-step, as long as I could; wrestling and wriggling with the fact I was alive, contemplating and resisting the fact of being awake: for there was very little evidence, to my self at any rate, that I was anything but both.

I should be guided henceforth by the finite polarities of necessity: of needs: of eating: of resting: of actual or simulated reproduction.

And what were my wishes then?

191

Did I wish to become rich?

I must work then like a beetle; curry favour with relatives of my own or someone else's, having done so await their demise; learn very rapidly to swindle like a gentleman; sound no false notes; send out false bills; seek furbished rectitudes and not be found out. All these things guaranteed nothing; all these things, in spite of every effort, I could never really learn.

I would never then be rich.

Did I wish to become famous?

I must hob-nob pointedly and poisedly with the right people; toe the right lines with the wrong feet; strike sharply—but on no account to burn—when the iron was at its hottest; know the know-how and the what-not; conform but not too closely; cut loose but not too far; eccentric but not lunatic; original but not subversive; social and swim but not drown in it; purposeful with no real conviction: then I would go far.

None of these things I practised; none of these things possessed me.

I would never become famous.

Did I wish then to store up Treasure high in Heaven? To be pious, respected, an example upon Earth?

I abominated all religions, cheating easy refuges, re-insured escape hatches, grease to make the wheels go the wrong way round.

I could never be religious.

Did I wish to be a great lover, indulge myself fully in the delights of the table and the beaded brimming glass? Run a mile in six minutes? Swim the seven seas?

Yes. But my wheezy aching body played traitor to me in these things now, in the far past, in the all too evident future.

Did I wish then to drift along hoping always for the best, fearing constantly the worst, in the sly stream of events to the inevitable grist mill, the slow sad sewer to the certain sea? Yes! Yes, that was it! There flamed my great overweening ambition! There was the culminating zenith of my nadir, my *ne plus ultra* to obituary or tomb . . .

Did I wish to live then? Or did I not at all? . . . Yes, yes, I

wanted to and longed to and loved it and feared it and hated it
and welcomed it; as all of us, as everyone, as no one else at all . . .
'Very well then' I said to myself, 'hop it downstairs!'

# 49

I STOOD up warily. My right foot touched the crinkly note where
unknowingly I had let it fall. I gratefully bent and took it for my
own.

I must move now. I must place one foot down before the other.
Down before the other, one after another, one after another
repeatedly.

I must go downstairs.

Which I did.

It was quite easy.

Near the door, just at the door before the opening outwards,
the night air, fresh from the street and the sea and the mountains
near by, came in to me. It rushed spouting and sparkling right into
my blood to my head. As I drew breath I drew courage: at last,
at last the courage to move, the courage to change, if not then
myself (for selves are not changeable) then at least my condition,
the environment round me—from a frog on a rock to some frog
in a pool, from the frog in a pool to some frog in a stream—
swimming, swimming at last, directed at least partly, in the all
transporting current.

So I went out: two steps and I was out!

No sounds, almost. No steps certainly. Just the sea-breeze in
the wide leaves: magnolia and banyan.

The great square was empty and I wanted to run this way and
that in it, skipping and jumping to make free of it; to be free in
it; altogether; myself.

As it was, finding a small polylateral shard I had sometime or
other put or neglected in my pocket I dropped it down before me
and started hopscotching it across those patterned cobbles in the
general direction of the small public gardens far away on the
other side.

This was delightful: I had the town to myself!

But not at all: my laboured wheeze-fed hopping and the skitter of the shard on the stones soon roused a distant dog to his barking and a startled cat streaked like negatived fork-lightning, hissing from one gutter to the next. These two beasts, each in their turn, attracted and inflated other idiotic bow-wows, other and many miaouling tabbies, so that soon the night was shattered with their hawking and their spitting and two depressingly deliberate figures, their leggings and boots already audibly creaking, drew near inexorably from the far off shadows. I continued with my hopping as they approached.

'What are you doing?'

I gave another hop; rather a good one, I thought.

'You can see for yourselves, *Messieurs*, I am playing at *marelle*.'

'None of your cheek now. Who are you? What are you up to here at this hour?'

'I am on my way to a meeting; a very special meeting.'

They doubly-winked sagely, the fools!

'Ah, I see. But we've cleared them all up this evening as a matter of fact, so you're wasting your time. Your papers, please!'

Wearily I dragged from my inside pocket a sheaf of uncredentials I kept just for this purpose. They perused them very carefully and handed me them back.

'He's probably had a bit too much,' one said to the other in a patois they did not know I knew. 'He looks fairly all right. A bit touched evidently. Let's leave him. We've enough looneys in the fiddle-box for tonight already; and with all those bloody *poules* it's a regular bloody hen run.'

'Move along now. Clear off. Get along home to your bed!'

And they left me.

I was most surprised and not a little grieved that they did not even try to take me with them. This might have led somewhere; I might have led *them* somewhere. Now that line was lost.

After one hundred and fifty-three hops my shard collided with the dim cement coping holding the low green slightly-rusty iron railing formed of a series of semi-circles crowning straight bars, of the municipalized flower-beds set around the trees, shady in high summer, dapple-shadowed now by and from the tubes. In these thus circumscribed and circumstanced beds thousands upon thousands of *Primula malacoides* set out in right regular rows, their farina-white stalks and lacy pink flowers shaking as if palsied in the slight night breeze, cast myriads of fine criss-crossed shadows on each one of their neighbours, who cast it on their neighbour, who cast it on their neighbour, who cast it on their neighbour *et sequitur* until they cast it in the end on the sown artificial-looking lurid green grass at the edge and the end of their territory. With their swaying, the whole lot of them swaying, swaying with their shadows and trembling also with them, they formed a huge diaphanous pale pink haze, ever shifting, fugaceous, chronically ephemeral, a pale pink sea; soon I was hypnotic in their all-atremble ocean and was forced, just in time, to look up to prevent myself drowning in it.

I did so, staring straight ahead of me down a dark steep side-street, and there at the end of it, inlaid against the black night sky, illuminated by its significantly placed necessary working-lights and portholes, I saw the samson posts, mast, derricks, ventilators, white glittering superstructure and shadowy flaring hull of a ship; a big ship.

This was what I wanted.

I set off delighted.

I hopped along still but not after my shard which was safely back in my pocket.

I skipped along and in the dark street in spite of those leather-louts of cops lots of girls were lurking. I wondered should I ask them did they know my Yvette. No, I thought, later will be time enough: when there's no time it will be time enough. So I skipped along past their good nights respectfully, regretfully, and came out on the quayside with the ships stretching port and starboard, some sleeping, lights tunnelling here and there only, their derricks still and donkey-engines silent: others, floodlights glaring from their cross-trees, at work loading and unloading, tallying and stowing on through the night, sailing in the morning.

I walked straight over towards the ship there before me, a four thousand-ton newly-built curved-bridge-fronted intermediate cargo liner, her scarlet simmering funnel high between the crates and bales stacked there for loading, until I reached the edge where the stone quay ended and a strip of dark water stretched between it and the towering steel hull spotted and streaked with red lead; pimpled with rivets. There in the inky channelled slit, tarnished with bilge-oil, bobbing with floatable refuse, a small wooden lighter lay moored and from it as I watched nine rats ran leaping to the quay, scurrying into cover amid the piled cargoes. In the inky channelled slit, in the small wooden lighter, I saw two children crouched also, eating the remains of long stale fish, sharing with the rats, running the backbones through their mouths as others might mouth organs, dragging and sucking off the putrescent fish-flesh with their teeth and lips. When they saw me they too leapt, crying out alarmingly; and all along between ships and land other figures jumped, scurried from the lighters, leapt from floating larders, cowering and slithering, seeking for the shadows; surely starving creatures of my newly starry night . . .

The sight of them terribly unnerved me: guilt, regret, impotence, nausea, ran seething in my stomach with the terror of and horror of starvation; its dehumanising onslaught; its perpetual treadmilling threat. That I should stuff myself, that I and others should guzzle—and then my turning stomach remembered and I realized that I could not remember, nor myself nor my stomach, when last I had put food in it at all: and covering all my horror and all its linked anxieties there came roaring and crushing the coercive urge to eat.

A startled black-headed gull, disturbed from its roost on the ship, fluttered for an instant in the glow of the floodlamps, its loosely-flapping wings appearing, disappearing, reappearing, in and from the surrounding dark.

*All birds that do not sing make me hungry; all those that do make me sad.*

This one made me both.

Evading all these problems, putting aside my inside, I turned away sadly seawards along the edge of the docks, several times tripping, twice or thrice falling, over tautly stretched hawsers fast to their bollards. Their rat-discs shook and jangled, casting leaping shadows, calling vast attention; but none was ever paid. I was soaked to the knees with warm condenser-water gushing from the ships' sides, inadequately shielded by the wooden traps hanging on ropes from their rails. When I came to a great bow I looked up at the mudfluked anchor clutched in her hawsepipe and passed on then under her shadow, dodging her high-flying gangway, ducking under or tripping over her numerous moorings, to a lowly triple-expansioned short-sea steam tramper, her gangling funnel loosely sifting coal smoke to an even blacker sky, her old hand-luffed open-pulleyed derricks loading aged horses by canvas hoisting-slings from a pitiful group who stood there dejectedly, straw-flecked dried manure on their flanks and their black weeping tails, awaiting their turn—to the next ship still, busy unloading carcasses, each wrapped and sewn in their white muslin shroud; all for our bellies in their time. So back again we were; badly back too: nausea surged and I set off once more. . . .

Everyone was busy earning out their eating: no one ever noticed me and so I passed along to the next vessel, a white painted modern Scandinavian-built fruit reefer brilliantly illuminated, silent at its resting.

Christjesus I was hungry.

I must eat! I must eat!

I looked about.

Through the bales, barrels and crates piled high above me, far in beyond them where dockside turned to city, I could peep the dimmed lights of a café; and when I listened carefully, turning one ear in that direction, closing the other to the water sounds, I heard company and music.

My stomach now screaming I found myself running across towards that light house. At least I could drink: furthermore I might eat. I was ravening to do both of them copiously.

When I got there it was obvious the place was well peopled by residents for the night and my entry was the signal for many hostile looks. Who wants an intruder when they're nicely settled; well sozzled; pleasantly warmed; filled to the brim with enmity and friendship?

'*Messieursdames*,' I said, bowing foolish-obsequiously, walking

197

over to the bar, 'can you possibly let me have something to eat?'

'Nothing but eggs hot. Some *oeufs-sur-le plat* if you wish,' said the tired, wiry barman.

'Splendid! Magnificent! Six please, at once, with some ham if you have some.'

'I beg your pardon, sir.'

'Please cook me six eggs with ham if you have some and give me some bread and a litre of *rouge*. I have not had a bite or a sup for simply ages since the ... since before ... Well, I don't know before what.' (I was commencing to shout.) 'Come along, quickly now! Please give me six eggs and some ham—if you have some.'

'As you wish, sir, as you wish. Bad for the liver though you know: an assault on the digestion: ruin the sump altogether.'

'You can leave my digestion to me, if you don't mind' (I was still bawling), 'if I have any left for lack of exercise of it, and give me some brandy, a double one and *Perrier*, for I must catch up on these half-plastered sailors of yours. Hurry up ... !'

I felt in my left trouser pocket: the note was still there. Excellent this moment as far as it went if no further.

I raised my filled glass to the scowling company.

'Good health to you all, gentlemen!' I cried freely and fiercely.

But they looked cross, very cross, resenting altogether my unsolicited testimonial.

I drained the glass, the gaseous liquid bursting its bubbles in my throat. The watery fire deluging and grasping at my empty inside passed straight to my blood, thence to my head, in a fountain of warmth and new life. I was ready, however bogusly, for anything or nothing and I knew it well too. The six eggs followed (without the some ham) and great hunks of that morning's baked bread gurgled down with the wine.

By the Lord, I felt fine-fettled!

# 50

So I walked out smoothly along the pavement past the flashy ship-fronts with their cranes and cowls, jiggerstays and riding-lights, ventilators and radar masts, king-posts and FWTs, boot-toppings and MacGregor hatchcovers, trucks and keels, and up back along the re-inviting street to the tube-lit square.

When I got there it was all changed and I was too.

I looked up at the fifth of fifty-seven: no light there.

No girls to ask from.

No persons questioning.

No hopping-scotching.

No life at all.

But mine!

Mine!

I crossed again the patterned cobbles, retracing as best I could walking the way I had previously hopped.

I left 57 on my left hand. I walked straight on.

I hurried along, retracing and advancing, and when I came to the fifth corner there was a group of girls still standing. I stopped automatically before I had time to think and they all came cluster-ing round me with their smiles full on and their clothes full off, gesturing and winking at *Les Home-Sweet-Home Studios*' as the faded and damp-spotted black glass, gold-lettered, armorially-shaped name plate euphemistically labelled the dark hallway and dim stairs adjacent.

'*Tu veux faire l'amour? Viens donc vite.*'
'*Comme tu es gentil. Viens donc vite.*'
'*Allons! Montons!*'

They treated me kindly as a cross between a lost *tou-tou* and a lecherous love-starved monkey and they were possibly quite right.

'Girls,' I said, holding up a traffic-policeman-like arresting (but slightly trembling) hand. 'Listen! I am sure I should enjoy a love-bout with you all but that's not what I think I'm now after.' They giggled, wishfully uncomprehending, convinced obviously that I was not only hybrid of the above-mentioned fauna but plain dotty to boot, 'Listen,' I went on, 'I am looking for someone and I want to find them badly and you may be able to help me. She's called Yvette . . .'

They all burst out laughing.

'Yvette!' 'What Yvette?' 'Whose Yvette?' 'Michou's?' 'There are many, you know.' 'Yvette who?' 'Won't I do?' 'Won't I do?' 'Won't we do?'

'Shut up now!' (they all screeched with laughter) 'and listen. She came from the country ("They all do") and she was dark and she was tall and her brother ("Ooh! Ooooh! *Quelle histoire, le salaud!* What's wrong with us?" "He wants his Yvette, does he?" "Won't we do?" "Well, I must say . . .") . . . and her brother ("Oooooh!")—Please, please, won't you help me? Do you know an Yvette and if you do where is she?'

'Well you know we can't stand here talking and laughing for the rest of the night or the *flics*'ll be after us again, the bastards,' said a plumpish pseudo-blonde. 'What about coming up for a while anyhow? Then we can see about this Yvette you talk of. Have you any money?'

It was then I put my hand in my left-hand pocket and found to my astonishment that the note was still there. In my eagerness leaving that café I had walked out unnoticed and unnoticing without paying them.

'Yes, yes . . . I've plenty,' said I like a fool, taken unawares. 'Anyhow some, I mean, enough,' I finished lamely, hedging.

'Come along then,' said the plump one, taking me firmly by the arm, 'and you too, Dédé. Come along and let's see what he's got, this Yvette-chaser.'

Before I knew where I was or could do anything about it or run for it (if I wanted to) I was being politely but firmly marched along that dark passage and slowly (for I was suddenly dragging with tiredness, apprehension and general unwillingness) up those stairs to the first floor only where (again before I had decided what, if anything, I could do), a respectable governessy Madame was receiving us most graciously in an over-furnished hall and all in a rather dim twinkling ushering us into the very room itself.

There a large soft-looking bed with fairly immaculate sheets made me long to stretch out on it and go to sleep that very instant minute.

'Five hundred, please, for the room,' said the governess, whilst the girls fussed and primped themselves uselessly before a large mirror behind a greyish-white marble-topped faked Boule side-table.

In the age-old, time-still-honoured, pre-coital ritual, they set the taps running.

I yawned most truthfully and sat down on the bed.

'I am very sorry and I do not want to insult you, but I have no desire to make love,' I began. 'Not yet, anyhow,' I timid-tactfully amended. 'I am dead tired. I've been walking for miles—maybe years. Here,' I went on, handing them helplessly or hopefully the five-thousand-franc note, 'that's for the two of you whatever you do do or don't do; but please, I beg of you, tell me where I can find this Yvette I was speaking of. I feel certain you know her. Do you or don't you? Tell me.'

But ignoring me, if by no means my note, the girls went on undressing and when they were naked, semi-automatically stripping themselves, fully ready now in their work-a-day clothes, they came and sat down one on either side of me and there in the damp-blotched mirror I saw my own unwashed, unshaven, scratched and bashy face, tousled hearth-rug hair, skewed tie, soiled collar, crumpled jacket, and flanking me the pale and the dark one, pretty enough, pretty enough indeed with their bare shoulders and warm-centred breasts, bodied full plainly.

I damn near burst out laughing: I was highly inclined to shed maudlin tears.

'Listen, girls; tell me what you know,' I persisted, half-heartedly encircling their warm naked waists with my scratchy-tweeded arms, then withdrawing them, no welcome for them; none at all, thank you. 'Where is she? Where is my Yvette?'

'*Your* Yvette? Ha, that's a good one! She's as much yours as we all are: as long as you can pay her, she's yours, that one, and not a single minute longer, I'd say.'

'But you see it was not here I met her; it was not here I knew of her or saw her ever at all but in the country somewhere not far from this city. I left her. I walked off and left her. I deserted her and I want to find her, to make amends, to put the clock back, wind it up, set it right, hear it strike, tick its tock! Do you hear me? Do you hear me?'

But they were not listening: not at all. Thinking me more than half off my chump they paid no attention to my protestant ravings.

They were not listening: inexorably their game went forward, not mine which was no game, but theirs which was the real one. Brass tacks not half nuts, and probably do him good anyway; value in their own coinage for the money I had given them.

And I, being tired, still a little drunk from that fine double brandy, still fairly well adrift, still searching my way as always, now found and guided by them only, eventually and gratefully surrendered to their cheery indomitable embraces, laughing and crying and fleeing and sinking and blissfully, momentarily fading and dying with and by and for and in them . . . And afterwards, yes afterwards, when I was lying on the bed, satisfied in spite of myself, exhausted from our antics, staring up at the high ceiling, they hurriedly dressing in their walking-out well-baited clothes, I exploded:

'Well damn you both, anyhow. You might at least tell me if you know. Is she alive?'

'Oh yes, I'm sure she's alive, all right; don't you worry, mister. Come back again soon for a nice little while and we'll have her here on tap for you: not dear, either; she's a real bargain and does anything you want. Bye-bye!'

So they went out and left me there freshly stranded, a new old wreck on the sad soft sandbank of the topsy-turvied sheets.

I dragged myself upright. Began to dress. My bashy face mocked from the flown-image mirror. Sweat-soaked shirt and filthy collar, crumpled up trousers and disembowelled tie, herring-boneless jacket and heel-absent socks, ditchworthy lace-knotted shoes—I was a fine sight; an encouraging detritus; there and then and always.

# 51

BUT off I went, scarecrow of scarecrows, ostrich of ostriches, king-gull of gullibles, out into the hall—saying a polite good-bye, nay *au revoir*, to the governess whose go-between services I had never really wanted but was none the less indebted for and whose avaricious rent had nearly cleared me out.

Down the stairs—the stairs—the *stairs* again, my flaccid tail limp between my weary worn legs; forced again and faced again with approaching new daylight.

The streets were stirring; trolleys, drays, vans, trailers, lorries, handcarts, barrows, *triporteurs*, all converging towards the market laden with their wares: leeks and avocados, lemons and cauliflowers, carrots and capsicums, live rabbits and cheeses, to provide the wherewithswallow to live; to love; to defecate and die.

Here was a new day afoot and awheel; and I passed through it against the tide now, burrowing and sidestepping in the purposeful flood, shuffling meaningfully forward in my vague precise direction. Had I not a way too?

Thus I came to the fine public park and sat on a hard green seat in an oval clearing covered with white gravel, faced by an improbably hideous fountain, surrounded by cactus-beds and palings. I slumped there then, my head lolling backwards until I stared at the ever-lightening sky and the handlike fronds of a stumpy phoenix-palm playing five finger exercises in the chilly morning air. I slumped there and my head fell back, my throbbing thyroid bared for some avid surgeon's scalpel. I slumped there and dozed. Giddiness and tiredness assailed me.

When I was next conscious of living my face was lying on the sharp-gravelled ground to which my left cheek was painfully and cunningly contiguous; whilst the rest of my body appeared, however incongruously (was it?), to be horizontal also.

What, however, distinguished this, my ever new awakening, from my sixteen thousand one hundred and twenty-three others, was that something more desperate than usual was wrong with what was left of my head.

I never believe the accuracy of my senses except in a case of burning; which is really just as well. But it did seem to me as if something peculiarly heavy was clutching at my hair with sharp prehensile claws and that this something was, furthermore, *promenading*, and by your leave, on the limited area of my sideways available scalp. As I horribly felt (but dared not open my eye to watch) these claws proceeded to that part of my skull immediately adjacent to my right ear and one of them, chillingly cool and fearfully wiry, placed itself sharply in and on my earhole and earflap itself . . .

I was done for: talk about the rats: this was the end-up surely and no mistake . . . and then to my increasing panic, my cowering internal horror, some sharp and horny object made a rapid dab at my lips, into my mouth, vibrating on my teeth: repeated *staccato*: repeated *staccato*: and madness crept like a suppurating caul, mistily but certainly, up and through my brain.

I collected all my remaining breath to scream as best I could.

'Coo-coo,' went the clawed one, 'Coo-at-the-little-coo,' he went again, and flapped and flapped, stretching his soft wings, dowsing me with his air, his feathers faintly creaking there so near me. And I opened my tight-shut upper eye within half an inch of the downy opalescence of a puffed-up plump town-pigeon's breast.

I leapt to my feet and a cloud of them clatteringly scattered.

So I was not a scarecrow after all! Not prostrate and sleeping there anyhow.

*All birds that do not sing make me hungry! All birds that do make me sad.* The coo-coo and the fat breast, the opalescent feathers and the softly-burbled song, made me both.

There was the dazzlingly bright sun: the sky was hand-polished blue: the day was well on and I was in and with it.

I brushed the crumbs, droppings and gravel off my further-tumbled clothes; rubbed the gritty sleep from the corners of my blinking eyes; took the stones out of my left then my right shoe;

buttoned up my flies; parted unevenly my matted hair with an almost toothless comb; readjusted the pigeon-plates in my always toothless mouth; re-hitched the belt of my half-masted trousers; refreshed with some difficulty the saliva in my drought-encrusted throat; rolled my eyes to the sky, my tongue on my plastic palate, my last coins in my pocket; and set off without further ado for the Central Municipal Bus Station.

There, without the slightest hesitation or fluster I went to the right window, purchased a full-length ticket to its furthest destination, tendered the right change, thanked the ticket clerk, walked bolt-upright to the rear door of the same-coloured rightly-labelled vehicle, climbed the steps and sat down in the selfsame seat (was it?) as at least once before.

The collector checked my ticket, called all aboard, struck his bell, blew his whistle, shouted to the driver, and we were off.

Whilst I, home again, laying my head longingly against the ever-trembling window, closed my eyes and fell peacefully asleep.

# 52

WHEN morning came, if it *was* morning and if it *did* come and was not, on the contrary, already well there when I was awaked or half-awoken, it was raining, not half raining, but pouring cats and dogs.

I sat up abruptly. The wind had loosened one of those windows controlled by a screwable bar: it was thrashing loudly and soggily against the frame.

There I was, there I was . . . There was no escaping it at all.

It was *a* morning after the funeral.

It was *a* morning after the Concerto (was it?).

It was *that* morning anyhow and Maggie, God blast her, was knocking with the tea.

With the tea in its teapot with the little faded violets, the teacup on its saucer with their little faded violets, the sugar bowl also with its little faded violets and the little faded-violet-studded plate.

'Good morning, sir. It's a terrible morning. It's God's judgment. It was a terrible end. And the poor dog is gone.'

'I am glad to hear it, Maggie, as I've said once before, haven't I?'

'Oh sir, you should be ashamed of yourself: the Captain's favourite. McMawk, he used to call him, when in specially good form.'

'As I've said before and repeat again: I am glad they are all gone. I hope they all stay away.'

'Oh the poor Cap'n. Oh the poor Cap'n. If he heard you, do you hear me? He'd be turning in his grave.'

'He isn't in one, thank goodness. How long have you been saying that Maggie? How many times have you said it? How many times have you repeated all these worn shibboleths? How long have I been laid here recovering from that ducking? How long have I lain or sat or stood since I fled from the sea and those dreadful people and that scarifying meddlesome, though he had his use then, dog? Answer me that, Maggie, answer me that!'

'I don't know, sir, really I do not. The time has gone by and a terrible time it has been with me too. But I do know this, sir: it has been raining every single day. Every single day and all and every night and every single hour. It's God's judgment on you, sir, and I'm going. I've told you before, every day for the three months past and before it and I'm sorry but I give it to you again: a week's notice. My full week's notice! I'm going. Oh, the poor Cap'n. Oh the poor dog. I wonder what on earth's become of him, the darling.'

'Drowned, I hope. Good night.'

'The man's mad,' she whispered. 'It's morning, sir, not night!' she shouted. 'I've told you before, it's morning. Morning *not* night. Morning *not* night. Morning *not* NIGHT!' she drummed at me. 'Losing his reason,' she mouthed *sotto voce*, 'losing what reason the man ever had. IT'S MORNING NOT NIGHT.' *fff. da Capo.*

'It can't be always morning,' I yawned.

'It's morning now, then, not night. Oh, the poor dog! Oh, the poor Cap'n! IT'S MORNING NOT NIGHT. Oh, the poor Cap'n. It's morning I tell you and you should get up; you have lain there long enough and plenty. There's a lot to be seen to, a great deal to be doing; all the bills are unpaid; the unsolicitor was here too: he called twice. I told him you were too ill to see him on business. And the whiskey's finished.'

'What?' I cried, springing out vertically to a standing position next the bed and Maggie on the cold polished lino. 'What did you say?'

There was a violent crash on the door. It flew open and in bounded Mawk. He dashed up destructively, his paws at the full-height acclaim, knocked me flying, knocked Maggie flying, licked and lashed our faces.

'Take him away, Maggie. Take that beast away!'

His giant rough tongue was overstippling my stubble. His wide adplanted paws Eiffeltowered my straggled feet. No pretty sight met my upturned goggling eyes but Mawk's underparts over me.

'Take him away at once. At once, away! Or *I* am going, *I* am going . . .'

I got up, overturning the monster in my mastery, opened the door which had wildly banged shut, and shoved them both out very savagely. So they went. Maggie down the steep stairs pursued hotly by Mawk giving vicious wet tugs at her white starched apron-strings knotted at her navy-blue back. The apron fell down about her descending knees. She tripped then and toppled.

I went back to my room, slammed the door.

There was a roar as of unloading timber, a tinkling crash as she tried to save herself by grasping the pink-glass-bowled sand-blast-patterned oil lamp on its brass acanthus-leaved bracket on the wall, and down she went to deserved perdition.

And the dog must also (and at last) have fallen too; for there were some gorgeous high-pitched yelps that scarcely could have been Maggie's mingled with the generally delectable commotion.

I must admit I giggled.

The sounds bore up loudly to me, continued so temporarily, then gradually, finally and mercifully grew fainter and fainter somewhere far away, further away, furthest away—outside!

This time, I said to myself, they've really gone for good.

And so, perhaps, they had! So it might well be.

But the whiskey was finished . . .

Well, there was still some in that bottle there anyhow. I poured it, as long ago aforementioned, into that by now even more sordidly soiled pepperminty tooth-pasty glass and drank it and was glad of it as it flowed in me, fanning my weak flames.

So the whiskey was finished. His whiskey was finished . . . I might as well go.

When I got downstairs (down *stairs*) the hall door was open and now there was no sound. Maggie and Mawk, MacMaggie and MacMawk, the four of them were gone.

There was no sound at all.

Except the rain, of course.

Except the rain.

# 53

E X C E P T for the rain Inverdonich was empty.

MacMaggie had said it was morning. She was probably right.

The whiskey was finished: his whiskey was finished: Uncle Melchi was finished: I must be off.

I selected a stick once again from the blue faience stick-stand.

From the hooks I chose his deerstalker, my borestalker, and a tallstalker for tall stories.

I chose a sou'wester for the nor'east, a Raglan for the road, an overcoat for the underdog and a telescope to look well through the wrong end of. Thus accoutred, I set out . . .

On the dining-room table the remnants of many meals had stood.

I went to the larder: it was bare.

I went into the kitchen and it was empty also with the fire coals settling in the Zebra-polished range.

I turned on the taps, both taps running full: and the hot and the cold ran rattling in their washerworn sockets as they always had done. They wept for us; they wept for us all.

I left them both weeping.

I went into the hall.

I went into the music room.

The parquet complained. The dead dog sang. Long-uttered notes trembled and new flies buzzed. But the fire did not crackle in the dead man's hearth; the roses did not shed their frowzy petals to the Brasso-polished fender or the hearthbrush-tidied grate. *Mrs. Karl Drushki* was no longer in her shellcase and *Caroline Testout* had gone with *La France*.

And a wet wind flapped, flapped, flapped.

I crunched the dripping gravel, went down the sopping grass, went down to the foreshore, went down the slippery jetty where the salved boat posed, poised on its own image, cut by the circles of the ever-falling rain.

It was full tide. It was full *out*. It was *marée basse* . . .

I pushed off.

The oars were there this time, rainslippy but seizable; and the thole-pins were well oiled. Inverdonich's absurd brown-painted over-fretworked gables pointed at the low grey sky just above, sank deeply in their *alter-egoed* image in the dark, rigid, still rain-circled sea; each drop musically, too musically, sounding above the spinach-green inverted laurel hedge.

I could hear the water falling in the unbailed pool of the soiled bilge towards the stern. I could hear the water falling on my hand, on my head, on the thwart at my several sides, in and on the sea, on and up the hills, on ling, bilberry, oak, hazel, birch and the coniferous plantations in their stupid marching rows. I could hear the water falling on the water falling in the waterfalls and cataracts and spuming white cascades, dripping as it wept from the green-weedy shores to the sea-weedy sea. I could hear nothing else.

I pulled at the sculls. I made for the village. I rowed for the pier.

We passed the buoy for which Mawk so much had lusted and I cast my *memento mori* bunch of fine-chopped tobacco leaves on the vacant tray of water. My butt for all buts.

We passed Blair's shed and its slip with its rusty rails from which boats no longer swam; and Archie's creek where the sand-eels were wriggling and Hermits-in-Trocus greatly relished their young; well-known fixed landmarks of stream and of dream. We rounded the point.

The village was empty. No one was about. No one I knew.

No one I knew was about. The fires were not smoking. No
smoke rose from their chimneys. The rain had quenched all . . .
. . . but at the pier: at the pier lay the Royal Steamer, R.M.S.
*Planet* or *Comet* or *Gannet*, scarlet funnelled as always, ready for
the journey, for my all-the-way-back.

Domestic ducks quacked, guzzling and gorging, bill-filtering
themselves greedily at her dripping galley drain.

*All birds that don't sing make me hungry*—but there's no need now
to go into it any further, for all birds, *all*, make me sad.

I sculled, suckled by the rising tide, to the yellow new-planked
landing. I got out and went ashore. I did not make her fast, nor
knot nor take her painter. I left her to sail.

I walked up to the kiosk to buy my new ticket.

There was no ticket-seller for the rain had quenched all.

I would buy it and bare it and use it on board.

I crossed on the gangway, the green-and-gold gangway, the
R.M.S. gangway, to her holystoned caulked teak deck.

I had muffins and crumpets and strumpets and limpets and fillets
and pullets and millet and mullet and lo-its and—stow it—for tea.

And the paddle-floats thumped, the oscillators oscillated, the
steam-whistle celebrated, the gulls wheeled, flying—and on we
went, dying. Do you hear me?

We passed along passing back, gold and black and scarlet—
gold-leaf, coal-smoke and Rowan—goldie, dark waters and my
own heart's blood.

On the water rings ran.

In my head spent songs sang.

Carrick Castle, Ardentinny, Kilcreggan, Kilmun: Blairmore,
Inellan, Arrochar, Cove, Kirn: Dunoon all too soon. Across then
to Gourock past the Cloch under the Misty Laws; white train-
puff feathering the olive grassy greyness, downhill towards high
tea at Wemyss Bay.

We rounded Princes Pier and I looked. There on slipway . . .
on slipway No. 5: the *Clan* . . . the *Clan MacDougall* on slipway
No. 5 . . . *began to move!* A ragged cheer full of holes trembled
from a crowd of yardsmen, shipwrights and boilermakers
clustered on the fitting-out-berth extension.

My God! They were launching her and I was on the bilge-sections. They were launching her this minute and the blueprints not dry. Gently increasing her ever slow momentum, her anti-fouling unsalted stern broached the water, her twin screws for the first time and last being turned by, not turned in, the here-polluted sea, straightening up as the water bore her, straining to her utmost at the fulcrum from her stress, her bows grinding dust gustily from the undergreased launching-ways, her wooden cradle flying, sharp-splintering, to matchsticks . . . the waters took her and the tugs swung her and we went our different ways.

# 54

W HEN at last I got back to Hector the foreman in the drawing-loft, he was twirling his latest Jacobean acquisition between his Capstan-stained fingers and his up-and-down strained thumb.

'Well, your uncle was as bad as that Becket fellow in the school-books, an unconscious—No, that's not it—an unconscionable—hell of a long time dying: one year and nine months. I am afraid we shall certainly have to dock you this time. Get over to the board there and thank your lucky stars we are still short of draughtsmen.'

I began to move off.

'Eh! Here! . . . Did you know I've got a son? I married Jeannie.'

'Who's at the telephone now?'

'Ah, a sonsie new girl who you would not know.'

'But you do.'

'Get along.'

I sat down at the board: my instruments were rusty: ditto, terribly, my skill.

I sat down at the board and I soon fell asleep.

# 55

S KIDDLE-DE-DAD, skiddle-de-dad: that's what it kept murmuring: skiddle-de-dad, skiddle-de-dad.

Nothing very new, of course; nothing at all forgotten and even less learnt: 304D on the long straight stretch from Donabate, on across the estuary, over the fat mullet, frightening off the pochards, diving under the eiders, on through the cutting, skirting now the brickworks, passing through Portmarnock, rattling at the Junction, rushing Raheny, skipping Clontarf, slowing down past Fairview, all the way home.

The Begrudger was at me.

I scrabbled for my pasteboard.

But the Begrudger, Mick, the eternal perennial Begrudger, would not leave me alone.

'You had better get out, sir. You really had better. She is going to the scrappers. She is going to the scrappers down below at Hammond Lane. Sure we're *dieselized* now; didn't you know?'

# 56

'For God's sake, Mick. You can't cod me that way. I know well enough the buses this long time are diesel—none of that dangerous petrol any more since the party was burnt at Tramore, thirty-two of them, wasn't it?—and far more economical. But it's another tale with trains. Do you really think that after all my travelling I do not know the difference between one and the other? You'll be telling me next they're the very same thing.'

'So they are, very nearly, only one is on rails. And you're long on them too; much too long, you are, sir. Come on along out, she's due for the scrappers. Look at the empties!'

The Begrudger waved his right arm around and up and down, his gesture embracing the entire compartment from overladen bulging net racks to cluttered filthy floor.

'Just look at it! Don't you know you're not let put heavy articles upon those racks?'

'A bottle is not a heavy article.'

'No, but that gross is. That load'll bust them altogether shortly. But I suppose it does not matter greatly now on account she's for the scrappers, and a rack here or there's no importance any longer; though it's not right surely and no way to send her off. I never saw the like in all my long experience and we've little time now before she's gone.'

'What's all this about the scrappers? She cannot have aged that much. Surely to goodness she's game for another stretch yet? What's the time, anyway?'

'It's well past one and I'm due for my dinner, but I'll have to get you out first or they'll take you away. Come along!'

But I still refused to *get* out, only leant and *looked* out, the Begrudger standing back from the window, hands behind him, feet well apart on the spit-flecked dingy worn tarmac as I did so, dispirited as before by the doors of the carriages hanging listlessly in rows like the wings of dead birds used for scares.

It was then that I thought, after long times not thinking, of the crockery-merchant's bag; and its contents and his chair and his chat; and the appointment I should keep. It was well after one, but time enough till three.

'You'll have to get a trolley for the corpses then, Mick. But there are one or two live ones here yet; Bushmills from the border, Perse's and Powers, Jamesons from Portmarnock from the old man's house itself; and sandwiches too, all fresh from the counter in Dundalk! Look, Mick, let's finish them. Come on along in!'

Well he tried, but he couldn't. I had forgotten about the job with the hacksaw I had done so long ago and neatly on the door.

'Jesus Christ! The damages you've done to the Company's property beats cockfighting,' he said, peering in more carefully this time at the dreadful destruction I had wrought in my residence, twisting the severed handle back and forth vainly all the while. 'It's lucky enough for you she's bound for Hammond Lane. Can you not let me in from your side even? Have you the whole bloody lock jammed up and broken?'

'A minute, Mick,' I said, and opened up. And for the very first time in all my long journeyings (though we were sadly halted now) I had living company in my siege-stood compartment; living company I had gone to great extremes to avoid.

Admittedly the place was a shambles: every king his castle, mine was tumbling down. Moraines of spent bottles, screes of yellowing newspapers, sloped from rack to groaning seat, from seat to buried floor; on all available space and on all unavailable also; a pigsty, a slobland, though cleared well enough round, below and above my old corner-seat on the side next the sea; except for the ash of the thousand dozen hundred assorted cigarettes and all their butts not flown out of the window when the weather was clement, which topped or smothered all. There were burns in the threadbare upholstery (where visible) from those I had puffed when I'd fallen asleep or those which had dropped from my ignorant fingers, voyaging within voyage, when still wide awake. There were fresh holes in the old tongues, new ones in the grooves. Spots, stains, spews of all sizes, viscous or volatile, and of liquids and in colours too numerous to mention, spread or sprinkled paper, wood or glass. Of the six window-panes, three were badly cracked.

With both arms and much difficulty I removed some of the detritus from the seat opposite mine so that Mick could sit down: and he sat, pernicketily brushing the filthy mange-plush surface with energetic flicks of his worn-from-clipping hand before he did.

I reached over to my right where I knew the last stock rattled (latterly this jangling had nearly set me mad) and drew out a full Jameson, a quart Bushmills, four baby Powers and a bottle of stout.

'Thick or clear?' I asked Mick. 'There's plenty of cloudy knocking around somewhere from the summer. That's when I'd a thirst!'

'God, I'll have a nip of the hard. You seem to have more than when you started, I must say. What about some water?'

'Never mind that. There's plenty outside.'

And indeed it had started to rain.

We took a Power apiece for the start off: and then we took another.

'Ham or cheese?'

'Didn't I tell you I was going to get my dinner? I don't want to spoil it. Drink's one thing; whets appetite. Sangwiches another. Though I'm not the sort of man never eats with his meals.'

'Come on now, Mick, there's no hurry away from here, is there? When are they taking her anyhow? And why?'

'She's used up. It's all diesels now. Glass all round and not a pick of privacy. But a grand view; Oh Lord, a splendid view! Nips up north before you can say Dev and back again before you'd say Craigavon.'

'Why's she slower coming down?'

'Customs at the border, looking for books and articles. But they're streaked lightning both ways.'

'When'll we have to go?'

The Begrudger took out his half-hunter railwayman's watch, cut straight from the pages of the old *Wide World*, and sprung open its lid. He examined it ponderously and with such great attention that no one would have thought he had set eyes on it before.

'Eleven and three-quarter minutes more to go. We'd best get out of here,' he sighed.

'And what about the corpses?' I sighed sadly also.

'Ah, leave them! There's no use at all in clearing her up now.'

'And the fulls?'

'Put them all back in your mother's old goatskin bag and take them with you. It'll be the holy hour when we get out of this and they'll come in handy: more so still later when they close up for good.'

'We'll make a hole in them first though. Tell me this: why don't they sell her for a house?'

'Sell what?'

'Carriage of course. Makes the neatest little, ugliest little slug of a bungalow or shop God ever saw! Lovely out at the Burrow or up at Sallynoggin for Ice Cream and Cigarettes, taking the loneliness off the countryside!'

'Can't be done now at all. They're mad after trams. Two storeys; and all lovely green.'

'Well, here's to my last few minutes of peace then! Here's to the immortal soul of 304D, may it rest in pieces! Amen!'

Uncorking, I put the Bushmills to my lips, drained a good slug, passed it on to Mick.

'Lord, but I don't care for this stuff. Damned side too sweet.'

'I like it though. My Uncle Melchi loved it. It's all the same in the end anyhow; and good stoking when you're face to face with death.'

'Death?'

'The death of my carriage. Dear old 304D, will there ever be another one like you? Not likely, I'm afraid, the way things are going now. Nuisance and refuge, presence and absence,' I maudlinly stroked the frayed red seat, the feel of it on my hand sending shivers down my spine like cheap chamois gloves. 'Home from home, Rome from Rome, Mudlin' from Dublin, Mawk from Dundalk, Rablon from . . .'

'That's enough! That's quite enough! You had better come along by the way you're talking . . .'

> '*I know my love by her way of talking,*
> '*And I know my love by her way of walking . . .*'

I sang. The sweet Air did me good.

'That's enough! That's far more than enough! And we've had all this before. Come on along out and get along across the city or you'll miss your appointment. They are closed up now and there's no danger. You had better be off and on your way!'

Mick was vexed; very vexed. I had no choice.

And so at last, at long last, I stepped out onto the platform of my native city, sprinkled with gob, well wet with rain, a public convenience if ever there was one.

I had packed my mother's bag with all full bottles left except the stout, wedging them with newspapers so they could not break or jangle; and on top and between them the old paper bag with its crockery, reached down from the corner of the rack below which I had voyaged those many mile-years. I took my mac and my hat, left the door hanging limp like the others, and walked away, never turning round, down the sooty tunnel of grimy glass-roof which was dry, towards the far barrier next the bowdlerised bookstall, and the bar that sometimes wasn't. Behind me I heard

Mick at his banging: five jangly, two resounding, one (the next one) my own and dully final. Gone, my escape or main chance.

I did not look round but continued towards the barrier.

I walked past number two tank hissing and resting, ready for the sheds when the other pulled out.

It was then I remembered my pasteboard.

I put down my bag, leaning it against my knee, and I searched and I searched and sure enough I found it. Multi-punctured, colourless, shapeless; and soft as a piece of old crochet.

Mick was at the train, he was not at the barrier. Across his sentry's cabin stretched a leather-covered chain, protecting thus his sitting-polished seat.

So I turned back.

I went back towards Mick; back towards the train.

He had finished his banging and was now sauntering towards me, his arms overgrossly encumbered with the balance of the stout, as many worthwhile empties as they possibly could embrace, his pockets full too. He was flustered when he saw me.

'Here, Mick,' I whispered, 'take it. I've finished with it now. Turn it in. It's all up.'

In his effort to take it some of his prizes fell, two fulls bursting, scattering froth and glass particles on the platform and his trousers: some empties bounced: and my ex-passport, my valiant golden key, fluttered to the ground amidst the mess.

'There it is!' I said. 'That's my ticket—broken bottles! Froth! It's no good now; you may leave it where it lies.'

But in any case Mick could not stoop.

# 57

*WHY didn't I catch it, though? Why did I not go on?*

Maybe I could get——

As I watched there was a chuff, a suppressed sombre chuff, and 304D, my *Alma Mater*, my *sine qua non*, my *reductio ad absurdum*, my *quod erat demonstrandum* (if I know no other Latin) began to slip off silently, without fuss, to its funeral in the rain . . .

I could not let it go. I simply could not leave it.

By-passing immobilized Mick in an agony of effort, I took a few fast running leaps, seized the door-handle of the very last compartment, succeeded in opening it, and dragged myself in. Gasping I plumped down, my bag on the seat beside me.

304G: it might not be the same but was very much akin, pristine clean but for one cracked window after fifty years a-rail in normal service.

I could not face my city but would see this to the end. I could call about my crocks some other day.

So I sat in my condemned cell: a new one, unsullied, but just as much condemned; and the rain crept on the windows, seeped on the blackened ballast between the shiny wet rails, as we trundled, flanges groaning, to the sidings near the locos where we stopped.

There was silence now but for the furtive drips: no milk cans, door-slams, whistles, crunchy gravel, shouts, tickets-pleasings, steam, or any station. Just the furtive drips. And very, very distant indecipherable commotions from far away outside. From my all-condemned world.

In this condemned cell of a house within a hearse, we halted. Time halted too. I looked out: dirty wet slate roofs, dirty wet streaked yellow bricks, the tram company's chimneys steady smoke, O'Casey's prodding church.

I could just hear the cries of the Racing Special sellers in the rain-sodden street, pinned to time thus and place. Beyond the sheds along the squirming river, at intervals behind the seagull's ridge-tile perching, peeped the masts and black-topped funnels, raking green, buff and scarlet, of the Liverpool, Holyhead, and Glasgow-bound boats, wisping occasional belches of banked furnace-smoke. Not too soon their sailing.

The sky was aerial mud.

Thank God I had my bag and plenty in it. Though still hyphened to the living warmth of companioned drinking, my strength was ebbing fast. So I took out a full one very carefully, uncorked it similarly, similarly and plentifully reinforced.

Must see this out somehow to the end: must see us both out.

A silent first-year herring-gull, brownish-grey smudge against smudge, flew crabwise near me across the worn-out sky above a sooty roof; shied at some sight he could, I could not, see; made off towards the docks.

After an interminable age when I had finally decided there was really no more life in the old box, it stirred; jiggling backwards this time, back, backsliding to the back-sidings of the decrepit and dis-guarded next the huge cut-stone penal-timed masonry wall and two old MGW twin-axled passengers with their roofs ripped off and their windows boarded blind for carrying turf; not laden, however, with this country-cousin fuel, so sad and so sodden in the town, but empty of everything, even this.

And the rain fell vertical over all.

A ship's siren bleated mournfully, fleeting to the sky a wisp of once-warm steam: prows pointed for a far sea, stern trembling for a port.

I took another swig.

The light in the sky was failing: there would be no light switched on this time when the light of the sky had failed. But that was a good while off yet. I wondered if I could stick it.

I took another swig.

For the carriage and my own deaths grew steadily coincident. No travelling now, no waiting, no movement; no railbeat, no heart. I dozed miserably, half snoozing, half sozzle. Images of a pseudo-brightness flitted in the crypto-dark end-alley of my buffer-stopped all-up mind. I wakened and slept. No sound but the drips; no drips but many millions.

I tookanotherswig.

Interminable convolutions of colourless colours and flaming blacks prised open and swallowed the vortexed tunnels of my place that had been eyes; so I sat on my skull with my buttocks wide open to assuage my lost mouth.

But it would not do.
None of them would do.
Nothing at all of any kind would do.

For myself no escape.

So I waited.

For something to happen. For anything to happen. For movement, for change.

And at last something did.

# 58

AN afternoon diesel (all glass and no privacy), a few lucky ones over-despondent in its freed cage, ground out from Platform Four for Howth and Ireland's Eye . . . white sea-washed gravel near the Martello tower . . . a big stretch for guillemots . . . further for razors . . . on the Stack Rock, never quite grasping them, but a puffin's beak nip in her burrow instead just beside, indeed beneath, the old green tartan rug with the airman's red blood on it from nineteen-fifteen or the jam from Maggie's sandwiches which ran up your sleeve. A fine day there, a great place for a boat and a girl if the wind blew strong and southerly after landing, cutting off retreat, if the rain very likely was not brought along with it, discomforting all fun, cowering beneath a cheap showerproof far too small for two, isolate for one, water after jam up your sleeve, down her neck. God, how I hated that road along the always-absent sea, nothing but mud and shelduck and curlews maybe, in the teeth of the ever-east wind past the black nuns in their cow-red convent and the back of the grandstand in everlasting shadow in the pub where the whiskey on race-days would kill or cure a horse . . .

But the flame would not last.

Old Aunt Hen plagued with poachers and lovers, infuriate on Sundays when we all sat indoors lettering out her notice on the rather too-rough board: MANTRAPS AND POLYPODIUMS SET HERE. By Order. Illegal the former, God alone knew the latter; safer to stay out from the ferns growing freely in her gentle mossy wood. Rory eaten by the crocs in the River Murrumbidgee leaving nothing but his boots; worse if they'd started at that very end instead, leaving nothing but his head. Never shall we know if . . .

But the flame would not heat.

A train from the North, steam and proper this time, fairly full, all standing ready, longing to be out with their contraband cargoes, creams for contraceptions, English Sunday papers, *Hot Women*, *True Crimes*, Huxley, Graham Greene, and poor Marcel Proust . . .

But the flame would not light.

Only the box, within and without. No bolt, rabbit, rat, mouse, or gnathole.

No hole at all.

The flame had gone out.

# 59

THE flame had gone out but the rain was stopping, the sky lifting: a weak pale sun slanted between the trucks.

Incipiently there were noises of couplings and clinkings as our knacker-train was fashioned rusty chain to rusty hook.

Semi-inanimate, part yet not quite parcel, I lurched in my seat as buffer struck buffer, hitching the unlidded, an echoing tanker leaking brown oily water, three deliquescent cattle redolent o damp dung, two flatcars falling asunder, the remains of a 4-4-0 tender-loco (its leading bogie passed on before) staggering crippled and unpleasant on its disconnected drivers, firedoor agape, bronze and brasses swiped long since as adjuncts for the foundry.

Then the whole procession, 304 leading in front or behind, dreeled out onto the main-line embankment in the fine sea-breeze off the mudlarking swans' ooze, glimpsing the bay from my tumbril, sniffing the far sunny coast down to Dalkey; and back again jerking, uneasily reluctant, screeching and groaning through the GSR platforms so distant and tactful with their *fir* and their *mná*, 'permitted' in Irish but NO SMOKING plain, by bridge over the swilling street, the brighter sun now glinting on the noisy stone sets roaring with the hard rims of green twin-horsed postvans striking sparks on dark winter evenings through Store Street for sorting down the road. Cutting through the backs of the blank-windowed houses, carriage-length over Talbot Street, dangerous to touch the wires, deadly to run the rails, people upright and walking to the Pillar there for sausages, back for the Mills and McHugh himself right under, diagonal over Gardiner past the plumbers' drainpipes, chimney-pots and roof-tiles far down below, we obliterated Gandon with our skeletons and chuff-smoke, his copper-dome shrunken and windows too squared since the burnt paper falling on the summer-flowered garden in 1919, but saw him further on set off splendidly by the goldening sun and vermilion-red funnels of *Carrowdore*, *Clarecastle*, late of John Kelly, now home with empties from Manchester, flame against the grey, unloading their rimmed barrels into puffing Liffey barges as we waited on the bridge for the all clear from Tara.

Up the river, west and sad, the town's sore centre, mauled and maimed Carlisle-O'Connell, from one thing to another until nothing was left but the river-light spanned by the Metal Bridge and the orthodox towers of Uniform Stout with *Clonsilla* bound to them. The stop-signal jangled and our railroad was clear through the underground murk of the overhead station past the back of the bath's ever echoing voices, the back of the poor's fronts, the affront of the poorer's backs, trundling over Brunswick-Pearse, cutting once more . . . but I had had enough.

*Stop this funeral, I had had enough!*

I had always longed for it; now was my chance!

Abandoned in this box: neglected, deserted, bound for the scrappers; for imminent, certain, deliberate destruction; if ever there was an Emergency, here, surely, was one.

I reached up for the chain and pulled with all my might! . . .

Nothing whatever happened, nothing whatever at all.

The convoy went on, there was no sudden braking.

But the whole chain came running out, quite slowly running out, like the chain from that awful cuckoo clock I should never have meddled with, meaning to wind it, strangling for ever its cuck and its oo. It came on running out, patched red where it passed through the once used compartments, the rest of it black and encrusted with grime, never having seen, since its clean bronze was long ago threaded in its dark secret tube, the bright light of day. It came on running out, piling itself impertinently in a neat heap on the dirty planked floor between my feet.

# 60

THERE I was in the siding.

I had an idea of running for it, not knowing whither; but the whiskey had laid weight to my legs. I pressed my face, my pressed-tongue face, to the cracked-glass window so that a small red welt grew diagonally on its haggisy surface.

Through the window I saw a mountain of dripping small coal.

I turned away and I finished the bottle.

I finished the bottle and all the bottles ever made, filled, corked, or stoppered; of all colours or sizes; of glass, stone, pottery, metal, lapislazuli, crystal, leather or other skin; amphoras, carboys, *bonbonnes*, demi-johns; hockshape, chiantied, alembics, tureens. I finished the decanters, jugs, pitchers and jars . . .

He had said it was better to keep to the side streets.

And so I did.

When I came at long last to Mrs. N.'s door the name-plates were changed both in colour and text.

Where there had been silver, there was now brass. Where there had been N. there was K.

I rang the bell all the same and a smart arty tart came tripping to open up:

'Have you an appointment?' she said before I spoke.

'I have one with Mrs. N. I am her uncle, son and nephew.'

'She died long ago.'

'And her daughters?'

'Married, dead, or buried.'

'And her son?'

'She had none.'

So I went out into the square and from the square to the canal and from the Canal to the Dodder and from the Dodder to the Park and from the park to the garden and from the Garden to his window.

223

At the window there was the sound of music and on the drawn blinds the shadows of bows.

So I went to the door and I rang.

'Is the Captain in?'

'No. He is flying all this week. Night-flights, you know.'

'You may be right,' I said, 'though I hardly should have expected it. Maybe that is what he's at almost all the time now. It accounts for his absence, do you hear me?'

'I beg your pardon?'

'Never mind. How's his nephew?'

'Very bad. Not expected to recover.'

'Ah, I see.'

So I went back through the garden to the Park and from the park to the Dodder and from the Dodder to the Canal, and from the canal to the mews and from the back to the bell-spangled front.

I rang the right bell and was promptly let in.

'They are very uncomfortable,' I said.

'So are most things, Ha Ha Ha! Open up . . . wider . . . wider . . . and let me see. Ah, Yes . . . My goodness, to be sure. Well, I never! You are growing a whole new set of wisdoms, complete! You'll never be comfortable with them. This will *never* do . . . But don't worry: wait until I ring Doctor Hacket: just a whiff of gas, just the smallest little whiff, and we'll soon have them out . . .'

But at that instant the knacker's axe, striking cleanly through the filthy wood of my celled compartment, split my sleeping skull too.

For my day had passed.

And I heard or saw no birds.

Spéracèdes, France
*January 1955–January 1957*

# An Afterword

Why should we attend to *Cadenza?* It is a book of memory, termination and death, written with an Anglo-Irish arrogance worthy of Beckett, an arrogance that leaches out of these things the sentimentality and hideous falsity that they usually encourage. The novel comprises a chain of loosely connected stories having to do with the hero, one Desmond; these stories exist in an arbitrary fictional time and are ordered and combined (or not combined) as instances of memory, fantasy, and what may as well be termed dream. The actuality of the novel is the present but as we read we discover that the past is also the present. We have then no firm grasp on time and nothing in the book allows us the comfort of an "and then" chronology. The train in which Desmond has hidden himself is one that moves through a space that has been converted into time at the author's bidding so that we find ourselves in a kind of fictive fourth-dimension. This sleight of hand permits the author to concretize, so to speak, the temporal, so that what seems lost is not but is recovered in its entirety.

Although the work is an utterance at the invisible edge between life and death it is written in a scintillant comic spirit. Cusack's comedy is, however, of the classic Irish variety, that is, black and then blacker. In *Watt,* Beckett speaks of the "laugh that laughs at that which is unhappy." Desmond and Celia caught *in flagrante*—what could be "funnier"? The drunken French priest, the singing of an Irish Republican song at an Orange Christmas party, the scene in which Uncle Melchizidek's corpse falls overboard — all these things are material for burlesque, if not what is depressingly called "humor." But in *Cadenza* these occurrences are inseparable from loss, unhappiness, misery and death.

Yet nowhere in the novel are we allowed the specious deliciousness of the tragic. The Irish are not good at tragedy and when it appears in Irish literature it almost always rapidly disintegrates into the mawkish, the sentimental, and the maudlin. I have always suspected that this lack of tragedy stems from the Irish vision of the world as eminently *fair,* or, to be clearer, the Irish think of life as a stew of bewildering and impenetrable events, an inexplicable "cosmic joke." Given such a vision, how can there be a tragic if one expects, at any minute, to be knocked flat? What can possibly be surprising about man's propensity for evil, the tragic flaw, sickness, pain and death? This sense that life is what it is and is no great bargain at that is not a good one for tragedy. It is perhaps pertinent to note here that the Irish writers whom we have taken to our hearts in the United States, e.g., O'Connor, O'Faolain, O'Flaherty, Behan, have a great gift for what my mother called "snots and tears," i.e., the tragic gone awry. But it is hard going here for a writer such as Flann O'Brien; his bitter and anarchic comedy, rooted in squalor, meanness, death, and torture both physical and mental, is not our dish. O'Connor writes of one of his stories, "The Martyr's Crown," which is about a virtuous woman who prostitutes herself to a British officer in order to save members of the IRA during "the troubles": "It is probably as old as history, but Mr. O'Nolan [O'Brien] must be the first writer to have treated it as farce." One feels the thin edge of disapproval in the remark. Cusack is in the O'Brien tradition but we prefer an O'Connor, whose very titles ("My Da," "My Oedipus Complex") often have the ring of our "civilized" humorists' pallid feuilletons. Such titles could have come from the pen of E.B. White.

So. The past informs this entire work but the past is the present, it is the same past that Maurice Blanchot speaks of when he says that in Proust events "can be brought back by the tide of time, not as memories but as real events... recurring in another moment of time." It is a sophomoric truism that the present instantaneously and without surcease becomes the past: Cusack has exploited this fact and places his dead events on the same temporal plane as living events — which are, of course, also dead in a snap of the fingers. My last word, "fingers," is as much a part of the past as are those things I did and said and wrote yesterday, a year ago, ten years ago. Yet as I write, the word "seems" to be more present than what I wrote ten years ago and I assume that the reader also thinks of it as being in the present. Yet we know that although it "just" happened it takes its place with everything that is gone. Cusack, in managing his work so that the past and the present are one, implies that if the past is dead and the present is the past, it too is dead: it simply does not exist. Given this proposition, the idea of fictional realism suffers an enormous blow. If presently occurring phenomena are not *really* here and now, and if they are as actually irretrievable as the phenomena of a decade past, what indeed measures or can measure present reality? And if memory and fantasy are interchangeable, why cannot the *present* instant be memory, or more pertinently for Cusack, fantasy? Cusack tells us once again (we cannot be told often enough) that all fiction is a lie and lies most egregiously when it pretends to remember *the facts.*

The past and the endless dying present are of a piece: we call this "life." As we live we die, and the present, in such a view, is negligible if not contemptible. When Desmond remembers the sweetheart of his youth and the blissful lovemaking they enjoyed before discovery, he remembers it as a brilliant fictional scene of excitement, fulfillment, and depression. He has polished it perfectly in his mind so that he *makes love* in a pattern of his own devising, he retrieves that afternoon in absolute totality. It is more than memory. It is the actuality of what has ended and will never end. And he will make love to her again, surely. *Cadenza* insists on the stupidity of reality, or, more exactly, insists that to remember our lives is an act of creation. Williams writes, in *Paterson,* "Anywhere is everywhere," to which Cusack might reply, "anytime is every time." Nothing disappears.

GILBERT SORRENTINO